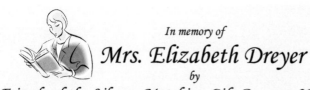

In memory of

Mrs. Elizabeth Dreyer

by

Friends of the Library Matching Gift Program 2004

SIERRA BARON

Half a million acres of gold was a lot for a man to handle, even a hard-fighting man like Mike McGann. But when he learned that he owned it, he aimed to keep it—and his aim was pretty damn good.

Only suddenly he found himself the target for every gold-hungry gun in the territory, and before he could stop it the Rush was on—for Mike McGann's land, and his blood . . .

SIERRA BARON

Tom W. Blackburn

GUNSMOKE

This hardback edition 2003
by Chivers Press
by arrangement with
Golden West Literary Agency

ISBN 0 7540 8222 9

British Library Cataloguing in Publication Data available.

Printed and bound in Great Britain by
Antony Rowe Ltd, Chippenham, Wiltshire

For Gary my son

• ONE •

The *Susan Winthrop* was in at Monterey three months and nine days out of Boston, a record trip.

Mike McGann stood content at the landward rail with a number of other passengers who were passing a spyglass among them. He noted that he drew a fair measure of respect from them all. He supposed one or two, by simple arithmetic, might have figured out that his winnings at cards during the trip were enough to pay his fare twice over, and that he had never mentioned another means of support. Perhaps some might have long since scented the hemp and tar which yet clung to his hands and so know his previous voyage to these waters had been before the mast.

McCracken moved over to stand moodily at Mike's elbow. Most of the original leathery tan had faded from McCracken's face during the long voyage, but time had done nothing to lessen his hatred of the sea. In this hatred Mike had sympathy for the Texan. He had himself been born within sight and sound of the sea and he had hated it through the bitterness of his childhood. He had served enough long shipboard months as an unwilling sailor to sharpen his own hatred to something McCracken could never know. Still, it had brought him to this—to California—to what awaited him here.

Mr. Jeffers had completely captured the attention of the others. He had a way of doing that. It was something that came naturally, with no apparent effort. Somebody had said he was a lawyer. Mike didn't know. Gold showed in Mr. Jeffers' well-kept teeth and in the great yellow chain across his waistcoat and in the gem-studded circlets on two of his short fingers. For an old man he kept his mind and his body in fine shape and people listened when he talked.

5

"A new Eden," he was saying. "As many as four crops a year—maybe more. And anything will grow. They say it's a stampede, by wagon, ship and afoot. But if half they say is true, it's nothing to what they will soon be seeing. The American farmer has worn out his land. He needs new soil, and he'll think nothing of crossing the continent to get it."

"Stock has a future here, too," Mike suggested. "Livestock—cattle."

Mr. Jeffers waved the suggestion aside.

"The farmer is the future," he insisted. "Always has been. And already enough of them have come in to crowd that Swiss colony up the Sacramento from Benicia—what's his name's place—the one that bought out the Russians."

Young Benson's attention shifted from the shore to Mr. Jeffers at this. Mike supposed Benson was not actually as young as he looked. He was mild, modestly dressed, and soft-voiced. Perhaps the illusion of youth came from cheeks heavily fuzzed with a downy beard. Shaving was made impossible for him by a violent pustulation of acne. He was alert enough, Mike knew. Benson played a good hand of cards.

"Sutter," Benson supplied for Mr. Jeffers. "At New Helvetia. Captain John Augustus Sutter."

"Captain Sutter—yes," Mr. Jeffers nodded. "Thank you, my young friend. As I was saying, Captain Sutter's place. They will engulf him. Poor devil, he has too much land."

"No man can have too much land," Mike said quietly.

"Sutter has," Mr. Jeffers said with a sharp glance. "Too much either to police or defend. History will repeat itself. The have-nots will close in on the haves. A universal law of human behavior. Maybe of equity, too. I've never been quite sure."

Alice Abernathy handed Mr. Jeffers the spyglass in his turn and he peered eagerly off through it at the town ashore. The woman smiled tentatively at Mike. He did not let his own expression change. As far as he was concerned, she was a damned bore.

"I'm just dying to know what wonderful secret is keeping Emil here," she beamed to the group in general. "Something absolutely magnificent he's building, of course."

She paused uncertainly and then beamed again.

6

"Emil is an engineer, you know."

"Is there anything we don't know about Emil?" McCracken growled from the rail.

Mrs. Abernathy sniffed. Benson moved in beside her and looked off at the town.

"I've been thinking," he said. "It might be smart for all of us to land here. They say fog can hold you up for days off the Golden Gate. Might be able to make better time overland."

Mrs. Abernathy paled at this and turned to face the group with defensive briskness.

"None of us would do that! In a strange country like this?"

She turned appealingly to Mike.

"You've been here before. Tell them how foolish it would be to leave the ship before San Francisco."

Mike was saved the necessity of an answer by Jeffers.

"The ship is not going to San Francisco, madam."

"What?"

"Ask Captain Ellis."

"But Emil is waiting there for me!"

"The Captain's return cargo is waiting here. His owners have ordered him to sail for home from Monterey."

"But he has an obligation to us! Our—our passage contract. I'll see the consul ashore at once!"

"There isn't any consul," Benson told her with a shadow of amusement. "This isn't a foreign port any more. Just good old U.S.A. There isn't anybody to see."

Alice Abernathy tried to draw herself up against catastrophe, but her eyes were frightened. Mike felt a grudging sympathy.

"You'll be comfortable and safe enough in Monterey," he said. "And Benson is right. Your chances of getting to San Francisco or Benicia overland faster than by sea are good."

"If you could be of any assistance, Mr. McGann, I'd be most grateful—and Emil, too."

"I'm sorry. I'm not heading for the Bay country."

Both Benson and Jeffers eyed him with surprise.

"It must be something extraordinary to make you forego the Sacramento Valley," Mr. Jeffers said.

"It is," Mike agreed.

"She must be a beauty," Benson suggested archly.

"She is."

Mike did not feel it necessary to add that he spoke in both instances of the Princesa, and that she was not a woman.

Alphabetic juxtaposition put Mike and Larry McCracken into the third longboat to pull away from the ship. It was already dusk, thickened by a lowering fog.

"This ranch of yours, Miguel," McCracken said as the ship fell astern. "Bought it, you said. Ranches don't buy easy and they come high. You didn't tell me how you got it."

"No," Mike agreed.

"It don't figure," McCracken persisted. "A bum off the Boston docks ships out to California as a seaman, intending to clean the pockets of everybody aboard his ship at cards. I get that. So you do that, your last trip, an' have more luck than you're entitled to. Right?"

Mike nodded. McCracken scowled.

"That lands you here pretty well heeled. Legal and logical, so far. You had enough of sailorin' and wanted to buy somethin' here. I get that, too. There's times a man can't stand it, wantin' to get his hooks into somethin' that's his—somethin' he can look at an' feel an' own. Somethin' that'll make him an honest dollar an' keep him from starvin'. I know about that. But when it came to buyin' in, why in the name of the beautiful blue Lady of Guadalupe did it have to be a ranch?"

"A switch was pulled on me," Mike answered, "I had three thousand dollars. I looked around here and found an old house I figured I could make over into a business place, cheap. I found a man I thought could make a good buy for me, so I gave him the money."

"What kind of business did you have in mind?"

"A tavern."

"Rum and women—that kind?"

"They make the most money."

"Sure. But the ranch?"

"After I'd made my deal with this Angus Peyton, the skipper of my ship found out I planned to jump his crew and stay here. Him and the rest aboard didn't know I'd spent the money I'd won from them, and they wanted it back. They shanghaied me aboard again. It was a rough

8

go and they messed me up some. We'd been at sea a week on the way back to the States before the Captain gave me the deed this Angus Peyton had sent out to the ship for me just before she sailed. It wasn't a deed to the old house. It was to the Princesa, instead."

"That's the ranch?"

"An old Mexican grant, about a hundred miles back in the mountains."

"Probably ain't worth five hundred dollars, that far from a shippin' point or a market," McCracken said thoughtfully.

"I know," Mike agreed. "Peyton must have pocketed the rest of the three thousand dollars I gave him. Picked up this old grant someplace for a song and probably tipped off my skipper to haul me back aboard."

"The Princesa," McCracken muttered. "Women is always trouble, Miguel."

"The deed says ten leagues of land. I like the sound."

"How much land is it?"

"I don't know. Maybe half a million acres."

"Half a million!" McCracken whistled. "How's it look?"

"How do I know? I've never seen it."

"What's the difference? You wouldn't know what you was lookin' at, anyway. Water—soil depth, root depth—storm cover—season—stock. Why, hell, you an' a ranch is like puttin' a boy to bed with a hungry woman. You wouldn't even know where to begin."

"You'll show me."

"Not till I've seen the place an' made up my mind. Till then, I'll take a hundred dollars off of you."

"For what?"

"Expenses. A horse, a saddle, a blanket, and a woman."

"In that order, Mac?"

"What's the matter with it?" McCracken asked truculently. "Do I get the hundred?"

"When you've earned it. There's a load of freight coming ashore from the ship. I picked up what I thought I'd need for the Princesa in Boston."

"Boston! That's a great place to outfit a ranch from!"

"A team and wagon's got to be found. Local supplies have got to be picked up and the lot loaded. A week's work at one thing and another here."

"That's for you, Miguel. I'm heading for the ranch. If

9

I like it, I'll wait for you there. If I don't, I move on. You take the risk on the hundred."

Mike scowled, momentarily distrusting the instinct which had attracted him to McCracken when the Texan boarded the ship at Vera Cruz on her southward swing for the Horn. But the fellow was a stockman and Mike knew better than anyone the incongruity of his plans. He counted out five double eagles into McCracken's hand.

"You're an easy mark, Miguel," the Texan grinned. "You know that, don't you?"

"It's the way I was raised," Mike told him.

The boat bumped against the quay and they were ashore. Heavy odor lay over the waterfront, boasting that fishermen dipped much of Monterey's living from the sea.

A group of men were standing against the custom house wall, huddled in their *serapes*.

"You are from the ship, *señores?*"

Mike stopped, nodding. The man who had spoken pushed out from the wall.

"They look for a man from the ship. One who calls himself Miguel—"

"Who's looking for Miguel McGann?" he asked.

"Señor Peyton, at the Yankee House."

McCracken saw Mike's expression change and stepped close.

"The same one?"

"Couldn't be two of them."

"Probably wants to return the boodle he took off of you."

"Sure," Mike said wryly. "His conscience is bothering him." He nodded to the brown man. "Thanks. I'll see him."

There was still considerable evening foot traffic, soft-shoed, liquid in motion, liquid in sound. Mike turned into an alley he remembered, cutting through a block. It was lined with narrow doors. Although none were now in evidence, it was Monterey's street of women. As they reached the far end of the passage, the door of a detached adobe shack opened. A girl came out and looked at them—a girl with a sad, pretty face and magnificent shoulders, exposed from tip to tip by the round, low-cut neck of a voluminous blouse. On impulse, Mike tipped his hat as they passed. McCracken looked back.

"Now why in hell did you do that?" he asked.

"A thing of beauty is a joy to behold," Mike answered.

They emerged from the lower end of the alley into a square faced with older buildings. Directly across was a former residence, now freshly plastered, fitted with new doors and windows, and garishly lamplit, within and without. It was a bright, clangorous oasis in the quiet dark of Monterey. A sign across the entire second floor advertised the Yankee House.

Mike pointed.

"There's Peyton's place. The bastard! That's the old house I wanted him to buy for me. That's even the name I was going to open under."

"Fast on the shuffle, ain't he?" McCracken grunted. "Come on. I'll buy the first drink."

"Later."

"Thought you wanted to see this Peyton."

"He wants to see me. That's what the man said. Maybe tomorrow. I want to do some thinking."

"Company's no good for that. See you in the mountains, Miguel."

Mike nodded. The Texan moved on across the square and shouldered into the Yankee House without looking back. Mike remained where he was, staring across at this harvesting of his original dream. A brassy piano was clattering within—the kind of a piano he had planned to import when he could. Anger swelled in him. For the first time in many months his ownership of the ten nebulous leagues of the Princesa did not seem the huge joke on Peyton he had labored so hard for a year to convince himself it was. Turning, he started up the street. He knew he had much to do before he met McCracken in the mountains and was certain that slipping a coin to the right party would secure a room at the hotel.

Almost at the end of the square, he passed a deeply recessed doorway.

"Señor McGann?" a voice asked.

Two *californios* stepped from the doorway. He thought one of them might have been among those against the wall of the custom house. The other was a stocky, immensely powerful man who trailed a short length of heavy, knotted manila cordage from one hand.

The man swung hard with this and the knots struck

11

Mike at the base of his ear. His knees buckled but he remained on his feet by desperately gripping one of his assailants. The knotted rope swung again. Mike lost his hold and fell to the walk. He was rolled over and he saw the face of the squat man above him. It was a terrible face, a scarred ruin, dark with an unaccountable hatred. A booted toe drove into his ribs. Breath exploded from him. He fought for air; it would not come. Only darkness and the boot again, dispassionately kicking the life from him.

• TWO •

Someone big had Mike by his collar, holding him up with one hand. Water had been poured over him until his hair hung in his eyes and his shoulders were soaked. He pawed away the hand at his collar, his legs stiffening, and opened his eyes, to see that he was in an unfamiliar room.

Red-faced from anger or exertion, an old man in a wide-shouldered, tight-fitting embroidered suit faced him. He was big, with a handsome, curly shock of white hair, a straight figure, and a large, blue-veined nose jutting from his florid face. He was Spanish.

"Where is it?" he demanded.

Mike raised his eyes past the old man. In the background, floating like a painting against the whitewashed plaster of the wall, was a girl with an arrogant regularity of feature and a startling cameo beauty. Mike coughed and the spasm sent agonies cutting through him. He turned his head and saw the man with the scarred face, the man with the knotted hemp and the boots.

"You dirty son of a bitch!" Mike said.

The back of the old man's hand slammed across his mouth.

"*Yanqui* pig! My daughter is present!"

"Want me to tell you what she is, too?"

The open hand struck again.

"Where is it?"

The man with the scarred face stepped close and pushed Mike tight against the wall at his back.

"I am Fiero." he said softly. "Use your tongue foolishly again and you die."

He ripped up the tail of Mike's shirt. broke the lacings of his moneybelt, and flung it on the table in the center of the room.

"What you want is there, *patrón*."

Mike watched the old man feverishly open the pockets of the belt. What he was looking for was not money, for he ignored the coins he spilled in his haste. Mike knew, then. They sought the deed to the Princesa. The anger he had known in the square before the Yankee House came flooding back.

"Where's Peyton? He wanted me. Now he's got me, hasn't he guts enough to come out where I can see him?"

The old man found the carefully oilskinned deed.

"You think we do this for Angus Peyton?" he asked, seeming surprised.

"Who else?"

"You do not know us?"

"No."

"Nicolo Delmonte—my daughter Felicia."

"Delmonte? The family that used to own the Princesa?"

"Señor Peyton took it from us a little more than a year ago," the old man said, "for a bill I could not meet at his suttler's store—a bill for a few hundreds of *yanqui* dollars."

"A thousand *yanqui* dollars, to be exact," the girl cut in.

"Yes, so little as that," the old man agreed bitterly. "And he transferred the *rancho* immediately to you, as we learned a few weeks later when we secured funds and wished to redeem it. Hardly news to you, *señor*."

"You damn bet it's news!" Mike said. "And if he only credited you with a thousand dollars, he made a nice profit. That deed cost me three thousand dollars—and I thought I was buying something else, at that."

Nicolo Delmonte studied him carefully.

"It is possible, I suppose. Angus Peyton is not noted for his honesty. If I remain dubious, *señor*, forgive me. Perhaps later we can make amends for Fiero's faithfulness in bringing you here when it was reported to him you had at

13

last returned to Monterey. He has watched many ships. Meanwhile, we can easily erase the other injustices each of us has suffered. My daughter and I are willing to return the three thousand dollars you say you gave Angus Peyton last year. It means we must secure a loan, but I think it can be arranged. You, of course, will sign our property back to us."

"You'd make up the extra two thousand Peyton pocketed? Just on my say-so that I gave it to him? Two thousand dollars is a lot of money, specially here."

"I relinquished the *rancho* to Peyton for a debt. My honor demanded it. The Princesa has long been the home of my family, although we have forsaken it in recent years for Monterey and Felicia's education. I wish to buy the *rancho* back for sentiment's sake."

"Two thousand dollars is a hell of a lot of sentiment!"

"It is worth it, *señor.*"

"Not to me."

The old man looked at his daughter. She nodded imperceptibly.

"Five thousand, then," he said heavily. "I beggar my daughter's future to make the offer."

Mike shook his head. "There's more than a ranch behind this," he said narrowly. "A hell of a lot more."

The girl met his eyes.

"You know. No need to pretend, now. A *vaquero* brought us the news from the North. But how could you have known so long ago—more than a year? And Peyton knew when he talked my father into putting the Princesa up to guarantee his debt. But how? This I do not understand."

"Know what?"

"That there is gold in every stream bed on the Princesa!"

Mike blinked incredulously.

"Gold?"

"It isn't only on the Princesa," Felicia Delmonte went on savagely. "That is what has betrayed you. A *yanqui* named Marshall found it in the race of Capitán Sutter's Coloma mill. Already the word is all over the North and riches have been found in other streams. Treasure—that is what you and Peyton have stolen from us!"

Mike leaned against the wall behind him for support.

Gold!

Half a million acres of gold—his! This was why Peyton was looking for him, too. This was what came of believing in dreams, of trying to make the best of a swindle, of clinging to a faint faith in the luck of the Irish. He looked at the three before him and grinned.

Delmonte slowly thrust the deed back into the money-belt and began returning the coins which had spilled from it. He spoke over his shoulder to Fiero.

"It grows late and the *yanqui* needs attention. We brought him to this house. Therefore he is our guest. See to his comfort."

The old man took his daughter's arm and they left the room together. When they were gone, Fiero motioned to Mike and led the way through another door into a narrow hall and up a steep back stairway. At the top of this he opened a door and Mike entered a large, airy bedroom, furnished with handmade pieces which had the glow and comfort of long usage for all their sparseness and spartan simplicity.

Fiero excused himself with a gesture and left, locking the door behind him. He returned in a few minutes with another servant and a water-laden, body-shaped copper tub. He also brought toweling and a long nightshirt of laundry-softened Cantonese silk. He retired again, sullenly, once more locking the door behind him.

It was the first bath Mike had been able to take since boarding the *Susan Winthrop*, and he relished it. The nightshirt was a little too much for him. He took to the blankets of the bed without its benefit. Before he was settled enough to blow out the lamp, the lock on the door rattled.

Felicia Delmonte entered. She relocked the door and approached the bed with a small medicine chest under her arm. She put this on the bedstand and took out phials and lint for dressings. Without a word she went to work on his battered features with the lint and an aromatic lotion which stung violently. Presently Mike found his facial discomfort much eased. The girl repacked the medicine chest and looked at him critically.

"You are not handsome," she said at length. "You are not much. A big man, strong—but had you been born a *californio* I think you would have been a fisherman. A *vaquero,* perhaps. Or a house servant. I can count twenty generations of the Delmonte—many of them on the Princesa. In your own country you could not have been better than you would have been here. How can such a one as you believe he has the right to a great *rancho*—to so much land—even to any land at all?"

"In my own country . . ." Mike said, his jaw set grimly, "In my country I was less than a fisherman or a servant. I was born in the worn-out heel of a shoe. I was born with no right to a roof over my head nor a bed nor food and clothes. No right to a job. No right even to life itself. In my country there are no rights like that. Life, liberty and the pursuit of happiness, they say. But it isn't so. Just one right. The right to what you can get. And I've got the Princesa."

"You whine and expect me to feel sorry for you," the girl said. "No one is born in the heel of a shoe."

"It's a saying. My mother worked the day I was born until she fainted with the pains and they carried her to a back corner of the loft where she was stitching sail."

"Your father?"

"Dead at sea before I was born. And my mother when I was eleven years old."

"Your family raised you, then."

"Sure. My family. The tarts and toughs of the Boston docks. Aunts and uncles. I love 'em all."

"You hate very much what you've been."

"I hate what made me what I've been, if that's what you mean."

"It isn't," Felicia said. "And I think you lie. I think you're proud of what you tell me."

"Proud!" Mike felt his anger rising again. "Sure," he said. "I'm proud as hell."

"I know," the girl said soberly. "I was, too, when we had the Princesa. I want it again, that pride. I can't tell you how much. I do not even know if I could show you how much."

Mike eyed her narrowly.

"But you might try?"

She met his look evenly.

"I might."

"For the Princesa?"

She smiled.

"Even my vanity is not that large. A share, only. For my father. The *rancho* is very dear to him."

"Your vanity is still too large for me," Mike said.

The girl shrugged.

"Then I am fortunate. You would not appreciate the sacrifice. It makes little difference. You will not keep the Princesa, you know."

She did not take the key nor turn the lock as she went out. Mike glowered after her a little, then snuffed the lamp. The sound of gold was in his ears and the taste of gold was upon his tongue as he drifted into sleep .

In the cell provided by his order near the chapel of his service, Father Bartolo lay in a sleep of the body which left the mind yet conscious. In this consciousness he dealt sadly with the allegiances which had been demanded of California during his own span. Old Spain. Then Mexico. Now the none-too-Christian republic far across the mountains to the east. He was grateful for the oath-bound habits of his own life and the fact that his own allegiance was to God. It was small wonder old generosities had vanished in these troubled times. Still a priest had his functions to perform.

He thought of the daughter of the Balanare—Beatriz. Hunger and desperation would soon force her beyond his good counsels. He could not deny this, nor could he truly blame. But there was a livelihood for her in the North if she had but travel funds. And as he had done each night for many days, Father Bartolo resolved to make extraordinary efforts on the morrow to find a good Samaritan who would grant him the funds the girl needed. His conscience over previous failures thus eased, Father Bartolo permitted his mind to sleep, also.

In the cheapest room in the La Fonda hotel there was no sleep for Alice Abernathy. She stood naked before a peeling mirror, kneading the imprint of corset stays from her firm, full body. A knock sounded on the door and a man called a question through the panel. She leaped across to the chair bracing the knob and shrilled a frightened refusal. The man went away.

She relaxed and returned to the mirror and dropped on her nightgown. Pulling out the pins, she let her hair down in the long cascade Emil had always said was more

17

beautiful than nakedness. She crossed slowly to the bed and turned it back. It smelled of the mud odor of the room and last year's fog and dust and loneliness. Suddenly she threw herself down across it and began to cry.

It was weak of her. She was ashamed for that. But she was so tired. Tired of lying even to herself, day after day. There were so many of them. There would be so many more. Emil was not waiting for her at San Francisco or Benicia or anywhere. How long since she had heard from him? Nearly two years. Not since he had reached California. She could not believe that he was dead, but she was days—weeks—from any chance of finding him. Her money was gone and she was occupying a room for which she could not pay.

The man came back along the hall and knocked again at her door, repeating his Spanish question. She wondered if it would be so terrible in a darkened room if one said yes and unbarred the door. She held her breath so she could make no answer.

In the hall the aged *pensionero* of La Fonda shrugged and went on about his business. Even the woman of the *yanquis* were incomprehensible. One asked a civil question as was one's duty with a new guest: "All is well with you, señora?" At first a cry with no meaning and now no sound at all. It would seem there should at least be courtesy among their women.

Breakfast was on the Delmonte house veranda. Neither Felicia nor her father were in evidence. The Indian woman who served Mike was too far lost in her own language difficulties to cope with his. In daylight Mike was acutely aware of the evidences of poverty about him. He knew poverty too well not to recognize it in any guise, even in this dilapidated shell of former opulence. Beyond the ruin of the garden was a low wall shutting off an adjoining property. This consisted of a bare, debris-laden earthen yard behind another large house, the rear wall of which was deeply scorched by fire. Mike had just realized with a start that this was the back side of the Yankee House when Nicolo Delmonte came out to join him.

"You slept well?"

"Late, anyway."

"I, also. In the old days this was the usual hour to rise. I do not easily break myself of old habits."

18

He offered Mike a cigar and a light. The tobacco was rank but the courtesy which accompanied it had the integrity of long tradition. The old man's eyes roved aimlessly. He gestured toward the back of Peyton's Yankee House.

"So many changes," he said. "That was once a great house, the house of friends. The Balanare."

"Not so fond of your present neighbor, eh?"

"No," Delmonte said. "Ramón Balanare had many cattle in those days. I slaughtered over four thousand head myself, one season. Ramón must have done much better than that in his best years. Then the fire. Ramón and the señora dead in it. A servant saves strange things in a fire. A little silver hollow-ware and a few bottles of brandy. The Balanare had a daughter, near Felicia in age. She survived to nothing. She is about, but she avoids old friends. She lives as she can, on pride, I think. But she cannot go on forever this way. I do not wish such a thing to happen to Felicia. It is because of this that I want the Princesa again."

"We settled that last night."

"I know," Delmonte agreed. "For now. The good God alone knows who will have the Princesa at last. I am content to let Him judge. But you are a wealthy man. I saw last night the moneys you carry with you. Your credits must be enormous. I have need of five thousand dollars."

"From me?" Mike was incredulous.

"A man must turn where he can. And, as I have said, you have means. For this I would agree to defend your title to my *rancho* against any enemy. You will have many of them, *señor*. The news of the gold is spreading. Soon not only the Californias but the whole world will know."

Mike made no reply.

"To you five thousand dollars is not much," Delmonte continued earnestly. "To me it is my life, my honor. I am penniless and I owe an obligation in that amount. If I do not pay it, my daughter must."

"Gambling?"

Nicolo Delmonte nodded.

"A last wager to correct all mistakes. A horse—at Carmela. My own horse. Certainly he must win. But he burst an artery in the neck. It is the wages of my sins that I must lose the animal, also. Now there is nothing but this house and my creditor has no desire for it."

"Peyton?"

"Who else in California could afford to wager such a sum against the last and best of the great Delmonte horses?"

"Wait a minute!" Mike said sharply. "Last night you talked of paying *me* five thousand dollars for the Princesa deed. Said you could borrow it. Borrow it now to cover your loss to Peyton."

"A little difficult," the old man said. "Angus Peyton would forgive the wager and pay five thousand besides for a share in the Princesa, once it was back in my hands. So long as you hold the title he will give me nothing."

Mike surveyed the old man with a sick feeling which made him angry. Embroidered suits and honor and hired thugs and easy daughters and houses empty of furniture, long ago sold out the back door. Gambling recklessly still, on past glories. Broken-down families and flexible pride which could not pass up the Yankee dollars it professed to scorn. The great *haciendados*. The genteel traditions of old California. All gone to hell like a drab in her thirtieth year. He stood up and flung his half-smoked cigar away.

"I don't have five thousand dollars," he said harshly. "Not in money and not in credits. If I did, I'd keep it. Where I come from, only the crippled and blind are beggars!"

Nicolo Delmonte turned blindly and entered the house. Mike slowly crossed the shabby garden and let himself out the street gate.

• THREE •

Mike strode down the center of the street to avoid the denser traffic of the walks. His freight was on the quay, subject to a small lightering charge for bringing it in from the ship. He paid this and briefly examined the stacked crating under a shedlike adjunct of the custom house.

The Boston firm of Halstead and Farady advertised themselves as vendors to the world. They had been very sure of Mike's principal requirements on a California ranch. They were similar to those of a missionary venture in the Cameroons which they had outfitted a few months previously. Mike found his scale was necessarily even smaller. The missionaries had more money than he did.

Even so, the outfit had taken every cent he could scrape together on his return to Boston: tools, the uses and names of many of which Mike did not know for certain: a hardware assortment—nails, fasteners, lags, bar iron and flat stock; medical kit, bedding, ducking and lighter yardages, assorted cordage; saddles, bridles, horse equipment; tinned staples and oil, lamps, and a thick cyclopedia of husbandry which Mike had seen and asked to have included; and a small case of various items labeled "trading goods" which the salesman had insisted upon as a necessary in traffic with natives. Thinking vaguely of Indians, Mike had allowed its inclusion.

Six or seven hundredweight of supplies, making a very poor showing, were stacked under the shed roof, when Mike remembered that with them he intended to forge an empire. He had a moment of thinking he was pretty much a damned fool—until he remembered the gold in the creeks of the Princesa.

He figured the load was not too much for a light wagon, even in rough country. He made arrangements for the storage of the crates until he could pick them up, and he turned back to the town.

Midway up the square containing the hotel, he encountered young Benson. He didn't at first recognize him. Benson had bought himself some new clothes—*californio* clothes, including a flat-crowned, wide-brimmed hat. The clothes made Benson look bigger and not so young. They gave him a swagger, even when seated. But the big change was not in clothes and carriage. Benson had shaved, or hired it done. And he had been to a surgeon. The deep, festered pits of his acne had been cleaned with sharp steel. They lay raw, open to the air. But the improvement in his appearance was startling. However, perhaps even this was not the big change in Benson.

21

He was sitting on a bench before a small *tienda,* legs sprawled out in the sun, elbows hooked on the back of the bench. His eyes brightened when he saw Mike. He caught Mike's arm.

"McGann! I'm glad to see you! Sit down!"

Mike sank down. "You're drunk," he told Benson.

"So drunk I'll never be sober again," Benson agreed, amiably exaggerating a self-evident fact. "Mr. McGann, I've lived my whole life in the last eighteen hours. Or I've never lived at all till now. And look at my shave. Some barber, huh? An Indian. Regular artist. Carved me up with a needle made out of a sliver off a razor. Claims in two weeks he'll have me looking human."

"It's an improvement," Mike conceded. Benson didn't hear.

"Know what started me off?" he went on. "A woman. Last night. Wonderful. Thought I was wonderful, too. Not one word about my face till this morning. Then she told me where to find this barber. Name's Lisa."

"Better go back to her. Get out of the sun and off the street till you sober up."

"Never going back," Benson said. "Ought to be a law about going back to good things. Never the same. I always want to remember this. Lisa. Why, you got no idea what she did for me. . . ."

Mike rose and moved off, leaving Benson still talking.

Presently Mike stepped out into the square facing the Yankee House. He had deliberately been forestalling the inevitable meeting with Angus Peyton. Too often before he had been betrayed into headstrong, reckless folly by the dark, lightly slumbering giant of his own anger. He judged he had cooled sufficiently now.

He passed through the doors and into the main room of Peyton's establishment. Across the front ran a balcony giving access to street rooms on the upper floor. A stair ascended one wall to this. As Mike headed for this stair, a man rose from a nearby table and intercepted him; a powerful, easy-moving man from the States.

"Where you think you're going?" he asked unpleasantly.

"Up there." Mike indicated the balcony.

"No you're not, mister."

"Why?"

"Because I'm here to see you don't."

Mike grinned. He took a step toward the stairs as though to by-pass the guard. When the man reached angrily for him, Mike pivoted, striking cleanly with the full weight of his body and instinctive accuracy. The man slammed back against the wall, his nose a ruin. He fumbled at his belt. Mike was ahead of him, lifting out the pistol there and ramming it into his belly.

"Upstairs ahead of me," he said. "Tell Peyton he's going to have to hire bigger men than you if he wants to keep me away."

The dazed guard stumbled obediently up the steps. Peyton was waiting at the balcony landing. He was a big man, a little younger than Mike, with a broad, open face and sharp, intelligent eyes. A singularly handsome man, a little soft in the body, but powerfully made. The only change Mike could see in the past year was a little additional weight.

"Go clean yourself up, Sawyer," Peyton said to the guard.

Mike caught the man's arm as he started away and shoved the gun back into his hand.

"You may need this," he said.

The man took the gun and moved off.

"You're a lurid bastard, aren't you, McGann?" Peyton said with distaste. "Come on in. I've been looking for you."

"So I heard," Mike said.

He followed Peyton into a long, low room which was at once office and sleeping quarters. It was furnished in a style Mike had never before seen equaled. He thought he knew now where some of the fine furniture sold out of the back doors of the distressed old homes of Monterey had gone. It was the kind of room, the kind of surroundings Mike wanted for himself; the kind he had always wanted. But there were oddments among the furniture and decorations, the nature and usage of which he did not know. Obviously Peyton did. He pushed a pair of chairs up to a low table, dropping into one and leaving Mike to stand or sit as he elected.

"I hear you spent the night with the Delmontes," Peyton said, with a small, wicked smile. "Your face looks like it. I suppose by now you know as much as Felicia and the old man do about the gold on their old *rancho*. Nobody knows too much, yet. But whoever winds up owning the Princesa is going to be one of the most important men in California. This morning that means you. Tonight it may mean me."

"Not tonight, Peyton. Not any night."

"I can be patient," Peyton said with a shrug. "I've done a lot of thinking since the gold was discovered and I knew you'd be back."

"And I'm going to stomp hard. Don't get in my way, Peyton!"

"You haven't a chance in the world of surviving and holding your title to the Princesa," Peyton said wearily. "I'm not sure I would, either, and I'm better equipped for it than you. But there's a complimentation between us—though I warn you now I'll deny it socially till the day you die—and we might do it together."

"A partnership with you—in exactly what?"

"California. All of California, McGann."

"You're crazy!"

"I have imagination. So have you. Use it! Look at the situation. Courts and commissions will eventually have to discover that Spanish and Mexican titles to most of the valuable property here are valid. Bankers and speculators will find that much of the wealth—aside from the unpredictable factor of this gold strike—is in Spanish hands. And politicians, when they get us functioning as a state and start appraising voting strength, aren't going to be able to juggle district and precinct boundaries enough to prevent these same Spanish-Mexicans from being the single largest bloc in the state—if they vote together. Get their friendship and trust and you've got them. Get them and you've got California."

"I've got the Princesa. That's enough for me. And you sure haven't got the Delmontes. They're going to wear boots made out of your hide."

"I had to break them up enough for them to need friends before I could be one. Don't worry. I'll have them."

"And me and the Princesa, too?"

"To do what I want will take a lot of time—maybe five years—and more money than either of us can dream. This tavern of mine lets me operate on a small scale and gives me a legitimate business to cover up anything else. But I'm limited. With what the Princesa can produce in

24

the next few years, we can swing the whole thing and do it right."

Mike leaned back in his chair. Peyton didn't know what power was. To be able to do what he was going to do now was the real power. Mike exercised it with relish.

"No," he said.

Peyton stared at him a moment, face flushing, then sagged back.

"You're ambitious," he said. "You have to be."

"A man like you, Peyton, can't ever know the ambition of a man like me," Mike said slowly.

"You're an absolute intellectual bankrupt if you can't see the value of this partnership, McGann!"

"Partners are friends," Mike said. "They have to be. Men who can trust each other and who do. I don't trust you and you'd be a damned fool to trust me."

"Felicia and the old man will fight. Fiero will fight for them. He was born on the Princesa. He's worked for Nicolo all his life. The old man's a god to him and he hates Yankees. A bunch of drunken sailors jumped him one night when they were trailing 'Licia. Kicked him to pieces. You've seen his face. He doesn't forget. He's deadly."

"I can get kind of hostile myself."

"No?"

"No."

"I'm sorry, McGann," Peyton said. "Really sorry."

"Don't take it to heart," Mike told him. He rose. "These little disappointments may make a man of you yet."

He crossed to the door and let himself out onto the balcony.

• FOUR •

Mike entered the biggest suttler's store in town, blandly ignoring the fact it was likely the Peyton establishment. He ordered a saddle, a slightly built and sadly used wagon, and secured the promise of four draft horses and a saddle animal, due in from the country the next day. Horses and wagons were dear in Monterey and his moneybelt held barely enough coin to cover the purchases. He shrewdly retained the cash on his person until he had seen the horses in the morning.

Purchasing and bargaining done, he found himself hungry and tired and turned toward the hotel. However, as he was about to enter, he saw Mr. Jeffers and the Abernathy woman and young Benson at supper, and he knew he would be obliged to join them. This prospect rendered the accommodations of La Fonda too bleak for him.

A perversity turned him down the narrow little street of women. With the waning light, many doorways were open, framing smiles and invitation. He wondered which of these girls was the Lisa whom Benson had found and to whom he would not return, in order to preserve a memory. He was nearly back to the square facing the Yankee House when he saw the door of the small, detached shack at the end of the row of cells was open. The same girl stood there, the one he had seen when he passed through with McCracken. He did what he had done before. He touched his hat.

"Why do you do that?"

He gave her the same answer he had given McCracken. "A thing of beauty is a joy to behold."

"You do not say it right," the girl corrected. "A thing of beauty is a joy forever."

"Forever is too permanent. Actually I'm looking for something to eat and a place to sleep."

26

She eyed him carefully.

"That is all?"

"That's all," he agreed.

"Something to eat would be beautiful to me, too."

Mike moved toward her. She hesitated a moment, then stepped back into the shack. Mike followed her, closing the door behind him. She crossed to a smaller duplicate of the conically crowned fireplace in the public room of the hotel. Embers here imparted warmth to the shack's single room but gave off no light. Mike did not like the dark. A lamp stood on a rickety stand beside the door. He lighted it.

An incongruous iron Pittsburgh bed occupied one corner of the room. It was neatly made and spread with a coverlet whose faded colors made Mike think with equal incongruity of something he had avoided remembering for a long time: a wan woman with jet hair and ivory skin and crystalline blue eyes, lying in fever. His mother had been very beautiful, even in death; more beautiful and almost as young as this dark girl watching him from the bench beside the fire.

"What's the matter?" he asked her. "Is it your saint's day?"

"I do not understand."

"You aren't working. . . ."

"Working . . . ?" the girl frowned. "Because I live on a street of women, you think I am one of them?"

Mike grinned at her. "You are not one of them. You live here by accident."

"Yes," the girl said. Her eyes flashed angrily. "I live here by a number of accidents."

"What do they call you?"

"In Spanish, Beatriz. In *yanqui* . . ." she shrugged, "many things. You want to know the first *yanqui* words I learned?"

"Beatriz—Bea is easier."

"I tell you I am not an easy woman."

"Sure, sure," Mike agreed. "Got anything to drink?"

The girl studied him a long time.

"I have a little wine," she said finally.

She rose and went through a curtain into an alcove, returning with a tall, unlabeled bottle and a metal goblet of florid design, much dented by hard usage. She put these on the table.

"Are you not the one called Miguel McGann?"

Mike nodded, considerably surprised.

"You own the Delmonte *rancho*."

He nodded again.

"Angus Peyton is your enemy."

"He seems to be getting that reputation," Mike said.

"He is my enemy, too."

She poured the wine. Mike tasted it and found to his astonishment it was not wine at all, but a fine, high, heady brandy. No rum or whiskey he had ever touched could match it. His tongue wiped his lips appreciatively. The goblet in his hand caught and held his attention. He bore hard against a floral detail with a blunt thumbnail and a rose leaf bent.

"Silver!" he said.

"King's silver—from Potosi," Beatriz agreed. "Made by a Balanare in Panama, more than a hundred years ago."

The name stirred a memory. Balanare. His mind absently began to gnaw upon it as he lifted the goblet again. Beatriz Balanare. Neighbors to Nicolo Delmonte. The family whose fire-gutted home had become the Yankee House. Old Delmonte had tried to borrow five thousand dollars to save his daughter from following the path of this one.

"Why go to Peyton?"

"When one wishes water, one goes to the well. I needed money. There is Father Bartolo—this place here belongs to the Church and he lets me have it. But even the Church has no money. There was only Angus Peyton."

"And he turned you down."

"I have opportunity for good work in the North. I needed a little for suitable clothes and for travel. Peyton tells me he has waited long for me to come to him. He is amused. I have been stubborn. If I want money, let me earn it, first. And why go north? There is work here I can do well. Who knows—perhaps I will even enjoy it. He will put me in the upstairs of his Yankee House to please men. He will put me in the very room where I was born. This also amuses him. He will advertise the Balanare has come home and there will be a lottery for the first night. My anger amuses him, too. He laughs when I leave. He knows I will have to come back."

Mike scowled darkly. If the girl was telling him the truth, he did not like Peyton's humor. But this was not something in which to involve himself.

"When do we eat?" he asked.

"Money . . ." the girl said.

He produced a half-eagle he could ill afford. Beatriz took the coin and turned it over in her hand, studying both sides.

"I want enough of these to choke them. I want to see them strangle and crowd in more yellow coins until gold pours from their eyes and nostrils. I want to bury them in money. I want to bury them so deeply in money they are not even remembered. I want to sleep in money and bathe in money!"

Mike understood her bitterness and desire. And there was something wonderful in the thought of her bathing in golden coins and sleeping beneath a minted blanket.

He tossed off the rest of the goblet of brandy and peeled off his coat while she watched with widening eyes. He shed his waistcoat and shirt and unlaced the money-belt and opened it pocket by pocket onto the bed until a heap of coinage lay there and the belt was empty. A few hundred dollars, the dregs of his accumulation, multiplied the effect it created by the fact it had come from many small sources. He had already spent the larger pieces, so what was left was of small denomination. Beatriz looked at the horde in wonder.

"*Santa Maria!*" she gasped.

Mike laughed at her incredulity. She looked from him to the gold, and finally she laughed, also. Then she suddenly seized him and kissed him full on the mouth—a quick kiss with no woman in it, only elation. She ran into the alcove and returned with another tall bottle of brandy. She pressed this into his hands.

"There is no more Valenciano. Make this last. I promised you supper. I will be back quickly."

She seized up a small handful of coins and darted out of the door.

Mike put a knot on the fire and warmed himself before it, easing the cork from the second bottle of brandy. He had finished another goblet when Beatriz returned. She was carrying a basket of food. She took this into the alcove, along with the lamp, and set busily to work. Presently she came out with a pot to hang on the crane over the fire.

"Money buys much in Monterey," she said. "It is not

29

good to be hungry. The padres do not understand this. They give what they have, but it is food for the soul. Can a soul ache like the belly?"

"I don't know. I'm not sure I have one."

"Of course," Beatriz agreed. "You are rich. What need do you have of a soul?"

She began to hum a little as she minded the pot on the crane and began to set out a supper of some kind of chowder which smelled as delicious as the brandy had tasted. Then she sat opposite him and they ate ravenously and in silence. Presently the pot was empty and Mike leaned back, abrim with contentment for the first time in many months. The girl across from him seemed equally at ease. Perhaps it was only the physical comfort of the meal, but a tenseness was gone from her and he realized she was beautiful. She had a dark and gentle beauty, even a sad one; but without the softness of temperament an Irishman could not abide. There was hardness in her, if the need was for hardness. But she had no vanity in it, only a knowledge of its usefulness.

"How much do you need?" he asked her suddenly.

"How much?" She did not understand.

"Money."

She was startled. At first she could not believe. Then full realization of what lay behind the question came.

"You—you would let me have it?"

"How much?" Mike asked again.

He knew this was the brandy talking. He knew he was doing something he could not do. But he could not suppress it. Maybe it was the coverlet on the bed, or the long, desperate unhappiness in the dark eyes across from him. He wondered how often the possession of a few metal coins had determined the difference between a saint and a sinner.

"I—I think fifty dollars. But it is much money. . . ."

Mike rose and went across to the bed. He pawed carelessly through the heaped coins, finding two gold eagles and a new, mint-bright half. He brought them back to the table. Beatriz closed her hand over them and looked up at him.

"Why?" she asked.

"What difference does it make?"

"There has to be a reason. I—I have to know."

30

"Maybe because you didn't ask me what a *yanqui* pig was going to do with the Delmonte *rancho*."

The smile came again.

"I think I would like to know about the Princesa now. Sit down. Tell me. I want to listen."

She pushed the bench nearer to the fire and made room for him. Mike sat beside her. There was no wariness in her, no hardness. A measuring, perhaps. Interest, certainly. And because of this, he began to talk.

Beatriz was against his shoulder and his arm was about her. The lamp flickered for want of oil and went out, and still he talked. When he was empty of words and plans and came to an end, he found Beatriz was asleep. She roused as he lifted her.

"I believe you," she murmured.

She lay against him and he carried her to the bed. The coin-weighted coverlet was in his way. Holding her in one arm, he stripped it back, sending a musical metal cascade to the floor. He lowered Beatriz and stretched beside her, holding her gently close to him. The gentleness was foreign to his desire, but she had said she believed and he could not be otherwise. Until tonight he had not wholly believed in his plans for the Princesa, himself—and news of the gold had made them even more difficult to cling to. Now he could hold to them as he held to the girl in his arms.

Sleep was long in coming, for there was a great gentleness and awe to spend in the warm darkness of the little room.

Mike awakened with a throbbing head and the thick, dry taste of old grapes in his mouth. As his eyes focused, he discovered he was alone. Rolling from the bed, he discovered likewise that the coins he had scattered on the floor in last night's grandiloquence had been carefully gleaned. Not a one remained.

Beatriz was gone and the money was gone and he was a drunken sailor in a woman's room in a distant port, possessor of a hazy recollection of brief splendor and an ugly hangover and nothing else. Unsteady, seething with loss and fury, Mike was seized with nausea. He made the door and stood retching in the opening in undress. As the nausea subsided, a man approached; a small, handsome man, with a devil in his eyes which belied the brown Franciscan habit he wore. Mike glared at him.

31

"The wages of sin?" the padre suggested. "May I come in?"

"Alms?" Mike grunted sourly. "Maybe I could do with a little penance, Father. But I couldn't even buy breakfast!"

"The day often looks darkest at dawn," the priest said.

He stepped past Mike into the little room. Unknotting the cord girdling his cassock, he lifted this to reveal a fine pair of runner's legs and raw silk undersuiting. Unfastening Mike's moneybelt from about his own waist, he handed it across.

"She asked me to return it and explain," he said.

Mike hefted the belt. The priest's eyes darkened.

"The money is all there—except what you paid her as fee."

"Fee!" Mike said sharply. "It was a gift!"

The priest looked unconvinced.

"So she told me, *señor*. The rest of the money—she brought it to me, since she didn't know how long you would sleep and there are many prowlers in this alley."

"She could have waited!"

"You forget it is past midmorning. A party was leaving quite early for Benicia. She wished to travel with it. As I said, she asked me to explain."

"To get work in the North?"

"Yes. To get out of Monterey. There are many sad memories for her here. I would have sent her before but for the money."

"Where has she gone?"

"She left me no instructions to tell you that," the priest said.

"In other words, I've got all I'm going to get," Mike said.

The priest's eyes ever so briefly touched the bed in the corner.

"You've already had more than your right," he said.

Mike glared at him. He knew a priest neither hated nor envied his fellow man, yet the taint of hatred and envy was in the room. He thrust a finger into a pocket of the moneybelt and brought out a coin. It was a half-eagle, more generous than he intended, but he handed it across. The priest took it and moved to the door.

"Thank you, Father," Mike said.

The priest looked at him, said nothing, and went out.

Mike dressed swiftly and went back to the suttler's store. The horses were in from the country, but the draft team were different animals than the trader had anticipated, and their price was higher. Counting what remained in the moneybelt, Mike could not meet the price. He was forced to forego team and wagon and so leave his little pile of freight under the custom-house shed until he could find means to move it. Settling for saddle and saddle horse, he rode into the cypress hills back of the town, heading for the distant mountains where McCracken and the Princesa were awaiting his arrival.

• FIVE •

First there was a belt of green fog country, lifting back from the sea in gentle, rising convolutions to a distant line of blue mountains. It was a day's ride from Monterey to these. From their summits the land fell away again eastward instead of rising as expected, on toward the great peaks of the Sierra Nevada. This falling away was into a great bowl of a plain, green at this season with winter rains which spilled over the coastal mountains. But bones of old growth spoke plainly of arid months and brassy heat and seasons of drought.

To the north on a clear day was visible an area of tule swamp and backwater, lower tip of a bay system so huge it was an inland sea. San Francisco lay somewhere on this —Benicia and the Golden Gate. From this immense lagoon a broad snake of permanent green marked the variant courses of the San Joaquin; not the great Sacramento, since this was a land of distance and the Sacramento was much farther north and east. The San Joaquin was the only living water visible on the great plain of its valley and for two endless days Mike McGann and his horse were the only visible living creatures.

33

Far beyond the middle course of the sandy river, floating above a haze which hung over the vague eastern edge of the valley, there rose a different world: the granite core of the earth, thrust skyward to ice and snow; Sierra Nevada, mother of gold.

Toward this they all moved.

There were the Russian expatriates, unable to leave the land they had married when Baranof sold the Czar's Fort Ross farms to John Augustus Sutter; also early comers who had heard John Charles Frémont's exaggerated, acquisitive passion for the land of California a full year—or even two—before Jim Marshall found yellow metal in Sutter's Coloma millrace.

Wandering stock traders and horse thieves made a good thing of driving California horses eastward across mountains and deserts for sale to cavalry remount stations in Kansas and Missouri. Trappers, searching for one more valley from which to take beaver and one more canyon where the camps of their kind had never been before, came to the Pacific—to the end of America and of their trade. It was a frontier which had been their private challenge for two hundred years.

Seamen, escaping the purgatory of a return doubling of the brutal Horn, adopted this new land of soft-eyed women and gentle weather and untroubled equality. Wagon men followed incredibly close behind the trappers with their women and their children and their plows, carrying with them the seed of the soil and the seed of their bodies, to be planted wherever they should halt and raise fencing.

The lost and the fugitive and the forgotten halted at the barrier of the Pacific.

Up from the South they came, by the long route across Sonoran deserts; down through the great coastal timber from the valley of the Columbia; by sea and the high, bitter passes of the Sierra. The rest of the country had not yet heard of the gold. These were the lucky ones, and Mike McGann was among them. They had come seeking something else and they were here, and theirs was the first chance at the gold.

Four men were occupying the old Delmonte 'dobe on the ranch when Mike McGann rode out of a hot-foothill afternoon to the wide veranda of the sprawling six-room house. The place was half in ruins, and those who had pre-empted it had made no improvement. Two of the men were in the shade of the veranda. The other two came up from the wash below the orchard, where they were working gravel. They heard Mike out and looked at his deed.

"Don't have to read this to know it's worthless," one said. "Don't cover mineral rights. They're public property. We filed on 'em legal at the miner's court over to Freezer's Bar. Suppose you get to hell out of here."

All four wore guns. Mike asked about McCracken. None had seen a stranger of his description. Mike was worried about Mac, and he couldn't face down four guns. He got out.

Three miles above the house he discovered a dam across the stream which should have been running in the wash below the orchard. There were upward of a dozen men here, running the impounded water off onto a sandy flat, cut by shallow trenches and rigged with crude troughs. Mike inquired of them the way to Freezer's Bar and rode on without mentioning his deed. He detoured around two more camps before he reached the confluence of the Conejos and Spittin' Jim Creeks, as directed, and rode into the mired street of tents and shanties for which he was searching.

Some questioning along the street resulted in a session of the miner's court of Freezer's Bar in the principal canvas saloon. Three of the five men composing it drank his whiskey and listened to his case. He was told that one of the missing pair of judges was dead and his successor had not yet been chosen. The other was out working his claim. The soberest of the three hearing Mike was Smiley Palmer, a small, alert man with myopic eyes and an untrimmed beard. He took a badly bent pair of spectacles from his pocket and carefully read every line of the Princesa deed. He folded it carefully along old creases and handed it back.

"Mighty interestin'," he said. "What's it say?"

Mike translated as accurately as possible.

"What you want us to do?" Palmer asked.

"Plain enough, isn't it? Cancel the claims you've given out on my land. Run the trespassers off."

"Just where's this land of yours begin?" Palmer said

35

judiciously. "Nothin' more mixed up than the Mexican that deed's written in. Seems to me the meets don't meet the bounds."

"The boundaries aren't marked exactly, I suppose," Mike agreed. "If they were, I wouldn't know where to look for them."

"Tough luck, Son," Palmer said.

"You won't do anything?"

"We can't. You need a survey afore you need a court. We ain't actually judges, anyhow. Plain miners, tryin' to protect our rights and keep some kind of order. This ain't our line."

"It's got to be somebody's!" Mike protested.

"You got somethin' mighty big there if somebody hasn't sold you a piece of paper," Palmer said earnestly. "Get a survey, first. Locate and post your boundaries. Then get back to the Coast. Don't count on no camp courts like this one. Get those lardbutts in Monterey to puttin' us a government together. Write Washington. Raise hell. Get your title approved by a legal court that can make it stick. Maybe then you can run everybody else off. I don't know."

Palmer and his two companions stood up, court thus summarily dismissed. The proprietor of the saloon put himself between Mike and the door until he collected for the drinks representing court costs at two dollars and a half a throw. Palmer stopped beside Mike at the door.

"I hear they's a feller got a surveyin' instrument up Spittin' Jim Creek," he said. "Called the Dutchman, I think."

He and his two companions went on. Mike ordered a meal next door to the saloon and was halfway through a steak with relish before he discovered it was bear and the price was six dollars. A woman passed along the street outside and he blinked in surprise until he realized she was the first he had seen in the camp. A man beside him grinned.

"Ma Finney," he said. "Got five boys, workin' a claim together. Best one in the district. Real busted-nail miners, includin' the old lady."

"Freezer's Bar," Mike said. "Hell of a name!"

The man shrugged.

"Got to call her somethin'. Get out waist-deep in that

36

water and shovel gravel into a sluice or a Long Tom trough all day an' you'll see why-for the name. Them creeks is liquid ice."

Mike finished his steak and left. Three shanties down he bought a rifle, powder and caps. The rifle looked like a good weapon. The pawnbroker assured him it was, and he was getting it at a third of its going price in Kansas City. He pointed to a makeshift rack of weapons of every description.

"A pick or a pan or a shovel I can't keep," the broker said. "Can't even get my hands on 'em. But everybody hocks guns. They're crazy, too. A man with a little sand in his craw could get him more with a gun than a shovel any day."

"Somebody'll think of it," Mike assured him. "There's supposed to be a Dutch surveyor up Spittin' Jim Creek. Know where?"

"Sure. Up a ways is a side canyon drifting south. Take it. You'll hit a Mexican place. Ask there. They'll tell you how to get on to the Dutchman's."

"Thanks. Know the country, don't you?"

"Got to. I take risks on loans. Got to know the country."

"Ever hear of the Delmonte *rancho*—the Princesa grant?"

"Can't say I ever did. Where is it?"

"You're standing on it," Mike told him, and he went back out onto the street.

Riding up the Spittin' Jim, Mike saw further compounding of his problems. He had welcomed the gold, but he had not anticipated men would come in such numbers, so soon. At every turn of the stream, where rock formations entrapped sands, the banks had been hastily scratched over. Appearances indicated a hundred men or so were already in the self-appointed district centering on Freezer's Bar. They were now hurrying from one promising location to another, unable to settle down because there was no pressure of competition. Confused, excited, unstable, they found gold wherever they looked.

Smiley Palmer's advice might hold if this didn't change. A judicial order from a stable state or territorial government could probably dispossess a hundred men. But what would happen if the discovery kept on mushrooming?

What if there were a thousand men in the district—ten thousand? A government which attempted to oust so many, regardless of the justice involved, might topple itself. For the first time the full enormity of the challenge he had accepted began to dawn on Mike. He was a little frightened, but he clung to one thought. Many of the men of Freezer's Bar were on his land, and they had to leave it.

He turned off into the side canyon as the pawnbroker had directed and near dark rode into the yard before a low, flat-roofed adobe on a bench above a tributary trickle of water. A small orchard lay behind the one-room house, with old trees, carefully pruned and well-tended. Beyond this lay a few acres in field, winter growth turned under and the furrows not yet resown. Another planting made a regular pattern on a cleared patch of sandy soil a little downstream from the house. It was a slope certain to get the full impact of the blazing foothill sun. Belatedly Mike realized the scrubby, shapeless plantings were grapes, just leafing into first vine.

He dismounted at a rail some distance from the house and started across the yard afoot. He had gone several paces when a big dog came around from the rear and stood near the door. A deep growl sounded as Mike approached. He grinned at the wary animal.

"Hello, my friend," he said in primer Spanish. "I am late for dinner; that is why you scold?"

The dog's ears came forward and his head cocked to one side. His tail began to wag a little.

Mike heard a giggle and looked up. A woman stood in the doorway of the house, smiling—a girl, really, warm and young and attractive. Mike removed his hat.

"Animals are wonderful," he said, indicating the dog, now leaning in heavy affection against his leg. "They understand my bad Spanish. I think they like it."

"We all like it when Spanish speaks itself with a *yanqui*," the young woman said. "You will come in, *señor*? It is not too late for supper."

"I made a joke about the supper," Mike explained. "For my friend, here. I am trying to find the way to the Dutchman—the surveyor."

"Tomorrow," the young woman said. "It grows too late to go farther. Come in. Make yourself welcome to the house of Murietta."

Mike glanced about uncomfortably.

"But your—your husband . . ."

She moved aside. Another figure, a young man, joined her in the doorway—perhaps of the same stock as Nicolo Delmonte, for he stood very tall and straight. He was tall and proud and handsome, with a prideful, possessive arm about his young wife.

"I am Joaquin," he said. "Please to come in."

After the meal Murietta went out with Mike to put up his guest's horse for the night. They turned the horse in with several others in a small pole corral behind the house. Remembering how much the animal had cost him in Monterey and the number of strangers in the hills. Mike inquired of thieves. Murietta smiled.

"My friends do not steal. The others know Joaquin would kill the man who touched what was his. Thieves are no trouble."

"What about the gold, Joaquin—for you?" Mike asked. "Isn't working the creeks easier than farming?"

"It is a saying among my people that anything is easier than farming—unless one likes it," Joaquin answered. "But who can eat gold? It is only for getting rich. Is a rich man happier than me? If I have a full belly, can he put more food in his? Can he ride more than one horse at a time? Can he sleep with more than one woman? No, señor. It is better to be Joaquin!"

The *californio* led the way back into the house. His wife was making up a pallet across the room from their own bed. She had built the supper fire up a little against the increasing night chill. Murietta dumped Mike's saddle beside his own, back of the door, and gestured Mike toward two small benches flanking the fire. Mike dropped onto one of these. Murietta took the other, scowling thoughtfully.

"I have been thinking, Señor Miguel. Is it possible to see this deed you told me of?"

For the third time this day Mike produced the Princesa document. Murietta studied it at length before handing it back.

"You do not know the boundaries, of course. It would require much measuring to know the full truth. But how far into the mountains do you think the *rancho* goes?"

"It says 'to the line of the second hill.' Something like

that. I think it means to the second range of foothills—just short of the big range, the Sierra."

"Then this house is on your land," Murietta said quietly.

His wife instantly dropped her work and came to stand defensively behind him, her hands on his shoulders.

Mike had for some time been aware of the conclusion Murietta had just reached. All of the time the man had proudly spoken of his fields, his home, and his prized permanence here, Mike had known he was talking about things which did not actually belong to him. A feeling of guilt went with the knowledge. There was an air of perfection and happiness here. It clung to Murietta and his wife and even Tito, the dog. Now it must be destroyed. Mike nodded.

"I am afraid so. Near as I can tell."

Tears started to course down the woman's cheeks. No outcry. No vituperative protest. Just the immense sorrow of silent tears. Murietta pressed her hand comfortingly. Mike looked away.

"Look," he said suddenly. "Is there any sign of gold in that little branch out front?"

"I do not know 'branch.' "

"The creek—the little creek—is there gold in it?"

"I don't know," Murietta answered. "I've never looked. Water is all we want. Water is all we'll ever want."

"I know that!" Mike said harshly.

He stood up, his back turned to Murietta and his wife, so that they could not see his face.

"I'd say a section would cover all you've developed here—six hundred and forty acres—with the house in the center."

He turned back to face them.

"We'll figure out how the lines should run in the morning."

Dodging out from behind her husband, the woman ran to Mike. Not knowing what to expect, he self-consciously opened his arms to receive her. Instead she caught one of his hands and knelt before him. Mike would have raised her, but he didn't quite know how. Murietta surged white-faced from his bench. He seized his wife and jerked her to her feet.

"Don't ever do that again—to anybody!" he said raggedly.

He looked fiercely at her for a moment more, then the strained whiteness faded from his face. He bent and kissed her gently. She smiled and he pushed her grandiosely from him.

"Tonight we shall get drunk!" he announced. "Make your duties, woman. We have a friend in the house!"

Mike wondered if there was only brandy in California. He kept turning the flavor over on his tongue, hardly listening to Murietta, on the other side of the fire. Was it the same, or only the error of an untrained palate? Was it the Valenciano from a silver mug he was thinking of, or was it Beatriz Balanare?

"My grandfather came here first," Murietta was saying. "My father was born in a house now gone. In time the family left. My wife's uncle came to this place later, when it had been long abandoned. The two families did not know each other. When the uncle died, my wife's father took his house—which was this place—and raised his family. My wife was born in this room."

"In that bed," the young woman said pridefully, pointing.

"Her mother died and her father went to work for the missions, taking his family to Sonoma. I met her there and we were married nearly two years ago. We came back here because it was an old home of our people. It was in ruin, but my wife knows how to make a home comfortable, Miguel."

"It's yours, now," Mike said. "This—this brandy. I think I've tasted it before."

"How does it remind you?" Murietta asked with interest.

"Something I had in Monterey. Called Valenciano, I think."

Murietta and his wife beamed.

"We have old vines on the hill," Murietta said, "brought by the grandfather from Spain. We have cared for them and they bear well again. They are the true Valenciano grape, but there is a difference of sun and soil. The wine differs a little, and the brandy. I did not think a *yanqui* could tell the grape from it."

Mike did not think it necessary to explain there was a special reason for remembering the Valenciano, but he did

41

not realize he had fallen silent for a long time. He realized with a start that the fire had burned low and the Muriettas had slipped off to bed. He crossed quietly to the pallet prepared for him. He heard the snap of the fire; the scratching of the big dog across the door; soft whispers of movement from the other corner of the room. Spanish sounds—Yankee sounds—sounds of the earth. He lay contentedly in the dark, listening without embarrassment to the lovemaking between Murietta and his woman, remembering again Monterey.

Later, when there was silence and there was yet no sleep for him, he thought of the promise he had made the Muriettas. A whole square mile of the Princesa gone in his first day in the mountains. A whole section gone before he even knew the true extent of his possession. All for shaken pride in a dark-skinned man's eyes. For a woman's silent tear. For nothing, actually, but a meal and a bed and a bottle of brandy. Twice now he had paid well for such comfort.

He grunted in monosyllabic self-condemnation and rolled over, drifting shortly into sleep.

• SIX •

An hour above Murietta's, following the little creek, Mike rode out of brush verging into pine timber to an open park or glade of half a dozen acres. Unlike the lower valleys, the grass was green here. The hot foothill sun persisted, but timber softened it to pleasant warmth. From the center of the park a vista opened eastward through intervening ridges to the high, white minarets of the Sierra. On the far side of the park was a camp, a large tent pitched over a hand-slabbed wooden floor. Beside the tent was a pole shelter, a shade roof without walls, and the smoke of a morning fire rose from it. Mike rode up.

A man was at breakfast under the pole shelter. A woman came curiously out of the tent at Mike's approach. She was young. Spanish and pregnant. But it was the man who fascinated Mike. He wore cowhide *huaraches* on large bare feet. His single article of clothing was a pair of clean, faded khaki pants, whacked off at the knees. He was tall, spare, perhaps forty years of age. His features were neither strong nor regular. An overbite and prominent front teeth gave an impression of vapidity contradicted by widely spaced, deep-set eyes. He came out from under the shelter to greet Mike.

"Can I do something for you?"

"I'm looking for a surveyor, called the Dutchman."

"Dutch is what they call me. But I'm no surveyor. Light down for coffee."

Mike dismounted and followed the man into the shelter. The woman went to a fireplace of loose stones and picked up a tin cup from a cloth-covered stack of camp dishes on a flat rock. She brought the pot, also, and set both on the table.

"My woman," the Dutchman said. "Her name is Maria."

"Mine's McGann," Mike said. "I need a surveyor."

"I told you—I'm not."

Mike's eyes drifted to a transit, indifferently covered by a piece of canvas. "Whose instrument is that?"

The man grinned.

"I'm an engineer, not a surveyor. A free man and a happy one. I'm a philosopher. This is my world. I love it. No fears, no worries, no enemies. Monarch of all I survey."

"Interesting," Mike commented. "I have something in my pocket says you're not."

Sharp concern showed in the Dutchman's eyes.

"Says I'm not what?" he asked.

"Monarch of all you survey."

Separating the copy of the holographic deed he had executed to the Muriettas from the Princesa papers, he handed the latter across. The Dutchman looked at them, then whistled softly.

"This thing bona fide?"

Mike nodded.

"You do need a surveyor!"

"When can you start work?"

"Sorry, McGann," the Dutchman said. "No work for me. I was lucky enough to be in on one of the first strikes. Nothing fabulous, but enough to buy thirty or forty acres from you when you can prove your title, since I'm apparently on your place. Enough to keep me here."

"Where can I find another instrument man?"

"Connecticut, maybe—or New Jersey."

"Looks like I can't sell you any land, then. But I might make this piece here a bonus for a good, fast job."

"You actually serious about trying to validate title and hold this *rancho* of yours together?"

"Turn me down and see how fast I move you out of here!"

"It's impossible!" the Dutchman protested. "Sure—you can move me out. I'm not panning gold. But there's men all over these hills. What can you do about them?"

"Maybe lease claims to a few. Maybe even sell a few, if the price is right—I'm going to need money to operate. Run off those who ignore my title and my rights."

The Dutchman rose and came around the table to sit on the near edge of it.

"I'm going to tell you something, McGann. I've had a good, long, impersonal look at quite a bit of this hill country. And I know something about mines. That's why I can guarantee if you're successful you'll be sole owner of one of the richest areas of surface mineralization the world has ever seen. I give you my opinion, gratis— this country is in for the damndest gold rush there ever was. Make this land grant of yours stick and you'll be the richest man on earth!"

Mike could feel the man's honesty and his doubt of Mike, himself. He shrugged.

"Worth making a try for, then, isn't it?"

"No!" the Dutchman said, banging his fist down earnestly. "Write me off as crazy, but you're the one not using his head! Nobody has to be rich. Nobody should ever want to be. With just enough for physical needs, a man keeps his belief, his happiness, and his faith in himself. All the gold in the Sierra can't buy him anything more."

"I like money," Mike said.

"I know about that," the Dutchman said. "I came out here almost two years ago, when it became plain that young Army scalawag, Captain Frémont, intended to take over California for us. I've got a wife back in the States. A good woman, raised to figure in dollars and prestige. Thinking about tomorrow. No time for today. No time for me, the way I was, because she was figuring how to get me next to this man and that family and this contract and that job. I wasn't setting the world on fire, but we had a little. Trouble was, it wouldn't go halfway around, the rate she was traveling. It stung her pride and killed mine. I left her without letting her know and came to California to get rich—crossed in the fall of '46 with the Donner outfit. Ever hear of it?"

"I heard what happened to it," Mike said.

His skin tightened, thinking of the grisly story of the men and women snow-imprisoned in the high Sierra pass.

"I went through that to get rich," the Dutchman said. "A year ago I was destitute, dying. Skin and bones. Would have died, but for Maria here. Took care of me, showed me how to live for today. Took me for the kind of man I am, to hell with the money I could make or the house I could provide. A blanket and a tent were enough. They still are. When I stumbled on a gold pocket in midwinter, I knew what I was going to do."

"I'm interested in hiring you, not in your life's story."

"I'm selling you wisdom, man," the Dutchman protested. "And I'm proud of my story. I'm proud of Maria and proud of myself for seeing the truth. This summer Maria will have a child for me. My first in forty-odd years. We're living as God meant us to live. And you're talking of riches! If that transit was the only instrument in the world, I wouldn't run a line for you!"

Mike crossed to the instrument and lifted the cover. A name was burned onto the wooden tripod. He came back to the table.

"A woman came out from Boston the last time on the same ship with me. I could have her here in a week."

The Dutchman lost his color.

"Alice?"

"Mrs. Emil Abernathy. Wife of an engineer."

"I didn't figure on that." The Dutchman scrubbed a hand across dulled eyes. "She must have known I was escaping. Why didn't she leave me alone?"

"She's your wife. Maybe that's got something to do with it."

"Don't be stuffy! She must have heard about the gold."

"Sure," Mike agreed. "At Monterey. With the rest of us."

"I can't believe it!"

45

"I can send for her."

"No," Abernathy said. "She mustn't know. When do you want your survey started?"

"Know where the old Delmonte adobe is?"

"Tomorrow?"

Mike shook his head, remembering his unwanted tenants.

"Monday, then," Abernathy said apathetically.

He left the shelter and entered the tent. The Mexican woman anxiously followed him. Mike returned to his horse.

Mike made a dry, fireless camp on a ridge above the Princesa orchard. Until sleep came he could see lights in the house below. He slept restlessly with his saddle for a pillow and saddle blanket for cover, and his stomach growling protest over missed meals. He awkwardly resaddled in the morning, without purpose, and scowled down at the house. He knew what he had to do, but not how to go about it. Finally he slid his rifle beneath the saddle skirt and angled along the ridge to a down log, from behind which he had a clear view of house and veranda.

There were still only four men in sight. He calculated how fast he could fire and reload. He could get one for sure, the first shot. Probably another, if the loading went all right, while the first surprise still held. That would leave two. If they stayed about, he could keep hidden and maybe later get another. If they left he'd have to follow them. It was the only way.

Settling again behind the log, he pulled back the heavy, curling side-hammer of the rifle and drifted his sights into position. He gripped the stock firmly and bent his index finger about the trigger. He lay motionless a long time, sweating, while the men on the veranda talked among themselves, unaware of death. Finally Mike swore softly, eased down the hammer of the gun, and backed from the log. Turning toward his horse, he froze. Another saddled animal grazed beside his own. A voice spoke mockingly from off to the left.

"A damned chicken-gizzard, eh?"

Larry McCracken was leaning against a tree, surveying him.

"What's the matter?" the Texan prodded. "Your powder wet?"

"When did you get here?" Mike asked with an effort.

"About noon, yesterday. Really looked the country over, coming in."

"You see those men down at the house?"

"From the other side of the valley," Mac nodded. "Figured they'd sure see you and I'd better get over here before they swarmed you like a mess of hornets. They're working a claim below the orchard. If they've got gold, they won't like prowlers."

"So they told me. They've got gold and they claim they're entitled to mineral rights."

"Are they?" McCracken asked.

"No."

"Then why didn't you squeeze off that shot?"

"I was thinking . . ."

McCracken straightened and pushed away from the tree. A pair of guns hung from belts crossing his thighs so low as to seem uncomfortable and awkward to Mike. Mac had not carried a weapon on shipboard. Mike had not seen the guns before. He thought they looked a little ridiculous, the way they were worn. He thought McCracken looked ridiculous.

"You were thinking!" the Texan mimicked him harshly. "Miguel, they's some things you got to learn! See these . . . ?"

He slapped the two holstered pistols and both were suddenly in his hands, cocked, level and steady. Mike gasped involuntarily. McCracken let the hammers down.

"Walker Colts," he said. "So new the shine's still on 'em. They belonged to my brother. He served with Sam Walker, the man that showed Colt how to make this model, down on the border last year."

The Texan flipped his hands. The guns spun and dropped into the holsters with the same effortless ease with which they had been drawn.

"Nobody ever thought more of somebody else than I did of my brother, Miguel," McCracken went on softly. "He was a fighting fool. That part's in our blood, I guess. But he was decent, too, and too damned honest for his own good. Also, he was a thinking man. . . ."

Mac's voice roughened angrily.

"That's how come he was shot down with these guns on him and still in leather. When a man's got a gun, he doesn't think, Miguel. He ain't got time. He shoots or gets shot. Don't you forget it!"

The Texan spat.

"Had breakfast?"

"No."

"Then what the hell we waiting for? Let's go down and get some vittles on the fire!"

"They'll give us real trouble, Mac," Mike warned.

"Only four of 'em, ain't they?" the Texan asked. "Come on. I'm hungry!"

By the time Mike and Mac emerged from timber, the men at the house had moved down to their workings. They saw the two riders approaching and would have hastily retreated to the house, but Mac switched course to intercept them and they stayed where they were.

"You do the talkin', Miguel," McCracken said.

The men lined up behind a big placer-mining rocker which gave them some shelter. Mike saw they wore their pistols, even while they worked. One of the four stepped past Mike's end of the rocker.

"Now what the devil do you want?" he demanded.

"I told you," Mike said steadily. "You're trespassing."

The man looked at his three companions. They seemed to have reached some prior agreement on a course of action.

"Stubborn, ain't you?" the spokesman said. "Like to see that damned deed again—if you got it on you."

Mike twisted a little to get at the pocket containing the Princesa documents. As he did so, the quiet morning exploded.

The spokesman reached for his gun. His three companions jerked their weapons clear. Pistols fired. One fired at Mike. He felt a burn along his thigh. He also felt his rifle recoil in his hands. He heard McCracken's guns. He saw three of the men spill away from the rocker, one after another, and pitch down onto the gravel underfoot. He saw the face of the man who had fired at him, bearded and blanched and accusative.

"Jesus!" the man said thickly.

His hands were gripping his belly, but convulsive fingers could not keep his body from turning itself inside out through a great hole torn when Mike's rifle bullet

48

struck the man's ornate belt buckle, driving it back through flesh and viscera. The man fell to the ground with the others. Mike came down woodenly from his horse and put his rifle on the ground, McCracken came around his nervous animal.

"The bastards!" he said. "Aimed to really whipsaw us!"

The Texan knelt and methodically searched the pockets of the fallen men, putting the possessions of each into a separately spread kerchief. Mike clung to the horn of his saddle. Mac looked up at him with a critical, frowning afterthought.

"You actually carrying that deed with you, Miguel?"

Mike nodded.

"And you're supposed to boss-brain this outfit! If they'd nailed us and got that deed, nobody'd ever move 'em off this gravel. That's what they figured. You carry a copy after this and hide the McCoy where nobody can find it—includin' me!"

McCracken came back to his horse with the laden kerchiefs and hung them by tied corners from his saddle horn.

"Reckon you'll be workin' this gravel any time soon?"

"No."

"Good. This'll do fine, then."

He went back and rolled one of the dead men into the trench they had been digging near the rocker. Mike came around his horse.

"Are you sure they're dead?"

"I'll guarantee my three," Mac said. "And you like to blew yours in two. Quick work, Miguel. I was afraid he was going to get a hole into you afore I could get around to him."

"Couldn't we go up to the house, Mac?" Mike asked.

"An' leave 'em lay? You crazy? They maybe got friends around. Get 'em out of sight afore anybody shows up an' nobody'll know what happened. Besides, it ain't decent to leave 'em unburied."

The Texan rolled the last two bodies into the trench. Mike mechanically scooped gravel. The trench was nearly full when he thought of the kerchiefs on Mac's saddle. This pocket robbery of the dead sickened him.

"Throw that stuff in, too," he said.

"I don't understand you, Miguel," McCracken said.

"There's bound to be letters or somethin' up to the house with names an' addresses. We got to send that stuff home to the kin. It's the least we can do."

• SEVEN •

Dutch Abernathy's woman took over the house when they moved down to the Princesa. She cleared the litter left by the miners, as well as the wreckage of earlier vandals, calmly setting about the task of caring for her man, his employer and McCracken. Abernathy copied out the meets and bounds specified in Mike's deed and began his work. Toward the end of the second week, he freed Mike of the hard monotony of a stakeman's chores when he discovered a boy wandering hungry in the mountains and brought him home. Thereafter the boy did the engineer's running.

Abernathy worked the boy hard, as a man and an equal, but he taught him the reason behind every surveying task required, so that the knowledge began to accumulate and the boy began to show an eagerness for it. He said his name was Pepe. He volunteered no more than this and steadfastly avoided interrogation. He hung about Abernathy in adoration, as a dog might. And he served him well.

Mike and McCracken, relieved of responsibility in the survey, rode widely over the area they judged the Princesa embraced. The riding was at the Texan's demand. A man couldn't work a piece of land till he knew it. Knowing the land to Mac was knowing every rock and thicket and patch of grass.

One morning McCracken claimed to have seen livestock on a distant bench higher in the hills and left with laden saddlebags for what he called a look-see. Mike remembered his own original enthusiasm for the life of a *ranchero* and did not protest his departure. That original enthusiasm often brought a wry smile to Mike's face, now.

He had been thinking of the Princesa then in terms of half a million acres of land. Vanishing imperfections in his understanding of written Spanish and Dutch Abernathy's coldly mathematical pencil had reduced the dream to a much more realistic 44,380 Yankee acres. Actually it was no diminution, for Mike had surveyed the half million acres only in his mind's eye. The forty-odd thousand he had repeatedly ridden over. It was still enough land to make a man king—and it was salted with gold.

The gold had of course knocked the rest of his original concepts galley-west. Now the upstream dam was out, water was back in the creek. When McCracken left, Mike tried a little clumsy panning below the orchard, using equipment inherited from the four whose unmarked grave lay near where he worked. At day's end he had color and high hopes until Dutch refined the sludge to dust and estimated it at less than thirty dollars—ten cured cattle hides in trade at the exchange rate current when he left Monterey.

No more came of the effort than Maria's suggestion that the old ditches could be cleaned and water put onto the neglected orchard. There was, of course, more important work to be done, but most of it required money and supplies and Mike had a fear of launching it, so he cleared out the ditches for something to do. Maria went through the trees with him, showing him how to prune out dead wood and sucker growth. In a few days, with most of the weeds pulled, the orchard took on the same orderly, living appearance the house had assumed.

On the fourth of May, while McCracken was still absent in the higher mountains, Abernathy finished his initial survey. With Pepe's prideful aid, he spread a detailed map before Mike.

"You've got to make a choice," Dutch said. "Tex and I talked about it before he left, but neither one of us are sure how it is with you. There's plenty of both, but which are you really interested in—land or gold?"

"What difference does that make?" Mike asked sharply.

"A gold strike brings in a lot of people," Abernathy said. "A lot of people crowding into a new country makes the value of even unmineralized land climb—land that isn't torn up and stripped of timber and topsoil by mining—

land that probably nobody is going to question your title to, now, but which might eventually be worth more than gold. I can't estimate relative values for you. But you're going to have to decide."

"I still don't see what that's got to do with your survey."

"The description in these Spanish grants is pretty flexible, Mike," Dutch explained. "The area is specific, but the exact location of that area could be floated around quite a little. The foothills carry most of the mineralization. But if you're interested in growing land, the thing to do is to drift the whole grant as far out into the big valley as possible, away from mining scars—and mining trouble."

"That's legal?"

"Don't see why not. Boundaries are so sketchily described there's room inside 'em for a dozen ten-league grants. It's a question of what ten leagues you want."

"That's easy," Mike said. "The ten leagues with the most gold, Dutch."

"That's what you've got, then—to the best of my ability," Abernathy said. "Look at the plat, here. I've kept you to watersheds almost completely. Makes the outline look more like an octopus than a princess, but it includes all the potential gold sands I could crowd in."

Mike nodded satisfaction. Now, at least, he knew where he stood. He had the Princesa on paper. The next move would be to establish it on the face of the land, itself.

"Looks like you've earned your bonus, the forty acres up the hill you and Maria were camping on when I found you."

"We want that, of course," Dutch said. "But there's something else. I've talked it over with Maria. She understands."

"Well?"

"I've never had a chance to use what I learned in school. And Pepe thinks he'd like to turn into a hard-rock man. We don't know too much about underground work in this country. The British have had the experience, where we haven't. There's some pioneering to be done. I'd like to try a hand at sinking a shaft."

"And maybe dig yourself a little of that gold you've got no use for, eh?"

"Yes, for you. Wages are enough for me. You'll need somebody, Mike. You'll have to go underground sooner or later, if you stick to mining and you last. Placers can hold out only till the surface gravels are gone. I figure this free gold had to come from somewhere. I've already located a couple of likely outcroppings. I want to start tunneling for the mother lode."

"Go ahead," Mike said. "What can I lose?"

"It'll take supplies—money—a lot of them."

"All right—when we've got them. But you're going to have to keep your belt pulled in till then."

"You won't regret it, Mike," the engineer said.

"I don't intend to," Mike answered. "Don't you forget it!"

The next afternoon a battered wagon rolled in from Monterey on wheels loose-tired and shrunken from the long, arid crossing of the San Joaquin. Mike stared incredulously, recognizing the crating with which it was loaded—his freight from under the shed at the custom house. His attention shifted to the driver. At first he did not recognize him. Then he realized it was Benson, minus his acne and its scars and with a deeply bronzed, healthy coat of tan.

Benson swung lightly down and crossed to the veranda where Mike stood. "Surprised, McGann?" he asked.

"Sure. Shouldn't I be?"

"Right out of your breeches," Benson agreed. "Give little Benny credit for using his head. You needed this stuff, didn't you?"

"I wouldn't have bought it in the first place if I didn't think I did."

"That's what I figured. I was talking to a padre down there—a Father Bartolo—and he gave me the idea. He located me that wagon and team and got a price on it. I bailed this stuff out on the chance you'd keep me on after I got here."

"Sure Angus Peyton at the Yankee House didn't have something to do with this?"

"No," Benson said. "Why?"

"I don't like Peyton. I don't trust him."

Abernathy came out of the house and surveyed Benson curiously. Benson smiled at him and grinned engagingly at Mike.

"Give me the word and I'll hate his guts, too, McGann. I'm adaptable, like Alice Abernathy. You know, she's wheedled old Jeffers into taking her on to Yerba Buena with him. Ain't that a cozy combination, though!"

Dutch stirred. Mike motioned him up.

"My engineer, Benson—Dutch Abernathy."

Benson made the connection swiftly and lost his smile.

"What did you figure you could do up here?" Mike asked him.

"Keep your accounts. Keep them accurately and keep them private."

"You know how?"

"I think so," Benson said. "I worked two years for a firm of Manhattan accountants. I doubt if they've missed the two thousand dollars I stole from them, yet. That's pretty good bookkeeping, isn't it?"

"You stole the money you came to California on?" Dutch asked sharply.

"There's worse things," Benson said with malice.

"Maybe," Abernathy agreed.

He turned and went back into the house.

"Everybody's got a reason for what they do," Mike told Benson quietly, indicating the departed engineer. "Forget that woman on the boat."

"She is his wife, isn't she?"

"She was."

Benson shrugged.

"You give the orders. I'll take them."

"All right," Mike agreed. "We'll try it. But your first job's going to be to find some accounts to keep."

"Maybe I can do that," Benson said.

He stepped past Mike into the house as though he had belonged there from the beginning.

McCracken returned that night. He stirred up fireplace embers and turned Mike from his blankets.

"I want to talk."

"It'll wait till morning," Mike protested.

"Damn it, man, haven't you ever been lonesome?" Mac said. "I want to talk!"

Mike reluctantly followed him back into the main room. They sat on the floor before the fireplace. Maria heard their voices from the room she occupied with Abernathy. She brought them the coffeepot and a pair of mugs. "You have ridden late," she said. "Coffee will warm you." She padded back to her room. Mac looked after her.

"Dutch ought to take real good care of Maria. She can't keep on doin' for everybody here. It must be gettin' close to her time."

"Leave that to Dutch. What's this lonesome business?"

"You ain't going to understand, Miguel. It's grass. Grass and beef cattle. I've been all through the upper valleys. They're full of summer feed, for when the grass down here burns out. There's cattle up there. Quite a few. Old Delmonte stuff turned wild, I reckon. Enough to start a herd. Bring in blood stock an' you'd have top beef in a few years. Table beef—not hides an' tallow. And there'll be tables aplenty waitin' for it if what Dutch says about the pull of this gold strike is true. You got the makings of the most beautiful ranch a stockman ever saw!"

"Too slow," Mike said. "The gold's faster."

"I'll settle for beef and grass and a working saddle under me. Fat stock to work and a little crew to boss. That's what I want. Crazy as Dutch and his hole in the ground, I guess."

Mike studied the Texan. Mac's truculence had disappeared. He wasn't lonesome. He was excited.

"Benson—remember him from the ship?—came in today with a wagonload of stuff I bought in the East when I thought I was coming up here to be a rancher. Some of it ought to be useful to you. The clerk that sold it to me said a ranch couldn't run without it. Go ahead and see what you can do. We ought to be able to stand a little strain directly. And we can't have you lonesome, Mac."

"You mean that—that last—don't you?"

"I believe I do," Mike said. "Turn in. I'm sleepy."

Thirty hours behind Benson and the wagonload of freight, a messenger arrived on horseback—a young *californio*, bursting with importance. He asked for Mike and Maria pointed him out.

"You are the Señor Miguel McGann who claims ownership of the Princesa Rancho?"

Dutch and Benson appeared in the doorway, curious.

"Sure, I own the Princesa," Mike said. "What of it?"

"You are witness," the messenger said to Maria.

He thrust an envelope into Mike's hands, ran across the veranda, vaulted into his saddle, and spurred his horse

55

out of the yard. There was a long moment of silence, then Dutch Abernathy snorted explosively.

"You," he said to Mike, "have just been handed a summons. All legal, too—by a well-drilled process server."

Dutch was right. The document within the envelope was nearly as long as the deed to the ranch and equally stilted and flowery, although it was drafted in English.

Michael McCullough McGann was thereby ordered to appear on the seventh of June, 1848, before the alcalde of Monterey and a panel of citizen peers, sitting as pro tempore court of the unofficial Territory of California. He was directed to show cause why he should not be required to surrender as imperfect his title to the Princesa Grant, secured from Nicolo Delmonte, through agents, under misrepresentation of fact. Furthermore, said McGann was ordered to bring proof of his claim to such title and hold himself ready, under judgment of the court, to meet all damages and costs incurred by plaintiffs in this action: the said Nicolo Delmonte; his daughter, Felicia Delmonte Peyton, a married woman; and her spouse under the law, Angus Cyril Peyton, a citizen of California.

Mike stared up incredulously from the document and saw Benson watching him with amusement. He handed the summons slowly to Dutch and turned on Benson.

"You knew about this!" he said. "You knew it was coming."

"I was afraid it would get here ahead of me. That kid must have gone up to visit his grandmother on the way up."

"You didn't come up here for a job. Peyton staked you and sent you up here to take over."

"Somebody had to come," Benson said.

"Peyton—Peyton married Felicia Delmonte?"

"Two weeks ago. Priest, promises and presents. Big affair. You should have been there."

"Kind of a tight corner, Mike," Dutch said worriedly. "The three of them against you—father, daughter and son-in-law. With the law behind them."

"My title's a sight more legal than that marriage!"

"In a fair court, maybe," Benson agreed blandly. "But they're already talking about electing Peyton governor whenever Congress gets around to an admission act bringing California in as a state. And this court is hand-picked."

"You got barely time to get down there before the seventh," Dutch said.

Mike took the document and envelope from Dutch. He tore them twice through and dropped them to the ground.

"Don't suppose you want my advice," Benson said.

"No."

"Better listen to it, anyhow. You're making a mistake in avoiding a court decision. Until you get one, you don't know where you are. Right now you got nothing. Nobody has. The gold is anybody's. Anybody can dig it and you can't stop them. You can't even hire men to help you. They'd quit and start digging on their own."

"That what you've got in mind?"

"Sure is, before this place is overrun with ten thousand others, doing the same thing."

Mike pointed to a shovel leaning against a veranda pillar.

"Go ahead," he invited. "There's a pretty fair bar in the wash below the orchard. Try just east of an old rocker sitting on the creek bank."

Benson grinned impudently, lifted down a pan hanging on the wall, and started down toward the orchard. Dutch spat.

"Really snake-backed, isn't he?"

"Maybe. Or maybe just hard-headed. He thinks he's been pushed around. He thinks he can spit nails. Give him an hour down there on the creek and we'll see."

Presently Benson came slowly up through the orchard. He was pale. He put the pan and the shovel back in their places and sat down.

"Maybe you can keep her after all," he said. "If I stay, I get a piece of the Princesa?"

"If you earn it."

"And if I don't?"

"You won't own any of the Princesa. You'll be buried under it."

"Who was he—the one buried down there by the creek?"

"There are four of them."

"Who are they?"

"I didn't ask them. They were digging on my land."

"I'll earn my keep," Benson said.

57

• EIGHT •

The launch was hardly more than an oversized skiff, dirty as the roiled waters of her namesake river. She was desperately overcrowded. Here on the Sacramento it was possible to understand the forest of abandoned ships lying on the mud flats within the Golden Gate. It was possible to understand the deserted mud streets of San Francisco village. It was possible to understand the madness in the air.

Mr. Jeffers knew what he was witnessing. He knew the kind of country in which he was; a stolen country, taken in a thievery now doubly sanctioned in Yankee eyes because of the gold. Mr. Jeffers knew this was no flash in the pan. He knew it was the creation of a new era. Those about him also knew and believed. The wind blew in Mr. Jeffers' face and he looked upriver, thinking sadly of the long years he had spent at book and bar, in study and club and the growing office of his firm, erecting a business of words. In all that time there had been long sea voyages available and raw villages building in the far places of the earth, needing men of wisdom, of knowledge of the law, of steady counsel.

This he had nearly missed, but he wouldn't miss it now. He'd follow the wind to its source. He'd breathe the smell and become a part of it. This was history at birth and he would touch a little of the blood of its travail. Hat in hand, his big head tilted a little back on his thick and still powerful neck, Mr. Jeffers was determinedly beginning a new life at sixty-eight, looking up a muddy river toward its source in distant mountains.

A little farther along the deck Father Bartolo leaned against the rail and thought about his hunger. When a man took sacred oaths which left him only prayer and food and drink out of the bounties of the earth, he was quite often hungry. There was no dignity in too much drink, and prayer was a metaphysical satisfaction which occasionally left the appetites of the body ravenous.

Father Bartolo thought of the legendary bounties of the Swiss master of New Helvetia, which had already become Sutter's Fort and was now beginning to be known as Sacramento City. There was beneath his robe a letter to Captain Sutter from Don Luis Peralta, that old man who was wealthiest and wisest and most kingly of his people. It commended Father Bartolo, for the work he would do in the mountains, and the two who traveled with him to the Captain's hospitality. There should be a fine feast at Sutter's tonight.

Standing as near as she could to the benison of Father Bartolo's Franciscan cassock, Alice Abernathy was miserable. Mr. Jeffers had avoided her since they boarded the launch. She supposed an old man's interest cooled easily. And she had to fight a constant terror that she would be abandoned in this miserable country of mud and bearded beasts of men. One slender hope supported her. She understood Captain Sutter, at their destination, supported a truly grand establishment. Already inured to the exaggeration which seemed a part of the very air of California, she still hoped Sacramento City boasted a bath. She hoped that Captain Sutter could tell her something of Emil. Until recent months practically all emigrants arriving overland had passed through Sutter's. Emil was not a man easily overlooked in any company. Someone must remember him.

If not—Alice looked at Judson Jeffers' broad back. He had made no issue of it and she had carefully avoided even discussion, but she thought he wanted her. It could not be too unpleasant to be an old man's wife. Distasteful aspects of intimacy would be offset by infrequency. Of this she was sure. At least she had been sure in Judson's case until they started up this muddy river. Now she didn't know. A change had come over him, more of a change than mere removal of his hat to let the wind rustle his really handsome head of hair. He even looked younger, dynamic, more virile. Alice felt a little excited, thinking of this. She also felt ashamed, and guilt added to her misery.

The launch docked on a makeshift *embarcadero* at the foot of a mired track ascending a low hill to the stockade of Sutter's Fort. On the flats below were shanties, poorest and flimsiest of houses, in geometric rows on lots being parceled off at whatever they would bring. This was Sacramento City. Downriver, among the tules, were a scattering of Indian *rancherias*. Back from the river, spread across plots betraying the cultivated patchwork of once-planted fields, were the transient camps of men on their way to the mountains. Beyond these were even more fields, not overrun by thoughtless and uncaring men on the move, but rank with unharvested crops, gone to seed and utter loss. For all this evidence of agricultural industry, there was no sign of domestic animals. They had long since been slaughtered or stolen by the endless stream of hungry bandits heading for the gold creeks. The empire of John Sutter was doomed.

As Mr. Jeffers and Alice Abernathy and Father Bartolo stepped ashore, a sad-eyed young man approached them, hat in hand.

"I have the pleasure of welcoming you for my father," he said in a thick accent. "I am Captain Sutter's son."

The attention accorded Don Luis Peralta's letter by the master of New Helvetia pleased Father Bartolo very much. He and his two companions had been given a princely welcome by the Swiss. Now a fine linen-covered table lay before him and he was drunk. That is to say, his body was overflowing with the spirit of brotherly love, for it was blasphemy to declare a brother of the Franciscan Order in his cups.

Far up the long table, like a figure out of a child's nursery book—the figure of the Unhappy King—sat John Sutter. At his right sat his son, interested in something at Father Bartolo's end of the table. And no more beautiful soul had Father Bartolo ever beheld than Beatriz Balanare. Young Sutter's was not the only interest in her. The important *yanqui* lawyer, although careful not to offend the Señora Abernathy, was attentive to Beatriz with more grace than looked for in his race. And Sutter himself seemed grateful in her presence.

"In a time when I lose help always to the mountains,"

he said, "I have been very fortunate in the Señorita Beatriz. It is many weeks she has been with us now. What she has done with my kitchens! Such help with the women of the fort and the farms. I tell you, Mr. Jeffers, a man should not sit as judge on troubles with women. I have tried to make my court here fair to all, but without the *señorita* I would have been a bad judge many times."

"With the *señorita's* family background, she must have a wide acquaintance among her own people," Mr. Jeffers suggested. "Perhaps she has heard something of the whereabouts of Mrs. Abernathy's husband."

Sutter looked the length of the table. Beatriz looked at Father Bartolo, then shook her head.

"No," Sutter answered for her. "She is very conscientious. Hardly ever out of kitchen and warehouse. She sees no one. And she has not been here long enough. I think you must try deeper in the mountains."

"I'm very interested in the legal aspects of your predicament here, Captain," Mr. Jeffers said. "Matter of fact, aside from aiding Mrs. Abernathy as much as I can, I really made this upriver voyage to see if I could be of some assistance to you."

"You will forgive my bluntness, sir," Sutter said. "I need no help in interpreting the law. I need law itself. Gold has destroyed honor and decency. Those I have befriended desert and steal from me. My mills are idle and stripped of all that might be useful to the thieves in the mountains. My crops are unharvested. Strangers live on my land and slaughter my stock. My gold goes into a thousand pockets and I receive none. I am defenseless."

"I thought I might help," Jeffers said. "Pending statehood, it seems to me local governing groups are what is needed here. Through them law can be administered and order restored."

Beatriz Balanare leaned toward Father Bartolo.

"Father, I must see you. And the *yanqui grande*, later." She rose. *"Señora—Señores—*you will excuse me?"

Sutter was hardly aware of her departure.

"Go into the mountains, Mr. Jeffers. You will see. If gold can buy souls, it can buy local governments. Now, sir—Mrs. Abernathy—padre—it is not my hospitality but my time which runs out. I have many things to attend to tonight."

Sutter quit the room. Young Sutter spoke to Mr. Jeffers. "It should be explained. My father has already employed a satisfactory counsel. Mr. Peter Burnett. You will not consider it a discourtesy to excuse me, also?"

Jeffers shook his head and young Sutter followed his father. At the far end of the table, cloaked in the anonymity of his habit, which he had noticed before now seemed occasionally to render him invisible or at least unnoticed, Father Bartolo saw Mr. Jeffers take the Abernathy woman's hand in his own. He rose and moved unsteadily toward the kitchen.

Jeffers had not been fretted by Sutter's blunt refusal of his aid. But apparently his host suffered qualms of conscience. An Indian brought a bottle of French brandy and an excellent cut of cheese to the door of his room. Jeffers accepted them, shielding Alice from the eyes of the servant with his body. He closed and locked the door and poured brandy into two glasses on the massive sideboard across the room from the bed. Alice sat on a small bench, watching him.

"We should have gone to my room," she said.

Jeffers didn't answer. He sipped brandy and breathed the air. Both were good. A younger man might find Alice plain. He did not. He was glad he was not as young as he felt.

"We've traveled a good many weeks together since we came ashore," he said. "We've looked at a great many strange faces."

"I know, Judson."

"None of them was the face you're looking for. I'm beginning to wonder if there ever was such a face."

"I've begun to wonder, too."

"We can't go on indefinitely this way. . . ."

He put his unfinished brandy down. He seized Alice's arms, pulled her to her feet and against him, against his paunch, against his chest until he could feel the firmness of her breasts and corseting there. He kissed her. A forgotten taste, forgotten softness, forgotten fire. This died, but youth did not. And with this you were forever young. His lips still against hers, he twisted her a little and took a step. The bed was against their knees and they fell upon it.

62

"Judson!" she said.

There were tears on her cheeks. He tasted the salt as her lips hurriedly sought his again; hurrying, hurrying, and the skirt was so long, coming up in handfuls until his hand lay along a thigh which quivered to the touch. Then the door shook suddenly to an insistent knock. Restraints flooded back with the jarring sound and both rising cringed at their lost dignity.

Jeffers crossed angrily, unlocked the door and opened it slightly. The engaging, know-everybody little priest who had secured the letter of introduction to Sutter, was there.

"What the hell do you want?" Jeffers snapped.

The Mexican girl who had sat at the foot of Sutter's table moved into his angle of view.

"It is not Father Bartolo who wants to see you, Mr. Jeffers," she said urgently. "It is me."

Jeffers stared a moment, then was forced to a grin. Another woman, by God! He hadn't remembered this sort of thing as catching. He opened the door wider.

"Of course. Come in. Brandy?"

The girl shook her head but Father Bartolo nodded grateful thanks and poured generously from the bottle.

"The offer of help with the law you made to Captain Sutter," the girl asked Jeffers. "You would do the same for another?"

"Possibly. But where is another situation like this? How many barons are there in the Sierra?"

"You were in Monterey, Señor Jeffers. You have heard of the Princesa grant. And you sailed on the same ship with Miguel McGann."

"Oh, him!" Jeffers shrugged. "Peyton and his charming bride explained the felonious and preposterous nature of McGann's claims. The most bald-faced kind of appropriation!"

"Bride!" Beatriz Balanare said intensely. "A devil! The woman is burned out of her. Only the devil is left—in a woman's body. You listen to strange people, *señor!*"

"I do seem to have a flair for it," Jeffers admitted testily.

The girl flushed.

"I tell you true!" she protested. "Miguel was tricked into buying the Princesa by the very ones you listened to, but the money was his and the Princesa is his. Now they know of the gold, they would take it from him. I have friends near who watch and send me word. He needs someone who knows the law is not of the government but of the people—someone who knows how to make the law strong. He needs you. Help him and you will be a rich man."

At the sideboard Father Bartolo refilled his glass.

"Miguel McGann is a wicked man!" he said with immense conviction. "All *yanquis* are wicked. Miguel McGann needs God. You are not God, Beatriz."

"You are drunk!" the girl snapped.

"If you don't mind, Judson, I think I'll go to my room," Alice Abernathy said.

"Wait!" Jeffers begged.

"You understand what Micaelo has?" Beatriz demanded of Jeffers. "You understand why he must fight for it—why I must—why you must?"

Jeffers had never cared for intimidation and he was too old to be swayed by bribery.

"From what I can learn, he's got a gang of cutthroats with him. They'll be more use to him than I could be. Mrs. Abernathy is giving up her search for her husband. We're returning to the Coast in the morning. I'm sorry."

"You will be sorrier!" the girl said angrily.

She crossed to face Alice.

"His name is Emil Abernathy," she said carefully and distinctly. "He is called Dutch in the mountains. My friends there know him, see him often. He is trained for mines but knows mostly railroads. He is a crazy man. He doesn't like houses. Tents are better. He is forty-six years old this year."

Alice rose slowly. Her glass fell to the floor.

"Where is he?" she breathed.

"Take Señor Jeffers to the Princesa," Beatriz said. "Then I will tell you."

"She's using you!" Jeffers warned angrily. "Enough was dropped at the dinner table tonight for her to have invented the whole thing!"

"The Balanare do not lie," Father Bartolo said quietly. "They are an old family, very proud. They do not lie."

"It's Emil," Alice said. "I know it is."

Jeffers glared at the Mexican girl.

"I suppose you've already made arrangements for travel?"

"No. I have worried much over Miguel, but I knew of no help until you spoke at the table of the law. I will make arrangements now."

"They will go alone, Beatriz," Father Bartolo said. "You will stay here."

"I have stayed here too long already."

"Then make arrangements for me, also," the little priest said.

Beatriz opened the door and went out.

"I must go, Judson," Alice murmured.

Jeffers followed her to the door. She pulled him into the hall after her.

"It's going to be all right, Judson," she said. "I've been looking a little too long for Emil. It has all been a little too long. I want to find him now and tell him and be sure of my freedom. You will be patient? We'll find him quickly and have it over with. We'll hurry as fast as we can."

She kissed him and hurried down the hall. Jeffers went back into his own room. Father Bartolo took one look at him and brought him a glass of brandy.

"I'll be damned!" Jeffers grunted.

"It is possible we all may be if we go to the Princesa," Father Bartolo said darkly. "This love of Beatriz for this man—it is unholy. I am not sure it is even love. I do not like to think it is. I believe it is the work of the devil."

Suddenly Jeffers understood a little of the torment within the robed man beside him.

"Nonsense!" he said with the strongest conviction of his life. "No love is unholy. It is the greatest of God's miracles. Have some more brandy."

Father Bartolo looked up with great, moist eyes and shook his head.

"The bottle is empty," he said sadly.

• NINE •

Felicia Peyton did not sleep well in the mountains. Hers had not been a hill family and she hated the deep silence. She heard Fiero approaching long before he knocked on the cabin door at midnight. She had been waiting long in the silent dark before this. As she slid from her blankets she heard Angus rising in the next room in answer to the summons. She crossed quickly to her door to make certain the bar was in place. Pulling her gown over her head, she lit a dressing candle and glanced a moment at the reflection of her upper body in the small mirror on the table. She frowned at its richness of contour. Beauty to her was something other than this. She took up a wide, soft scarf and wound it tightly about her, smiling satisfaction at the trimmer lines it achieved. Angus fumbled at the door, found it locked, and knocked gently.

" 'Licia . . ."

"Un momento . . ."

She pulled on pants she had bought from a miner's wife who had made them for her son. The boy was half-grown and the pants fitted well. The box-cut legs made little of her woman's hips. They were coarse, heavy, durable miner's pants—men's pants. She buttoned them up and pushed back the bar across the door. Angus came in.

"Get any sleep?" he asked.

"No."

"Turn back in. We don't need you. Keep the bed warm for me. It's raining."

"I heard it."

She turned her back and pulled on the boy's shirt she had also bought and tucked in the tail. As she started past him for the door, Angus seized her and kissed her. He had done it in this fashion on their wedding night, too, and she had hated him then. But he was adept at love and her body had been stronger than her hate. It had been an unwanted passion, but overpowering. Now it was different. She had control again. She smiled hard satisfaction beneath the warm, moist insistence of her lips. He released her self-consciously.

" 'Licia, what's the matter? Won't you tell me?"

"Father and Fiero are waiting."

She went into the outer room. Nicolo was standing beside the exterior door. He looked only half-awake. She saw his unsteady hand and frowned. She knew he had again slept with a bottle.

Nicolo shook his head at her with passive disapproval.

"You are not my daughter. My daughter is the most beautiful woman in the Californias."

"You've been drinking," she told him coldly.

"An honest man does his business by daylight," Nicolo said. "Wine keeps a man warm at night."

Felicia opened the door and went out, her father and her husband following. Fiero had four men with him, huddled in rain-wet saddles. *Extranjeros*—strangers—rough, stubble-faced *yanquis*. They had been well chosen. Fiero could be counted upon for that. As Felicia swung onto her horse one muttered a question to another.

"Three men! Where's the woman? One of the bosses is supposed to be a woman."

She glanced at Angus. He had heard. She reined near him.

"You look unwell, Angie. Maybe you should stay behind."

"This is no work for you!"

"I like it."

She nodded to Fiero and put her horse in motion.

They rode up through the chill night past the huddle of tents on the Spittin' Jim sheltering their mining crew: the four families which yet remained of the forty which had served Delmontes for three generations; men loyal to Nicolo who had gathered again about her father, now there was useful work to do. They would patiently shovel the sands of the claims Angie had staked out and they would surrender every ounce of gold to their employers with a faithfulness which was more habit than innate honesty. But they would be no good for a night ride like this. They were a soft people. This was work for *extranjeros*.

Dropping down into Conejos Canyon, they turned downstream, thus avoiding the numerous claims and camps scattered along the Spittin' Jim between their cabin and the confluence of the two streams at Freezer's Bar. Secrecy was important. Felicia was grateful for the masking rain. Even before they could see the lights, the roar of the camp rose above the whisper of the rain and the chatter of the creeks. They cut into the dripping timber of a sidehill and cut wide around the brawling single street.

There was a concentration of claims below the camp. However, the one they wanted was apart by itself—a cooking shelter of poles and brush and a tent on a bar of creek sand from which its owner was slowly and industriously sluicing out a fortune. The *extranjeros* spread out in a silent, restrictive circle about the bar to keep blunderers away. Fiero shook a loop into his *reata*, dropped it neatly over the iron kingpin at the summit of the pyramidal tent, and spurred his horse back, pulling the canvas privacy down.

A voice within shouted alarm, silenced abruptly with awakening caution, and a blob of flailing movement humped about under the slack canvas until it reached the collapsed door vent and a small, balding man emerged, straightening to stare at them through the rain in his underwear. A frightened, ridiculous little man named Smiley Palmer—Judge Smiley Palmer—the law of Freezer's Bar. He was the friend of Michael McGann.

Angus rode forward.

"Know me, Palmer?"

The little man nodded warily.

"Then you know why I'm here."

"No," Palmer said. "No, I don't."

"Where are the claim records of your miner's court?"

"You ain't touchin' them!" the little man said. "We got order here. We got property and we've put a lot of work in on it. Them records is what makes it hang together."

"I know," Angus said. "Without them you haven't got anything. You're all mining on our land, Palmer. You're trespassing on my wife's *rancho*."

"It ain't your wife's. It's Mike McGann's."

"I showed you a court order declaring his title void."

"Issued by a private court of your friends in Monterey. Why, Mike didn't even appear!"

"He had his chance. He was summoned."

"Oh, hell, Peyton!" the little man exploded. "Our court right here's got more authority and justice than the one you used and you know it! Leastways we're tryin' to be honest. And we're backin' McGann's title. He's recognized every claim that was filed on the creeks afore a deadline last month. He's licensing anybody else that'll come in on a fair-shares basis. To hell with you an' your wife and the old man, besides!"

"Bring me the record books, Fiero," Angus said.

Fiero swung down and started for the tent, long knife in hand. Palmer barred his way. Fiero struck him a dispassionate blow on the head with the hilt of the weapon. Palmer fell. Fiero slit the wet canvas and burrowed beneath it, crawling out in a moment or two with a thick ledger tucked under his arm. Angus took the book and stepped over under the cooking shelter, calling over his shoulder to the nearest of the *extranjeros*.

"This is supposed to be a rich claim. Anything you find is yours. You've got five minutes."

The stubbled *yanquis* scrambled under the fallen tent. Felicia went into the cooking shelter. Nicolo, following her, helped the stunned Palmer to his feet. Angus tore pages littered with untidy writing from the ledger and set them afire atop the table. Fiero was recoiling his *reata*. Out in the rain Nicolo supported the unsteady Palmer.

"It is no good to be stubborn, *señor*," Nicolo said.

"No," Palmer agreed. "Reckon it ain't."

Nicolo brought him into the shelter. He watched the last pages from the ledger go up in flames. Angus turned to him.

"Why can't you see both sides of a thing, Palmer? Why can't any of you? You'll say this is taking the law into our own hands. You took the law into yours when you came here and organized a mining district and set up a court on land to which you had no right. You side with McGann when you know he's an opportunist. How do you know he'll stick to the agreements he made with you?"

"At least he made 'em. He could have taken the same stand you're takin' for the Delmontes. But he didn't. He knowed he was in trouble an' he come around to us to work out the best of a bad deal for us all. He'll stick to what he's promised."

"He can't, with the claim records gone."

69

"I know," Palmer said. "There'll be hell to pay, now!"

"If you'd left me any other course, I would have followed it," Angus said, "but I have to protect the rights of my wife and her father."

"Sure, I know," Palmer agreed. "And by morning six hundred others will know, too—including Mike McGann. He may be a bastard, but he don't hold still for a foot in the face. The boys have figured all along you people was his problem. It won't be that way now. By morning McGann's going to have six hundred new friends and you'd better be on your way out of the mountains while you can!"

The last of the flames on the table flared and died out as though snuffed by the quiet intensity of Palmer's warning. In the darkness the rain-damp air felt doubly chill. Felicia found Fiero beside her, the wet length of his *reata* coiled on his arm. She felt a rising tide of strange excitement—perhaps the spur of danger. She touched Fiero's arm and pointed upward. He nodded.

Palmer backed away from Angus, a wet little man in baggy underdrawers who could destroy them all. As he came within reach, Fiero dropped the tight, silent loop of the *reata* over his head. Snapping the free end of the plaited leather over a projecting roof beam, Fiero threw his whole weight upon it. The noose jerked tight about Palmer's neck and he was hauled into the air so his head was near the beam and his bare, muddy feet were a yard from the ground.

Nicolo pawed clumsily in a pocket and brought out a spring knife, snapping the blade open. Felicia gripped the butt of the quirt dangling at her wrist and lashed out with it. Nicolo halted to stare at her with a curious horror. She saw Angus start forward and she cut wickedly with the quirt again. He fell back, hand up to a weal springing up across his cheek. Breathing hard, Felicia wondered at herself, looking up at Palmer's body. Did she hate all men that she could so relish seeing one against whom she bore no personal animus suffer this anguish?

She stifled the thought and watched the swaying body until its movement was only an echo of death. One of the *extranjeros* came in out of the rain, looked up, and blanched.

"Jesus!" he murmured.

Felicia shivered. Now she was frightened. She was more frightened than she had ever been in her life. She was frightened of herself. She was frightened, alone and a woman. She wanted comfort, quick and encompassing comfort, strength against which she could lean, and absolution. She turned instinctively toward Nicolo. He brushed her reaching hands aside and stepped blindly out into the rain. She would have flung herself at Angus, but he was looking strangely at her, daubing at the faint tracery of blood her quirt had left across his face.

"Murder," he said softly. "That's what you wanted, isn't it? With all of us involved. With me involved. To hell with Nicolo. To hell with yourself, if you could involve me. That's what you wanted. Because a murderer could never climb where I've dreamed of climbing. 'Licia Peyton, ever-loving spouse . . ."

"Angie, please . . ."

He grunted and his hand flung suddenly out from his cheek. She spun out from the shelter with the force of the blow and fell in the mud. She rolled slowly over, her whole body retching. A hand gripped her arm and helped her to rise. She saw Angus and her father and the *extranjeros* mounting and riding off up the creek into the darkness without looking back. It was Fiero who was beside her, and there was a strange look in his eyes.

"The dead one would have made bad trouble for the *patrón?*" he asked.

She nodded.

"It is better that he is dead, then," Fiero said. "Come."

He led her back to her horse and mounted his own.

Six hours later another party rode into Freezer's Bar. They made a compact, tight little group, no different from any other on the trails except for that tightness. It was still raining. With hat brims pulled low and ponchos wrapped tight to keep out chill and wet, they seemed to lack identity. Yet twice before they reached the floor of the Spittin' Jim, men touched their hats or waved poncho-draped arms in recognition.

Mike McGann grinned. The Princesa was achieving identity. He glanced at the soggy figure rocking along in the saddle beside him. McCracken. Then Benson and Joaquin. Then Romero, who was Joaquin's friend and McCracken's helper with the stock they were purloining from the higher ridges. And Alexander—the Indian whom Abernathy had named for the emperor of the Macedonians, whatever that significance might be. Alex worked the orchard and the garden and helped about the house since Maria's child had been stillborn and Murietta's young wife had gone back to her own place. They were all supported by a little panning of dust from the creeks near the house and the high hopes which tumbled about in the firelit shadows each night after supper.

A man came riding down hard behind them, spraying mud in a wide fan. Mike hailed him.

"Where is everybody?"

The man's face was a hard, white mask as he answered in passing.

"Somebody kilt Smiley Palmer last night!"

Mike reined up sharply. Benson came up beside him.

"How much dust was Palmer holding for us?" Mike asked.

"Sixty ounces. And whatever he collected from the leases in the last ten days."

"We should have kept it on the Princesa," Mike said.

He sank his spurs deep. The others strung out behind him. Mike did not ride well, but he rode hard. The country taught this swiftly. Ride hard or walk. There were no other bridges across the Sierra.

They passed the man Mike had hailed and several others hurrying on afoot. Presently they rode out onto the wet, tracked sand of Palmer's claim. The big pyramid tent was down. The kernel of the gathering crowd was about the cooking shelter. Mike dismounted and elbowed through.

Palmer was hanging by a plaited leather *reata* from one of the roof beams. The record books of the Freezer's Bar Mining District lay pageless on the worktable, a restless pile of paper ash beside it. The crowd became aware of Mike and his companions.

"That rope's Mexican," someone said.

Eyes turned to Romero and Joaquin.

"The book was burned apurpose!" someone else said.

"Yeah! Ain't any of us got legal claims, now!"

"I figured our deal with McGann was too easy!"

Mike listened in astonishment as the crowd shifted from shocked apathy to hostility.

"Wait a minute!" he called out sharply.

They quieted a little.

"Now, where's the man with guts enough to walk right out in the open and say I had anything to do with this?"

"Wastin' your breath, Miguel," McCracken said softly.

Eyes lashed at Mike and turned uneasily to McCracken. Mac had left his poncho across his saddle and his two guns were low on his thighs. His eyes were bright and eager and challenging and there were few men before them who didn't know the Texan's hands were rumored certain death. A silence came and persisted uneasily.

"That's better," Mike said. "Palmer was my friend. I respected him as you did. He trusted me and I trusted him. I had sixty ounces of gold on deposit with him."

"You did have," a man corrected without sympathy. "There ain't a washed ounce on the claim. We been over his gear."

"Palmer was carrying deposits for some of us too, Mr. McGann," a miner pointed out.

The man's fierce appearance belied his cautious manner.

"I ain't makin' any charges, but anybody that took their own gold out'a Smiley's strongbox would have got enough belongin' to others to make it real worth-while."

"With the Princesa, why the hell would I be stealing gold?"

"You ain't going to make it, Miguel," McCracken breathed.

"Maybe not you, McGann," a hoarse voice cried. "But you got some mighty mean boys. . . ."

"I've got friends!" Mike corrected. "I've tried my best to make you friends, too, if you'd only see it. Don't worry about your claims. To keep our own records straight, Mr. Benson made duplicate records of the whole district. Palmer's book's been burned, but nothing's been lost."

"The hell there ain't. They're your records, now. They'll say what you want 'em to say."

A stir ran through the crowd—a stir as ugly as Palmer's dangling body. Mike felt an unreasoning anger begin to build in him.

"See what I mean?" McCracken murmured.

"Peyton and the Delmontes," Benson grunted. "They did it!"

"We've got two judges left." a big miner named Farrow bawled, turning to the crowd. "By hell, I'll serve for Palmer. Let's get a trial going!"

"Oh—oh," McCracken said in a swift monotone. "Start backin' for the horses, slow, afore they cut us off."

Mike started backing. The others moved with him. Farrow saw the movement and roared an order.

"Grab them!"

The miners started forward in a concerted rush. A gun barked and Farrow went down so abruptly that those behind trampled his body before they could halt. They spread out from him in a fan of alarm and looked at the smoking gun in McCracken's hand. Mike stared at McCracken, also. The Texan was slanted slightly forward on the balls of his feet like a man tensed to leap. His body was rocking slightly from side to side, taut as singing wire. He was breathing lightly and swiftly and his lips were parted in a smile of strange pleasure.

"Come on, you stupid bastards!" he invited with lashing softness. "You sheep-headed, whining sons of bitches that can't make up your own minds!"

The miners hung motionless, a few watching with aversion as blood darkened the rain-wet stain on Farrow's shirt. Joaquin caught Mike's arm and tugged. They backed a few steps and turned. Nicolo Delmonte was coming past the horses, reeling afoot through the mud. For all his drunkenness, he was still a magnificent figure. He had lost his hat or left it behind. He was plastered to the knees with mud and he looked as though he had been all night in the rain. He strode unsteadily past Mike and Joaquin without seeing them. The fan of miners, their uncertain span of attention now arrested by his strange advance, opened a way for him. He rocked on his heels before Palmer's body, pawing in his pocket. He finally succeeded in withdrawing and opened a spring-blade knife. He severed the *reata* and the corpse fell at his feet. The old man began to speak in a Spanish less slurred by alcohol than constricted by what appeared to be genuine emotion.

"I am a coward," he said to the corpse. "I wanted to cut you down last night, when you were pulled into the air. I wanted to save you from being hurt. But I am a coward. I am also Nicolo Delmonte, so I have come back."

He clumsily closed the knife and returned it to his pocket. Back in the stunned group of miners inept translators were turning the words to English. Few of the miners yet knew what he had said. He looked down at the body at his feet again.

"I am sorry. Now I will go home."

He started back through the miners. Some were beginning to comprehend. One seized him.

"Boys, here's our hangman! He says he could have cut Smiley down before he was dead, and didn't!"

"He's Angus Peyton's father-in-law," somebody added. "That means Peyton's outfit up the Spittin' Jim did it!"

"That's horse sense!"

They closed in on the old man. A miner bent and began to work loose the *reata* imbedded in the neck of the hanged man. Nicolo struggled without apparent fear or real interest, but with the instinctive resentment of a proud man who could not bear the hands of others upon him. McCracken pushed against Mike.

"Come on, Miguel—while they got another dog to bite."

"They're going to hang him!" Mike protested.

"Beats hangin' us, don't it?"

"No trial, no nothing—they were going to give us that much!"

"They wouldn't, once they was started. It gets in their blood and they can't wait. Like rapin' a woman. Rope fever, I've seen it before. Let's get out of here!"

"Come on, Mike," Benson urged nervously.

Mike hung back.

"The old man must have been in on it," Mac said. "Sure looks like Peyton's work."

Mike shook his head.

"Bluffing Palmer—burning the records—stealing the gold, yes. But not stringing him up. That's not Peyton."

"Let these jokers think so. Let's get moving!"

Nicolo was a tall trunk among the miners now. Mike saw the noose go over his head. McCracken turned and started toward the horses. Mike snagged one of his guns as he turned and then ran with it toward the group about Nicolo Delmonte. He shouted at them and shoved Mac's gun at the nearest man. The miner's eyes flicked wide, then he lashed out powerfully with one foot. Mud from the swinging boot sprayed Mike's face, and hard leather caught his forearm a paralyzing blow. The gun dropped

75

from his hand. He tried to retrieve the weapon, but the miner plowed into him, drove a knee to his belly and a hard fist with pile-driver force to the side of his neck. He fell face down. As he came dazedly to his knees, trying to clear his eyes of mud, a hand caught his elbow and pulled him up, passing a kerchief into his hand.

"*Madre de Dios!*" Joaquin gasped, almost in his ear.

Mike got the mud from his eyes. Old Delmonte was pulled under the same beam from which Palmer had hung. The old man's height was almost too much for the shortened *reata* and improvised gallows. The toes of his boots touched the earth in his spasms. There was no dignity now, no magnificence, no prideful love of a sad land which had always been kind. Only animal strangulation. But it was not this at which Joaquin had gasped his oath. Joaquin was looking toward the timber. Three riders were racing from it. The first of these, far in advance, was Fiero. The pair behind were the old man's daughter and her husband.

Fiero rode like an arrow into the crowd about Palmer's cooking shelter. Two or three men went down under his horse before it was dragged to a halt. He leaped from his saddle, bright steel in hand, to cut a way to his expiring *patrón*. Mike thought that had any of the miners been sane in this moment, they would have run from Fiero's terrible fury. But the fever McCracken had spoken of was hot in them and they fell recklessly on the *californio* with gun barrels and butts and smashed him down. They hammered and swung even after he had fallen, until they were sure.

Peyton and Felicia pulled up at the edge of the bar when Fiero went down. They sat rigid in their saddles for a long moment. Peyton suddenly wheeled his horse and rode desperately back for the timber. Felicia seemed unaware he was gone. Quite slowly she turned her animal and rode back the way she had come.

• TEN •

In midmorning, when the rain lifted from the muddy street of Freezer's Bar and the rope fever of an early hour was an ash of contrition in the mouths of the men moving quietly along the walks, Joaquin and Romero returned. They had ridden up the Spittin' Jim, beyond the upper boundary Abernathy had laid out for the Princesa, to Peyton's string of claims. They had found the crew of old Delmonte retainers there, but packing to leave.

"This would naturally be so," Joaquin explained. "With the *patrón* dead, what would hold them? For certain they would not stay for Peyton and his *señora*."

"If you knew that, why ride up there?" Mac asked lazily.

"To see if there was anyone in Peyton's cabin."

"Was there?"

"No. Both were gone. In a hurry. They took little with them."

"Where'd they go?" Benson asked.

"I would have asked the Delmonte people that," Joaquin said, "But there were four *extranjeros*—bad-looking *yanquis*—hanging around the claims and I wanted no trouble."

"Yankees, huh?" Mac said thoughtfully. "Wonder where they fit in?"

"With Peyton? Nowhere, I think," Joaquin answered. "The Delmonte people are deserting Peyton's claims. It is *yanqui* custom when a claim is deserted to jump it. I think this is what they do."

"Sure they aren't Peyton's men, too—holding down his gravel for him?"

"Who knows?" Joaquin shrugged.

"Well, it'll be a long time before Peyton and his wife dare show up here again," Mac said. "Looks like we'll have a breather and a chance to dig in afore they give us any more trouble, Miguel."

"I hope so," Benson said. "If that friend of Joaquin's that wrote him from Sutter's really has old Judson Jeffers on the string for you, Mike, we'll need a breather for him and me to get all the ranch books and paper work up in shape."

Mike nodded. "Say, Joe," he said suddenly to Joaquin. "Wasn't Dutch's wife supposed to be with Jeffers?"

"She left Monterey with him," Joaquin answered.

"Ha!" Mac snorted. "Maybe that's why Dutch didn't want to join this welcome party this morning. How you like that? The chicken-livered old bastard. He was afraid she'd show up, too!"

Joaquin saw something up the street. He rose and pointed. A high, hooded *carreta*, fitted with tall, shaved-spoke wheels instead of the solid wooden disks of the true Mexican cart, was turning into the street from the Sacramento Trail. Its two incongruous mules were droop-headed from a long pull and the canvas hood was splashed higher than the wheels with mountain mud.

"Romero and I saw it from up the canyon as we came down," Joaquin said. "It will be Señor Jeffers, I think."

Mike crossed the walk and pulled into his saddle. The others mounted with him, brightening now that the wait was over. They rode to meet the *carreta*.

Two men were on the seat. Mike ignored the smaller, who was driving, in his attention to Jeffers. The old lawyer was twenty pounds lighter than when Mike had last seen him in the public room of La Fonda, in Monterey. The sun had darkened his shipboard tan to a much darker hue. His clothes hung slackly on him. When he swung down from the cart to shake hands, it was with an elasticity and energy which completely belied his age.

"Welcome to Freezer's Bar, Judge," Mike said.

Jeffers pumped his hand enthusiastically, his eyes darting about him in appraisal. Mike looked up to the seat of the *carreta*. Jeffer's companion, the driver, had a brown Franciscan habit and sandaled feet. A tide of recollection surged.

"Padre!" he said eagerly. "I remember, of course, but not the name. . . ."

"You never knew it," the priest said.

"Bartolo," Jeffers boomed. "The only man in the world

78

who can navigate with a brandy bottle for a compass!"

Mike stepped up onto the wheel hub as the others laughed.

"Beatriz . . ." he said swiftly. "Have you seen her—heard from her?"

The padre shrugged.

"She is somewhere in the mountains."

Mike's excitement ebbed in disappointment. Jeffers tugged him back to the ground.

"If I don't find something without wheels to sit on pretty soon, I'll never be able to walk a straight line again!"

Both laughed. Joaquin and Romero rode out ahead. Alex fell in behind to bring up the retinue, and they started for the ranch.

The trail from Freezer's Bar and the Spittin' Jim was hard, and twice Mike suggested Jeffers walk the bad stretches, but for some curious reason the old man clung to the *carreta* seat. As they approached the crest of the ridge, Mike dropped back a little. Once, when he had first ridden the ranch with McCracken, they had reached the summit as the sun was setting and the San Joaquin was a bowl of fire from the Coast Range to the Sierra; an incredibly beautiful bowl of crimson and gold, with the green and dun of the Princesa lands sweeping down to it in a flawless symmetry of shadow and canyon and undulating hill.

When Mike came up behind the rest it was as he had wanted it to be. Mac removed his hat. Jeffers, staring, removed his, also, perhaps with a different kind of marvel. Joaquin and Romero and Alex crossed themselves. Father Bartolo sat immobile on the *carreta,* eyes closed and face slightly upturned. Mike sat with eyes wide, drinking it in. It made no difference that blood lay on the land and gold beneath it and Larry McCracken had killed a man in the morning's rain. It made no difference that Miguel Mc-Gann only saw God in times of wonder like this. It was beautiful and it was a fair welcome to the Princesa.

The sun sank lazily below the crest of the distant Coast Range like a slowly closing eye, and darkness marched across the San Joaquin toward the mountains where the Princesa lay. Father Bartolo shook out his reins. The *carreta* moved and the caravan started on down through the parks along Delmonte Creek.

Two men were camped in one of the parks. They had

signed a lease with Mike for one thousand dollars and one ounce in ten of their pannings, payable only if they found commercial color. Their names were Forrest and Haney. If they could accumulate a stake, Haney wanted to build a sawmill farther up the creek, where the haul over to the Spittin' Jim would be short. He was of a milling family, and as to many others, gold was but a means to an end. Both of the men came out of their tent as the *carreta* jolted past on the opposite bank. They waved.

It was an hour after dark when they reached the house. The yard had changed much since Mike himself had first seen it. Romero and Alex had found clay and had built themselves quarters on an old foundation—a low, red-roofed adobe building which McCracken called the bunk-house. Dutch had gotten Alex to help him build another small 'dobe place which was mostly roofed veranda, attached to two small rooms and a lean-to, where Pepe slept. Maria and Dutch lived in the two rooms. The baby was buried under a great pine across their dooryard.

The windows of the old main house were bright. Joaquin rode with the *carreta* into the dooryard. He said good night here and spurred off into the timber toward his own place. Dutch Abernathy came out alone to meet Jeffers and the priest. Maria and Pepe remained in the kitchen as became a proper family. Alex and Romero would have put up the cart and mules, but Father Bartolo insisted on seeing to these himself, so Mike gave the two hands a bottle of wine from the house and they went off to their own quarters. The priest came in presently and they all sat down to supper. Father Bartolo pushed back in his chair and rose.

"Bring another place," he directed Maria. Then he turned to the rest. "I have a great surprise for you. For one of you the greatest surprise of all. Excuse me a moment. . . ."

He crossed, beaming, to the outer door and returned with Alice Abernathy on his arm. He proudly led her to Dutch.

"Gentlemen, Mrs. Emil Abernathy," he said. "Sir, your wife!"

"Hello, Alice," Dutch said very softly.

"Hello, Emil."

Dutch rose and offered her his chair. She shook her

head. Maria had set the extra place between Mike and Jeffers. Benson leaped up to seat her there.

"I planned this all the way from Sacramento City," Father Bartolo said, chiefly to reassure himself the surprise was worth the effort.

"Bring Pepe," Dutch said to Maria.

She padded obediently off and returned with the boy. They took instinctive positions behind Dutch's chair. His face was without color. He spoke with great care, eyes on the plate before him.

"Alice, this is my son. His name is Pepe. I found him here in the mountains, where I've found everything else I've ever wanted or believed of value. And this is Maria. She nursed me back to life. She, too, has given me what I have always wanted. Our child died three months ago. We will have another. Here in the mountains she is my wife."

Stunned, Father Bartolo sank slowly into his chair. Alice looked a long time at Maria.

"You have been fortunate, Emil," she said at last. "I have been fortunate, too. Mr. Jeffers has asked me to become his wife. You've removed the last barrier. I'm grateful."

"Bring some of Joe's brandy," Mike ordered. "We all need it."

When Maria brought the brandy, Father Bartolo hastily swallowed a glass, muttered an excuse, and hurried back outside. The meal progressed and drew to a close. Dutch went into the kitchen without a good night. Alice Abernathy asked for her room and Mike led her to a chamber next to the two rooms Maria had prepared in advance for Jeffers. He went out into the night.

The *carreta* had been pulled up under a laurel on the dark side of the house. Mike saw Father Bartolo sitting backward on the seat of the cart, the flap of the hood open and his attention on something within. He remembered he had not provided quarters for the priest. He started toward the cart. Father Bartolo closed the hood and scrambled to the ground to meet him.

"I'm sorry, Padre," Mike said. "We have other rooms, but we are short of furniture and they aren't open."

"I am comfortable anywhere," the priest said. "Please make no trouble for yourself."

"No trouble," Mike assured him. "I'll put out some blankets in the living room for you."

He started away. Father Bartolo's sandals whispered after him.

"I want to speak with you, *señor . . .*"

"Sure," Mike agreed. Then, hopefully, "Maybe about Beatriz?"

"No," the priest said firmly. "About another woman. About this child who has lost herself in sin with Emil Abernathy."

Mike found he had drifted toward the orchard. The padre shuffled along beside him.

"Maria's hardly a child, Father," Mike said.

"We are all children. She lives in sin."

"She loves Dutch. Certainly he loves her. She is happy. Isn't that enough?"

"True happiness, yes. But first comes peace with God. Absolution, repentance, an end to sin. This is a great sin. It is a damnation! Like that night in Monterey . . ."

"Wait a minute!" Mike protested. "This got kind of personal all of a sudden, didn't it?"

"You sinned, also. I ask you to repent!"

"What's the phrase you people use, Padre—walking with God? I walked with Him that night. It took me a little time to realize it, maybe. But I do now. I don't know why you won't tell me where that girl is. But soon now I'm going looking for her. And when I do, I'll find her. You'll see some real sinning, then!"

Mike turned and started back for the house, leaving Father Bartolo alone in the darkness by the orchard.

Lamps were out in the living room. Only the fire glowed. Benson and Jeffers had apparently finished their brandy and gone to their respective quarters. Mike opened a chest and found extra blankets. He piled these on the floor near the hearth and went on back through the dark house to his own room. A fire glowed here, also, radiating warmth and the faintest of light. Mike was tired, angry with Father Bartolo and Abernathy's wife, and he wanted a drink. But he would not go back through the house for it. Standing before the fire, he let his mind drift over himself and the Princesa and the accomplishments toward which he had striven.

He had first seen what he believed to be half a mil-

lion acres of land, without value except for sheer size—
empty land which was his, alone, on which he could grow
in a self-fashioned image until he was as enormous as the
Princesa itself. Then, later, the gold, and the image a
golden one, shaped by his own hand. If this was the biggest grant in California, then he would be the biggest
man. If this was the greatest supply of gold, then he would
be the richest. If he succeeded in bringing life to all his
dreams he would be the best man and the strongest—the
wisest and cleverest and most brilliant. When occasion
required, he would be the most dangerous, and always
the most important.

But he had not counted upon the parasites. He had
needed a companion and an early strength and there was
McCracken. He had needed a time of peace, without op-
position, and there had been the enmities of the Delmontes
and Angus Peyton, with the bodies of Smiley Palmer and
old Nicolo already swinging high. He had needed direction on a ride and there had been Joaquin and his wife,
with a homestead to be confirmed to them. He needed an
engineer and there was Dutch, with Maria and Pepe—
with Alice, come looking for him. Jeffers, now—and the
little priest who hungered to be his conscience. Now, lastly,
a loneliness for a woman he had seen only once.

Each of them had, in his own way, destroyed the dream
Mike had wanted to build. Each in his own way was better than the best self-image Mike could fashion from the
dreaming. In a very real sense they were more the owners of the Princesa than he would ever be. He doubted
if his own absence would greatly affect the course of any
of them. But he could not survive without them, and
neither could the Princesa.

Of them all, Mike McGann was not the most dangerous
one. This was McCracken. He was not the cleverest. This
was Benson. He was not the best nor the wisest. This
was the little priest, or perhaps Maria. Nor was he the
most brilliant. This had to be Jeffers. And, strangest of
all, he was not the most important. This was Beatriz
Balanare, wherever she was.

He was not sure what first told him she was there in
the room. He grew aware of her only by degrees. An in-
definable scent, neither perfume nor musk, but a curious

blend of both—woman-smell. He felt a warmth too penetrating to have come from the dying fire, a sensation of the skin as though it was pimpling to a touch which had neither weight nor substance. Finally he saw her in the darkness, sitting in the tall leather lattice chair near the window, her face underlit by the glow of the embers on the hearth.

It was then he understood the little priest's tortured pleading by the orchard. This was the other surprise which had ridden onto the Princesa under the canvas hood of the *carreta*. It was a surprise in which Father Bartolo had no joy, for he knew she was waiting for Mike here in this room.

"Beatriz!" he breathed.

He was across the room and she was in his arms.

"Micaelo—please!" she murmured.

He released her and pushed her gently back into the chair and knelt and clasped her knees to him and looked up into her face. It was no angel's face. But a man did not love an angel. He loved a woman.

"You were at Sutter's?"

She nodded.

"I found Mr. Jeffers there and knew you needed him, so I brought him to you. I could not come until I could do something."

"You should have showed up differently," Mike said.

Quick hurt clouded her eyes.

"For yourself," he explained. "Damn it, Alice Abernathy rode in here with you. She knows you're here now. And the little padre—he loves you. It kills him to know you're here."

"A priest loves all men, Micaelo."

"Not like this. This one wants to make love to you."

She put her two hands down, clasping his face between them.

"We do not say that. We do not think it. There is more in love than making love. If Father Bartolo has love for me, I have it for him, also. He is a good man."

"He's a tortured little devil! You should have showed up in the open, by the front door, like Alice Abernathy."

"Was her man happy to see her?"

"Good Lord, no!" Mike grunted. "That's a hell of a mess!"

"It could be the same with us. How could I know? It is better to find out in the dark, in private, like this."

He came clumsily to his feet and lifted her from the chair and carried her across to the bed.

"I'll show you how much I've wanted you ever since I woke up with a hangover in your bed and found you gone. . . ."

"You are sure?" she asked.

He ignored the question and fumbled with her clothing. She protested, but only at his impatience, for she did not understand.

"I'll show you how much I've wanted you at night—every night—here alone in this room with me. . . ."

He moved at an unconsciously rushing, increasing tempo, not realizing his voice was rising in pitch and intensity and words were tumbling as he flung back the blankets and rolled her, naked, into the bed.

". . . How much I've wanted you whenever I've tasted Joe's brandy, whenever I've seen the moon, whenever I've smelled jackpines and heard the wind whistle. I'll show you . . ."

He collapsed suddenly, sitting on the edge of the bed, bending over her, scooping her shoulders into his arms, pulling her to a sitting position against him, kissing her. Then he pushed her roughly back onto the pillow and pulled the blankets over her, tucking them in securely against himself. He stood up.

"Good night, Bea . . ."

There was only her breathing for a moment, then she reached for and caught his arm and pulled him down again to the edge of the bed. She sank back onto the pillow, pulling him with her to cradle his face against the warm velvet of her breast. Her finger traced lightly over the closed lid of his eyes. Her heart beat beneath his ear. She breathed deeply and shivered.

"I am frightened, Micaelo," she whispered. "What if another *yanqui* with money had come along that alley in Monterey?"

He kissed the flesh beneath her lips.

"Buenas noches," he said.

"Buenas noches . . ."

She released him. He rose, crossed to the door, and let

himself out into the hall, closing the door softly behind him.

Passing through the kitchen he took down a fresh bottle of brandy and carried it with him into the living room. Embers on the hearth here had died to a red eye in the dark. He threw a pair of large pine cones from the woodbox onto the spark. They caught in a moment and there was light. Father Bartolo sat on the floor, a blanket wrapped about his shoulders. Mike took another from the stack he had provided for the priest and sat down, similarly wrapping himself. Prying the cork from the brandy bottle with unsteady fingers, he wiped the neck on the blanket and offered it to the priest. Father Bartolo drank stoutly and belched.

"She was there?"

Mike nodded and took his own drink.

"You did not stay long."

"No."

The priest studied the blazing cones on the hearth.

"You love her," he said.

Mike's hand clamped tightly about the bottle in his fingers.

"I love her," he agreed softly. "As much as you do."

Father Bartolo drew a deep breath and turned to look at him.

"A man could not ask for more than that, Miguel."

The priest reached for the brandy bottle and held it critically to the light.

"Got another one of these?" he asked. "This one isn't going to go very far."

A new order came onto the Princesa. Benson and Jeffers chafed until Mac found a horse and saddle to suit the old man, and they rode the courses of the creeks and often into Freezer's Bar. Shrewdly singling out a responsible breed of men wherever he found them, Benson began accumulating leaseholders on a percentage fee to the Princesa, so that the creeks were not deserted any longer. Jeffers listened over noon fires and at smoking rests along the bars to the men who were working the sands. If he heard what he was listening for, he said little about it.

McCracken rode widely, as long as the sun was in the sky. He began to talk of Princesa cattle in terms of herds, gathering strays from back canyons and deep brush, working them in where the grass was greenest and they were least likely to stray again. Romero rode with him and laughed at the Texan's enthusiasm in the beef count, for like Mac himself, the *californio* had learned his trade when cattle herds were not numbered in dozens of animals but dozens of thousands.

Dutch set up his old tent near the ledge he had staked out to work, and he burrowed in the rock like a marmot, starting his tunnel. He did not come back down to the house, although Maria remained faithful in the kitchen and Pepe remained with her in the little 'dobe behind the main building, going afoot each day to Dutch's mine to do his share. Alice Abernathy rode with Ben and Jeffers when they would permit it or sat on the veranda and looked at the mountains without interest. Beatriz divided the house with Maria, for there was instant kinship between them, and as Maria cared for the kitchen, she cared for the other rooms. Romero made furniture in the evenings and she cleaned through the day, so that in a little time there were no more closed rooms and a feeling of expansiveness pervaded the house.

A day came when Mike found Beatriz in the bedroom he had surrendered to her. She had a dozen of the little buckskin bags in which Benson had been accumulating the first trickle of payments from the leased claims piled beside her. Their contents had been dumped onto a clean sheet and she was running her fingers through the thin, combined heap of indifferently washed gold dust with the same high ecstasy with which she had once handled a heap of golden coins on a coverlet in Monterey.

"How much of this is yours, Miguel?" she asked, looking up.

"All of it."

"None of it should be."

He was startled.

"Why not? It came from my land."

"You dug none of it. You sold no leases. You broke none of Dutch's rock. You didn't help chase the beef. How long are the others going to do these things and give it all to you?"

"You think I'm not doing my share, is that it?"

"I think you are doing nothing. I don't think I understand you. In Monterey you talked of money. Much money. Here you have all the money in the world, if you'll take it—if you will work it just a little. The Princesa is a woman, Micaelo. You want to have and to see, but you are afraid to take. A woman cannot be treated in this fashion."

The next morning Mike set up the old placer rocker below the orchard, where he had once sent Benson to dig, and in the five weeks before Christmas he washed out just under two thousand dollars in dust. He recklessly sent this out to the Coast with a man from Freezer's Bar named Jonathan Spier, whom he hired as the *rancho's* freighter. And he married Beatriz Balanare on the first day of the new year.

A hundred and twelve guests arrived, although none but the Princesa supposedly knew of the impending ceremony and none but Princesa people were expected. Sixty men, including Ma Finney and seven of her eight sons, came in over the trail from Freezer in a driving rain, leaving the camp deserted except for the four Yankees who had jumped the Peyton-Delmonte claims far up the Spittin' Jim. That there were not six hundred instead of sixty in this contingent was due to the winter weather, which had forced vacation of all but the best claims and a general exodus in search of a more comfortable climate in the lower valleys.

Joaquin and Romero came to Maria's rescue in the face of this crowd. They slaughtered the fattest of McCracken's young bulls. It was the greatest of sacrifices on Mac's part. The whole carcass was roasted in a pit dug in the yard. Alex and Maria labored at the pit and in the kitchen. All were fed. The late sun came out, clear and warm.

Alice Abernathy worked almost to the moment of the ceremony, altering a dress from her trunk to a suitable gown for the bride. If she noted Dutch's absence, she said nothing. He had not been back down since the night of her arrival and he did not come down today. Jeffers and Benson, shrewdly capitalizing on the spirit of the crowd, gathered in the loose ends of their rides, circulating among the guests as freely as the brandy, securing signatures and marks on petitions Jeffers had spent careful days in drawing up. As a result, they could announce be-

fore the ceremony that this was the first wedding to be
held in newly formed Delmonte County, a political area
coinciding with the boundaries of the Princesa ranch.

There were some heated discussions on the name, with
the *californios* stoutly holding out for Delmonte County
because this had once been Delmonte land and would always be remembered so. Beatriz backed them and the
majority swung to her. None could refuse a bride. So the
vote went. Two of the Finney boys, Mike, Benson, and a
tall old man named Albert Johnson were elected commissioners. Judson Jeffers was elected judge. Father Bartolo, earnestly petitioned, gave over preparations for the
nuptial mass long enough to stand before them all in
prayer for the guidance of God in this enterprise of government.

Father Bartolo was thereupon toasted. And the judge.
And the commissioners. And Delmonte County, itself.
All with gay unconcern over the fact that recognition and
confirmation of the efforts of Jeffers and Benson must
await state constitutional organization, the election of
state legislators empowered to recognize and confirm, and
finally the long-delayed admission of California into the
Union by act of Congress of the United States.

The sun was almost gone when Father Bartolo finally
led Mike and Beatriz into the sight of God.

• ELEVEN •

On the first day Beatriz was mistress of the Princesa,
Maria surrendered the kitchen and moved up to the tent
at the mine to be with Abernathy and Pepe. Benson came
to Mike for permission for Jeffers and himself to move
into the little 'dobe under the jackpines, thus vacated. It
became from that instant the office of the Princesa and in
effect the courthouse of Delmonte County. Here, besides
the record of leases and fees and a new and more accu-

rate claims book, Jeffers began a careful compilation of basic county government law. Almost from the establishment of the office, a stream of visitors began coming to the Princesa. Many of them were men who were becoming in various ways a part of Mike's enterprise.

They came in part because friction among them was inevitable and they early learned Jeffers was a friendly, impartial surgeon who always cut to the truth. They came also because it was winter and lonely in the mountains and there was Beatriz at the Princesa, and companionship. They soon came to call her the Princesa instead of the ranch itself and the Yankees among them made it the Princess. Because most of them were a part of what was being built under the guise of county organization, they did not question their right to a seat at Mike's table whenever they were present at mealtime, but each nevertheless invariably waited for an invitation from Beatriz. She disappointed none.

Mac spoke of a brand and Beatriz sketched a crown for the Princesa. Mike watched amusedly while Mac earnestly argued lines with her until the design was simplified. Two days later the Texan rode back from Freezer's Bar with the crown made up in iron. It was possible for days thereafter to locate Mac by the thin pillars of branding fires on the slopes. Mac also spoke to Jeffers of stockmen's laws and these were drafted into the legal structure of the county. Encountering stragglers of beef now, Mike began to see what McCracken was building. The animals supporting his brand were becoming a living measure of McGann's growing domain.

Still Dutch did not come down from the mine. Amused at the engineer's stubbornness, Mike rode up to see him. Dutch came out of his tunnel, trundling a wooden barrow loaded with hand-broken rock. His bare torso was powdered with white rock dust. He spilled the barrow on the dump and sat on its upended edge.

"How you doing in the gravel at the orchard?" he asked.

"Too good to be taking time off," Mike told him. "Alex is spelling me today. Eight to ten ounces a shift, I figure."

"Your damned luck!" Abernathy said.

He scuffed his boot.

"Suppose you're wondering why I didn't come to the wedding."

"You explained once. You don't believe in weddings."

"It's not that. It's her—having her around."

"Alice?"

"Get her off the place and Maria and I will move back down."

"Can't very well do that," Mike said. "I need Jeffers. We've got to be ready when the spring run comes. The old man and Benson are working night and day, getting us legally set on our feet. I can't let Jeffers go and Alice wouldn't leave without him."

"I'm a bigamist, Miguel," Dutch said. "I know it. But I don't like having my nose rubbed in it."

"I imagine. But the Father usually has an answer. He give you any advice?"

"Sure. Marry Maria. But I can't do that without getting a divorce from Alice. Even that'd be against the padre's idea of religion. And the only divorce we could get would be through Jeffers. He's probably the only elected judge in the territory, whether the election's valid or not."

"He wouldn't stand in your way, that's sure."

"Hell, man, don't you see?" Dutch asked angrily. "I can't go to a man and ask him to pry me loose from my wife when I know he's going to take her the next minute."

"Aren't you getting a little mixed up as to just who is your wife?"

Abernathy clenched and unclenched his hands.

"Maybe I am," he said. "Why don't you get the hell out of here? I've got work to do."

Mike shrugged and looked at the mouth of the mine tunnel.

"There ought to be an easier way of getting that rock out of there than with your fingernails. We're getting some dust ahead. What do you need?"

"Nothing except to be left alone!"

The rains persisted intermittently. A few of those who had deserted the mountains early in the season came back to Freezer's Bar, finding anxiety over their claims more demanding than comfort. The county organization gained confidence because the unworked claims remained as their owners had left them. Jeffers and Benson contrived another meeting on the Princesa for all those who cared to vote and an oversight of New Year's Day was corrected by the election of Ed Finney, youngest and biggest of Ma Finney's boys, as the sheriff of Delmonte County.

A few days later there was a flurry of excitement when a man named Bascombe was killed on the upper Spittin' Jim by one of the four men who had jumped the Peyton-Delmonte claims. Mike argued down the intent of the other commissioners to send the new sheriff after the murderer. The Peyton-Delmonte claims were beyond the determined boundary of the Princesa, and consequently the county would be without jurisdiction. Jeffers reluctantly supported him.

A rain-soaked and pocket-worn letter came for Beatriz from Father Bartolo who had gone to Monterey. Peyton and Felicia were in the Delmonte place there, setting the finest table and easily the most sought-after host and hostess in the capital. The Yankee House continued with fabulous success and Peyton was building an addition to it. It was even rumored that he would soon displace Sutter as the richest man in California. This was, in the priest's estimation, very questionable, but it seemed likely Peyton was well on his way to becoming the most powerful man in terms of influence. He was the chief agitator for another convention to draft a state constitution and general feeling was that the call for convention would go out by summer at the latest. There was also a rumor that Peyton and Felicia were expecting a child, but Father Bartolo had no verification of this. Felicia had not been to confession since her marriage.

Of principal interest to Mike was the fact that a shipload of English mining machinery had arrived, consigned to a syndicate which had become insolvent since placing the order. The freight was on the beach and could be had for a small sum. Also of interest but probably little fact was the report again that Captain Sutter was bankrupt and some Monterey merchants were considering bidding in his enormous stock of goods.

Beatriz did not read all of the letter aloud. Mike did not know what further gossip it contained. But he knew what he wanted to do. He took Beatriz out to the office and showed her the pine box Alex had built to serve as storage for their growing revenue. The hoard looked substantial now; three hundred ounces from the leased and licensed claims and nearly two hundred more from Mike's personal workings below the orchard—all at a going price of nearly fifteen dollars an ounce reported from Sacramento City. Seventy-five hundred dollars more or less. Mike stacked the little ten-ounce buckskin bags in three approximately equal piles.

"This one we spend," he told Beatriz. "This one we keep. And this one goes to the boys who have earned it."

"Just who?"

"Dutch, Mac, Benson, Jeffers. Five hundred dollars apiece, their wages for all the months they've worked. But I don't want them to know now. It's not enough. I've got to make it grow for them."

Beatriz looked at the piles.

"Just divide what came from the leases then. Not what you panned out at the orchard, too. That's for us—just for us."

"They share in everything," Mike said.

She looked at him levelly.

"They are friends. I know what they've done for us. But I also know they have realized from the beginning they would make themselves rich doing it. It's bad business to give them more than a reasonable share."

Mike rose and put the gold back in the box.

"I brought you out here to show you, so you'd understand. You get pleasure out of seeing how I do. But I didn't bring you out here to say no to what I tell you. The Princesa is mine."

Her lips compressed. She turned and went out. When he followed her back into the house he found she had gone to the bedroom. She did not answer when he knocked. It was their first quarrel.

McCracken left for Sutter's Fort to acquire the best of the Swiss's beef stock and whatever else might be of use, if it was true Sutter was selling out. He took a thousand dollars of the "spending" money with him. Benson and Spier took the wagon and headed for Monterey with another thousand dollars and orders to buy powder, general supplies and the beached machinery. Benson protested that the machinery should be first identified and its usability determined, but Mike overrode him. If it was designed for mine use, Dutch would discover some means of utilizing it.

Haney and Forrest came down from their leased claim

on Delmonte Creek with good news. They had hit good color. They believed in a few weeks they could pay off their licensing fee and commence making substantial contributions to the Princesa coffers. Forrest was excited, but Haney had been thinking of timber and a mill again. He thought that if the big spring and summer rush everyone expected came, milled lumber would be worth more than gold. If he could sell his half of the lease, he'd put what it brought him into a mill.

Mike went to Beatriz for her advice. She shrugged.

"You wanted to see Dutch and Mac and Ben and the Judge grow. You wanted what you set aside for them to multiply and make them rich. Buy Haney out for one of them. You've already spent most of what you saved for us. We can't afford to spend any more now."

Mike was angry at first that she should hold resentment at his division of the money, but as he thought of her tart suggestion, he fell more and more into accord with it. Haney accepted the five hundred dollars Mike had set aside for Dutch and parted with his half of the Delmonte Creek claim. But Haney had been figuring in detail and he thought it would cost perhaps twice five hundred to buy a mill, even one of Sutter's abandoned rigs. Faced with this, Mike used the five hundred he had set aside for Benson to buy a half interest in Haney's projected mill, and he agreed to send Indian Alex up to work with Forrest on the claim while Haney rode a borrowed Princesa horse to Sacramento City for his mill iron.

Beatriz said nothing until arrangements were made and Haney was gone. Then she confronted Mike earnestly.

"In this house, Miguel, the word of the man is not all the law. I will not see you be the fool my father was!"

"You want me to call Haney back?"

"No. But remember gifts do not make a man rich. The giving makes only a feeling of richness which is empty. And we are not going to only feel rich. We are going to be rich!"

"All right," Mike said. "All right. So damned rich you'll vomit at the sight of gold."

He went out to the corral and mounted a horse and rode out of the yard. In a mile he was ashamed of his flare of anger. He knew he could not understand the passion of Beatriz' feeling. What he wanted he had never known. To him freedom seemed a gift of great wealth. Perhaps even the greatest. As Dutch had once told him, a rich man could eat no more food than a poor one. And Joaquin had said the same thing. Theirs was wisdom. But he was married to neither of them. Bea would be easier on the subject when there was security on the Princesa. Until then he supposed he could give up the intoxication of self-aggrandizement through generosity.

Turning back toward the house he encountered Romero, starting off on another collection tour of the leased claims, a duty devolving upon him in Benson's absence. They passed with a wave. A little farther down he encountered a cousin of the Castros, southward bound from Sacramento City. They stopped to talk. There was little news from the Coast. The steamship *California* had anchored off San Francisco with 365 gold-seekers from the East. This was only the second week in March and these were the first to arrive. The inevitable rush had begun.

When he got back to the house, Mike found Ed Finney and Joaquin had been there in his absence. They were starting off on a deer hunt into the high snow country and Judson Jeffers had asked to go with them. Mike was not pleased that Alice and Bea had permitted the old man to do so, but he supposed there was no real harm in it. The sheriff and Joaquin were expert mountaineers and knew Jeffers' limitations as well as Mike himself did.

He felt a little uncomfortable about dinner alone with the two women, but it went off well enough and their discussion of the afternoon seemed to have left no real imprint on Beatriz. Alice retired early to her locked room, as she had taken to doing more and more in recent weeks. With the house quiet, Mike and Beatriz also went to bed at an early hour. They did not have a fire and the chill moved in on them, so that Bea snuggled close. Grateful, Mike held her tightly. Presently she spoke of Alice Abernathy.

"I do not understand her, Micaelo," she said. "She seems content. But Dutch does not come down from the mine and Mr. Jeffers lives in the office. Still she is content."

Mike chuckled.

"Maybe she's got a secret," he suggested.

"Maybe," Beatriz said. "The other morning I went to

call her to breakfast. She didn't answer my knock, so I opened the door."

"And she was in bed with Indian Alex!" Mike interposed.

"No silly! She was cleaning fresh mud from the floor near her window. And her shoes were dry. Honestly. I looked to see. How could she get mud on her floor before anyone else was up and keep her shoes dry."

"Jeffers, then," Mike said. "And you should have seen him on the ship coming out here! An old man. Now look at him. Off hunting in the snow. Climbing in and out windows. Having the time of his life! If he was ten years younger, I'd be worrying about you!"

"Worry anyhow," Bea suggested. "It is good for husbands. But I've never seen any mud on Mr. Jeffers' floor. If he tracked it in one place he'd track it in another."

"You don't know everything that goes on out there in the office."

"Ben does. He would know."

"Maybe he's sharing the old man's secret."

"No. You must do something about this, Micaelo."

"What?"

"This sort of thing is shocking. Father Bartolo would be upset."

"His worst fault is not minding his own business. Don't you start it!"

"Yes, Micaelo," Beatriz agreed.

"I'm your business. You've been neglecting me."

"I have not!"

"You are right now. You're talking too much!"

Giggling a little and wholly unchastened, Beatriz ceased to talk.

Very early, two mornings later, Judson Jeffers galloped into the Princesa yard from his hunting trip, shouting for Mike. Half-dressed, Mike hurried through the house to meet him in the living room. Beatriz followed to light a lamp. Alice also came out, hair tousled and body carelessly covered in her haste. Jeffers had been riding as hard as he knew how. He was exhausted and his age sat heavily on him in the lamplight.

"Murietta!" he said shakenly. "Finney's waiting for you over there, Mike. Get over to Murietta's as fast as you can!"

"Joaquin?" Beatriz asked sharply, softly.

Jeffers shook his head like a stunned, wounded bear.

"His wife," he said.

His chin dropped onto his breast and he began to sob along the thin edge of collapse, tears running down through the stubble of his hunter's beard.

"Give him a hot brandy," Mike swiftly told the women. "A big one. Then get him into bed, right away!"

He ran back through the house for the rest of his clothes. Bea met him in the hall as he came back.

"What is it, Micaelo? What has happened?"

"I don't know. Don't question the judge. Let him alone. Let him get hold of himself. I'll get word to you, soon as I can."

Jeffers' horse was not badly blown. Rather than waste time catching and saddling a fresh animal, Mike swung up and reached off through the timber, riding high and uncomfortable in the old man's stirrups.

It took thirty minutes to make Murietta's. The whole time he heard Bea's soft query in his ears.

"Joaquin . . . ?"

It meant a great deal. It meant the deep regard both of them felt for their quiet neighbor. It meant the first friends Mike himself had made in the mountains. It meant a man and his wife who lived as few did, in love and at peace with the world. They were gentle people, good people, friends.

There was no light in the Murietta house when Mike clattered up onto the bench where it stood. He rode straight for the door. Halfway across the bench, he was urgently challenged and he recognized Ed Finney's voice.

"Mr. McGann, don't ride up there! Over here . . ."

Mike reined toward the cutbank of the creek. Finney rose from it.

"Sure glad you're here!" he said with relief. "Joe's gone crazy. He'd shoot you down if you rode up like that to the door!"

"He's in the house?"

"With his wife," Finney said.

"What's happened?"

"Some dirty bastards raped Joe's missus to death."

"Stay here," Mike said grimly.

He jerked his horse around and rode up to the door of

the house. A little gray light was growing, the luminosity of false dawn. As he swung down, Mike saw the door was closed, but one whole plank had been smashed from it. Murietta's woodpile axe lay in the dirt almost at the sill. Half a dozen feet away lay the body of the big dog, head shattered by a terrible blow from the axe. Mike knocked.

"It's me, Joe—it's Miguel. . . ."

The broken door swung inward from the slight impetus of the knock. Mike stepped into the house. There was a stir across the room. A Spanish *fósforo* rasped, sputtered into a spark of yellow flame, and the wick of a lamp caught. The light revealed a terrible face above the lamp —the face of a man who was dead, although he breathed —a white, tense, bloodless mask of flesh, in which lay tortured eyes.

The lamp revealed so much else that was terrible: a room in shambles; furniture dislodged and overturned by desperate struggle; wanton destruction; a bed from which the legs at one side had been broken off by crashing weight, so that it tilted crazily. Across this sprawled the twisted nude body of Murietta's wife, beautiful still, but revolting for what had been done.

No animal ever died in this fashion. There was this decency in nature. The great, open brown eyes stared blindly from the horror mask of the bruised face as though in accusation at Mike for the blood in his veins.

"Welcome to the house of Murietta, Miguel!" Joaquin whispered hoarsely.

The mockery of the words was savage. Mike retrieved a blanket from the floor and spread it gently over the body. He touched an arm inadvertently and his stomach churned. The flesh was not yet cold. He turned to his friend, his hand reaching out in clumsy comfort. Murietta flattened against the wall behind the lamp.

"Don't touch me!" he said.

"Who did it, Joe?"

"Does that matter?"

"Come outside for a bit."

"No! I go with no *yanqui* again!"

"Joe—please!"

"You worry for me? Why? Am I child, to cry? Will that bring her back? Am I a fool to go crazy and destroy myself? Will that bring her back? Will I be a madman, not seeing what I see and not knowing what I know? Do not worry for me, Miguel. Worry for the *yanquis*. I am Joaquin, and they will come to know me!"

"Joe, it's no good, talking like that. . . ."

"They will suffer," Murietta went on intensely. "They will fear as she feared, until their guts are water. Get out of here, Miguel. Do not come back. Forget Joaquin as you will forget her. Do not try to find me again. You are *yanqui*. Get out, Miguel. It is hard not to kill even you!"

Mike saw the rifle then, clenched in the man's two trembling hands. The rifle shifted. It was apparent Joaquin was in whole physical control of himself. This was not hysteria. It was cold, implacably measured hatred. Mike knew his friend would kill him if he did not obey. He backed to the door.

Ed Finney was waiting uneasily near his horse in the yard. They withdrew in silence to the cutbank, where Finney had left his own horse.

"You got more sand than me, Mr. McGann," Finney breathed. "I wouldn't have gone in there like that for anything! Not after he knew it was Yankees and picked up his gun. But you can't blame him."

"Any idea who they were?"

"No. Four of 'em, from the tracks in the yard. Must have been here since afternoon—before supper time, anyhow. She hadn't started to fix a meal. An' I guess we run 'em off inside the hour. That's a hell of a long time for one little lady!"

Mike nodded, exhaling slowly.

"The Judge started to give out on us up in the hills yesterday," Finney went on. "Snow was deep an' the huntin' poor. We started down. Figured on makin' it back, so we kept travelin' after sundown. But the Judge got real whipped an' Joaquin figured we'd better camp it out, after all, back up on the hump a ways."

Finney stopped and looked off at the little house.

"It sure wasn't anything Joaquin wanted to do, because we could see a light down here from where we was. Kept gettin' later and later, but Joaquin wouldn't hit his blanket. Just sat off from our fire an' watched this light, wonderin' why his wife didn't turn it out an' go to sleep. That's what's killin' him now, I reckon—that he was just sittin' there, watchin'. After midnight, with the light still burnin', the Judge realized what was eatin' Joaquin an' made us start on down again."

"They were still around when you got here?"

"I wished they was!" Finney growled. "When we hit the spur off to this side of the Spittin' Jim. Joaquin was sure his wife was in some kind of trouble—sick or somethin'. We let off half a dozen shots to tell her we was comin'. They must have lit out then."

"There's got to be some way of running them down."

"Would be, if she was alive and could talk. Believe me, Mr. McGann, I'd round up every man in California, if it took me ten years, and drag 'em in here for her to point out the sons of bitches we want. Way it is, there's not much we can do. Tracks'll be lost, first main trail they hit. Too damned many could have done it. Just too damned many!"

Mike nodded. Finney gestured toward the house.

"Think he'll be all right?"

"He won't let anybody do anything. He means it."

"Might as well get moving, then. I got some questions to ask, down on the big creek. Maybe somebody else was by here an' seen 'em, or something."

Mike shook his head.

"They had the place to themselves or they wouldn't have stayed so long."

"Four of 'em—good God!" Finney swung stiffly into his saddle. "What the hell's the use of laws when something like this can happen?"

"I don't know. Be damned if I do. But tell everybody to stay clear of here. Joaquin wants to be alone. I think he'd shoot anybody on sight who rode up. Make it plain —leave him alone!"

"It ain't human not to give a man comfort."

"What happened isn't human, either. Make it real plain, Ed."

"Yes, sir," Finney agreed reluctantly.

He started down the creek. Mike waited until he was gone from sight around the first turn, then rode heavily in the opposite direction, back to the Princesa.

• TWELVE •

Jeffers was sleeping when Mike returned from Murietta's. The two women were huddled over the coffeepot in the dejection of an uncertainty already intuitively answered in their own minds. Mike dropped heavily into a chair and looked at Beatriz. His stomach churned again. He poured and swallowed a great gulp of coffee."

"Never let yourself be alone in this house," he said quietly. "Never! Do you hear me?"

"What was it, Micaelo?"

"Joaquin's wife was killed early this morning—before he got down from the mountains. Some men came by his place. They stayed all night—until his wife was dead."

Beatriz choked and her face drained of color. She crossed herself, then, and lowered her head. Mike went out to the office and sat woodenly there until Alex came down from Forrest's claim in mid-morning. He rose, then, wanting a service from the Indian. But Beatriz was before him. She spoke to Alex. He went to the corral and saddled her a horse. In a few moments they rode off together. Mike stayed within the office. He was grateful that someone on the Princesa could reach out to their stricken neighbor. It was best that it was Beatriz.

It was nearly dark before Alex and his mistress returned. No one asked where they had been. Life resumed a normal course, save that the name of Murietta vanished from their speech. Judson Jeffers remained in bed, wheezing in a high fever with pneumonia and requiring the better part of the attention of both women in the house. The Judge was little if any better when Haney and Larry McCracken returned from Sacramento City together. They brought with them the blade wheels, bearing, shafts and belting of a sawmill. They brought a dozen horses and a hundred hand-picked head of cattle, all the animals in

101

Sutter's vast herds Mac believed worth adding to the stock of the Princesa. They also brought contradiction of Sutter's rumored bankruptcy. McCracken reported the Swiss in unusually high spirits and certain the sale of his lots in Sacramento City would enable him to meet all his obligations with profit to spare.

Jeffers was a little better, showing the first signs of improvement, when Romero came in from his collection round with sixty ounces of gold. This, together with the reserve Mike had earlier retained, seemed ample to justify getting some of the immediate construction problems out of the way. Mike was surprised to discover Beatriz concurred. Construction was not expenditure of capital to her. It was investment, and she approved wholeheartedly. When Benson and Spier rolled in from Monterey with a big freight wagon, heavily loaded, instead of the light rig they had taken out, a dam was rapidly rising across Delmonte Creek, two miles above the house.

Benson had bought even more shrewdly than Haney and Mac. There was a stout steel safe for the office and a cast-iron stove for Maria, to be set up in Dutch's camp at the mine. There was a huge set of English tableware for Beatriz—enough to service forty guests in the Princesa dining room. A summer's supply of kitchen staples for both households was in half a dozen stout wooden boxes. There was a forge and smithy tools and a stock of bar and strap iron for repairs; also an assortment of hand tools for rock and two strong iron barrows. There was a quantity of powder and fuse. But the heaviest portion of the load was the beached machinery, consisting chiefly of the rigging and heavy iron for a two-stamp Birmingham ore mill.

Dutch came eagerly out of his mine to lay new lines and alter some of the first levels at the dam so the stamps could go in on one side of Delmonte Creek and Haney's sawmill on the other. Except for Benson, who was again busy with lease collections and accounts, they all worked on the dam. Mac rubbed Ben's fur a little over his bookkeeping, but Ben's efforts were making more and more sense to Mike—the necessity for recording the cost and income of each enterprise in detail, so that it would soon be possible to know where the greatest profits—if any—lay.

Two newcomers moved into Murietta's abandoned house. They saw the cross on the creek bank and asked who was buried there. They were warned and told the story. They did not take the warning seriously. Presently there were two crosses on the creek bank, for one of the men was shot from the timber one morning as he came from the house. His partner buried him and moved out the same day. There was talk of looking for Joaquin, but Sheriff Finney did not want to look and Mike McGann did not want him to. Who had fired the shot was a guess at best, for Joaquin had vanished and there had been no word of him since Beatriz and Alex had helped him bury his wife the afternoon of the day she died.

The street of Freezer's Bar was choking with men again, but there was a change in them. Many were still the old hands of the previous year. The others—newcomers— had sailed around two continents on crowded ships or crossed the mountains and deserts to the east on foot and by wagon for but one purpose—gold. They ignored Ben's system of claims for lease on the ranch. They refused recognition of Delmonte County, its court and its commissioners. They traded at Freezer and drank there, but they located far up the Spittin' Jim and the Conejos, beyond the limits of Dutch Abernathy's survey, where the land and the gravel and the gold were free and the law was their own.

In the last week in June Ed Finney rode down to the Princesa wearing a worried frown. Peyton and his wife had returned to the cabin on the upper Spittin' Jim and had taken possession of their old claims again. Mike remembered the four men who had wintered on the claims— who had supposedly jumped them—and he shared Finney's worry. Obviously the four jumpers were in Peyton's pay and had been from the beginning. Perhaps it was because of them Peyton and Felicia felt secure in returning to the district although Smiley Palmer's death was yet widely remembered.

"As one of the commissioners, Mr. McGann, you tell me where this puts me," Finney said. "If they didn't hang Palmer, they had something to do with it. Everybody knows it. So do they and so do I. And I'm sheriff. I should do something."

"No," Mike counseled. "You weren't sheriff then. Old

Delmonte was hanged for Palmer's hanging. Let it go at that. Forget old troubles. Plenty of new ones are on the way."

"Yeah, with Peyton back," Finney agreed.

Felicia Peyton's rumored pregnancy had apparently been false for she was reported striding the street of Freezer, slender as a lash, arrogant and masculine. But in this time an heir to the Princesa was on the way and as Mike watched Beatriz begin to thicken there was a new and wonderful excitement. They determined to say nothing to others in these early months. And to Mike, the building began to take on new significance. For the first time he realized the future would not necessarily end with his own death.

Alice sat often with Judge Jeffers as he grew strong enough to resume his county hearings again. She worked long hours in the Princesa office, recording leases, complaints, judgments, and registrations. Jeffers himself no longer had the flush of second youth he had first found in the mountains. He was, as Alice pointed out to Mike, an old man. Her treatment of him became more and more deferential but without the archness of the physical which had earlier marked their relationship. She remained untroubled and happy with her place on the ranch, as she had all through the spring.

After a flash night shower, Beatriz again found mud on the floor of Alice's room, tracked beneath her window. She made a joke of it again to Mike, but it was not really their affair.

Angus and Felicia Peyton paid an unexpected call at the Princesa, riding in alone over the trail from the Spittin' Jim. Their manner made it plain it was a social visit. It was accepted as such. Beatriz brought brandy to the men and commented with shrewd flattery upon the trim, flat-fitting riding habit Felicia wore. It was too masculine for Mike's taste. In fact, recognition of Felicia was difficult. He remembered quite another woman, full-bodied and provocative. But Bea made a convincing effort and Felicia warmed to it. In a few minutes these two who had been friends in girlhood were talking of the *californiano* days in Monterey and names neither had heard in years, and the two men had only to deal with the brandy and themselves.

"I'm afraid you make me out pretty much a bastard, McGann," Peyton said ruefully.

Mike smiled pleasantly.

"You don't need any particular help from me," he said.

"You remember the partnership I offered you?"

"If you're thinking of repeating it, save yourself the trouble. I might have needed your help in Monterey. I don't need it now."

"I know," Peyton agreed. "I underestimated you. Just the same, it's a pity. Felicia and I don't feel you really know us. That's why we rode over. We want to be decent. We want to be friends. Look at the two women. They have a lot in common."

"I suppose we do, too," Mike suggested wryly.

"I think so. Similar ambitions, at least. We both want more than money. Something to leave behind, maybe. Reputation and a name and a family. The chance is here —right here. We both know that."

"On the Princesa, you mean."

"Certainly. Felicia and I aren't bandits. Maybe not even the bandit you are, McGann. Look at it fairly. We both feel we have some right to participation. We're indirectly responsible for your being here. You can see that."

Mike let his smile answer.

"Your wife is one of the old families, too," Peyton went on earnestly. "The four of us could carve our names deeply into the cornerstones of this new state. I told you once what we could become. We still can."

Mike shook his head.

"There's logic to what I'm saying," Peyton urged. "The feeling Felicia and I have is logical. You've got to admit that!"

"Freely," Mike agreed. "A logical feeling and a common one. More and more people are getting the idea they should share in the Princesa, every day. I keep running into them."

Peyton smiled a little.

"I imagine." He sobered. "I realize you have some reasons for distrusting us. . . ."

"A few," Mike conceded. "Like Felicia must remember once in a while that in the beginning she and her father thought you and I had advance news of the gold strike and worked together to swindle them out of their ranch."

"She still believes that," Peyton said quietly. "She's

never stopped believing it. She married me and kept right on believing it. She holds me responsible."

"Very sad," Mike said without sympathy. "Which one of you was responsible for Smiley Palmer?"

"That . . ." Peyton shrugged heavily. "That's part of the reason for this call. So something like that won't happen again. We wanted to break up the organized district at Freezer in order to stir unrest and trouble for you. Sound enough, tactically, but Palmer was stubborn. Felicia became frightened and Fiero thought the old man was in danger. That's all it took."

"All four of you were there, and Nicolo was the only one with guts enough to come back."

"If you want to put it that way. I've never been one to believe suicide is the act of a brave man."

"I doubt if you know much about brave men."

"I didn't come to quarrel," Peyton protested. "You've got Judson Jeffers here. You trust him. Let him draw the papers. Cut me personally entirely out of it. Just fix it so Felicia has a share. That's all I want."

"I'm sorry, Peyton. I take care of my wife. You take care of yours."

" 'Licia married me because she hates me, McGann. She'll go on hating me till she has a part of the *rancho* again. If you think I'm begging, you're right. I happen to love her. I can't stand the hate. I'm desperate."

Mike studied Peyton. A fine sweat stood out on his forehead. There were nail marks where his overlapping hands clasped. He might be lying, but he was also suffering.

It was deep twilight and cooking smells were drifting from the kitchen. It was a measure of the obligation Beatriz felt to the hospitality of her house and the disregard in which she held these two unwanted guests that, although she listened pleasantly to Felicia's chatter of forgotten days, she extended no supper invitation. Mike rose and crossed to the women. Peyton followed him uncertainly.

"I have a question to ask you, Felicia," he said. "Think your answer over carefully. Do you love your husband?"

Felicia sat motionless for a moment. She glanced at Peyton, then threw back her head and laughed.

"Of course I love Angie! How could you ask? I love

him completely—passionately. I'm surprised he hasn't boasted of it to you!"

Mike looked at Peyton. The man's eyes were stricken.

"And just why did you ride over to see us this afternoon?"

"To give you a warning. Is that honest enough?"

"Warning?"

"To give me my fair share of the Princesa before I take it from you!"

"I think you had better go," Beatriz said.

"I'm sorry, Bea—so really sorry. But it will make no difference to you. I promise it will make no difference to you."

Before Bea realized what she intended, Felicia embraced her and planted a kiss on her lips. She broke free angrily. Mike took Felicia's arm and steered her toward her horse. Peyton moved heavily to his own animal and mounted. Mike returned to the veranda.

"I feel dirty," Beatriz said. "She is sick—wickedly and ugly sick, Miguel. I think I will go wash."

She went around the house toward the washstand by the back door. Mike cut through the house. Alice and Jeffers and Benson and Mac were already at the table in the kitchen and there was a great deal of delight among them because the enemy had finally come suing for peace. Mike let the conclusion stand without contradiction. He doubted that war was done—that it had even really begun—but he was learning patience, that most potent of all weapons.

• THIRTEEN •

Mike did not hear the fight begin. Beatriz roused him in the thin early morning hours when it was already in progress. He kicked from the bed, seizing clothing as he moved, and ran bootless to the kitchen, out into the yard, and around the corner to a patch of light beneath Alice

Abernathy's window. Alice stood in the open frame, a wrapper twisted around her, holding a lamp. In the square of light cast by this, Dutch Abernathy was killing McCracken.

The big Texan was livid with fury, but he was already badly mauled and his driving, deadly lunges could not reach the engineer. Hard as the rock he had been digging, compact and incredibly swift on his feet, Dutch was bounding in and out, side-stepping drives to seize Mac by arm or head, using the Texan's own momentum to lever him over hip or shoulder to a sickening crash against the hard 'dobe wall of the house, or a jolting spin to the ground.

As Mike watched, thunderstruck, Mack went down onto his face. Before his stubborn, spasmodically working knees could jack him up again, Dutch came in boots first onto his back, then punishingly down with his knees, locking his hands about Mac's throat from behind. Great cords stood up on the engineer's forearms as his fingers exerted crushing pressure.

Mike leaped angrily across and seized Abernathy's ears as Mac had taught him to seize the ears of an unruly calf. Twisting, he lifted the man bodily upward. Even then it was necessary to break Dutch's grip on McCracken's throat with a violent kick at the wrists. Mike pushed Abernathy flat against the wall beside his wife's window and turned back to help McCracken onto his feet. Benson and Jeffers, also aroused, came across from the office with another lamp. Mike was aware of Beatriz at his elbow.

"You damned fools!" he said angrily to the two men against the wall. "What is this?" And to Dutch. "What are you doing down here?"

Mac was still breathing so hard it was difficult for him to speak.

"That's right!" he gasped. "Ask the son of a bitch! What's he been doin' down here two-three nights a week —late, when he thought nobody'd see him?"

Mike looked up at the woman in the window. The excitement of the battle was still bright in her eyes. Beatriz touched his arm.

"I told you there was mud on the floor," she whispered.

Jeffers looked up at Alice Abernathy with malice.

"Maybe I can explain, Mike," he suggested. "I believe I'm supposed to be judge advocate around here."

"Keep your potbelly out of this!" Dutch snapped.

"Dutch has achieved a reconciliation with his wife," Jeffers went on, unperturbed. "He's been spending as much time as he could with her under the circumstances."

Alice slowly lowered the lamp to a stand.

"You—you knew, all the time?" she asked through the window.

The old man smiled.

"You have hardly been what I would call discreet," he said.

Dutch shoved truculently out from the wall. Mike pushed him back and turned to McCracken.

"Just what business is this of yours?"

"I warned him twice," Mac said.

"About what?"

"About Maria and the kid, up there at the mine. What you suppose this'll do to them?"

"Get yourself cleaned up and go back to bed," Mike told the Texan. "Dutch, we'd better have a talk."

He took Beatriz' arm and steered her back into the house. Dutch followed them sullenly. Beatriz lit a lamp in the living room and went back into the kitchen to poke up a fire and put coffee on.

"What are you going to do now?" Mike asked Abernathy.

"It's a hell of a mess." Dutch said heavily.

He leaned forward, bracing his hands on his knees.

"I came down here the first time to thresh it all out with Alice in private. She said she wanted Jeffers. I had Maria. It was all done but getting us unmarried. That's the way it started."

"Why didn't you wind it up that way?"

"You don't know yet what it's like when you've been married to a woman for years, Mike. You get so you remember the same things. There's a kind of language that doesn't even need words. And when its been a long time since you've seen each other, well . . ."

Dutch shrugged. Beatriz brought the coffee. Mike signed her to stay and made a place beside him for her.

"Then you've found out you're still in love with Alice?"

"I can't stand her," Abernathy said miserably. "She puts me in a box and nails down the lid. She always has. There's no freedom, no spirit of my own. She's jealous of my work, my time, my thoughts. It's just that I can't leave her alone. I've been over this a hundred times, trying to find a way out. I'd have sent Maria down here as soon as I knew how it was with Alice. But how could I? She's pregnant again."

"You've really diddled yourself into something," Mike said without sympathy.

"It seems a question of what's fairest, Dutch," Beatriz said quietly. "Fairest for Maria."

"She's a better woman than a man like me deserves," Dutch said earnestly. "She's given me more than I can ever repay. I want to take care of her, and the baby, too —if this one lives. You people owe me something. I want her to have that. More, if she needs it."

"What does she say, Dutch?"

"Nothing. We haven't talked. We never have. About anything. She knows where I've been going, but she hasn't said anything. She won't."

"Send her down to me in the morning," Beatriz said. "Take Alice down to the mine. I'll put Maria in her room. At least I'll know my floors will stay clean."

Mike walked out onto the veranda with the engineer.

"What about Pepe?" he asked.

"He's mine, Mike. He's staying."

"Alice may not want him to."

"I do!"

Dutch strode off into the gray light of false dawn.

It was too late to sleep again. Mike sent Beatriz to bed for the luxury of a sunrise between blankets and he went into the kitchen to start breakfast. Jeffers saw the lamplight and came uncertainly to the back door. Mike motioned him in. The old man sat down at the table and poured himself a cup of coffee.

"As a species, Mike, homo sapiens is the prize idiot of the animal kingdom!" he said.

"It's been a happy family here," Mike said. "I don't like this. Don't suppose you do, either."

"Me?" Jeffers laughed. "Never been so relieved in my life! For weeks I supposed Alice was keeping her husband's visits secret from me for some nefarious purpose."

"It was Maria that was worrying both of them. I thought you were in love with Alice."

"I was," Jeffers said. "She's a good twenty-five years

younger than I am, Mike. She'd have killed me inside of six months, and I wouldn't have died with my boots on, either."

"Then you'll stay on, without that—that added attraction?"

"Try and get rid of me."

"Good."

"Look, Mike," Jeffers said earnestly. "Ben and I were talking, earlier last night. That constitutional convention in Monterey the first of September. The real thing, this time, I think. And Delmonte County has to send a representative. I want to go."

"The convention's three weeks off."

"I know. But if I've already left the county, I can't be recalled."

"Recalled?"

Jeffers nodded seriously.

"You're baron of the grant, all right. Boss of the business end of it. But you're just one vote, politically. The new people pouring in on the Spittin' Jim are votes, too. If they turn against you, you've lost your control."

"You trying to tell me you want to get off to Monterey before they get together at Freezer and send somebody of their own?"

"They can do it, Mike."

"They won't."

"I hope you're right."

The old man sipped his coffee.

"You've heard about the gang of Mexican cutthroats that have been raising hell down on the other side of the Mariposas," he said. "Killing Yankees right and left and robbing everybody blind?"

Mike nodded.

"Their leader is Joaquin Murietta."

"Gossip. I heard that. Nothing to it."

"They're saying over in Freezer that his hideout is on the Princesa—over near the Minarets, someplace."

"Couldn't be a better place to hide."

"But you can't afford to give haven to a band of murderers."

"I'll believe Joaquin's a murderer when it's proved. Until then he's my friend and he's welcome to the Princesa."

Jeffers scrubbed his jaw thoughtfully.

111

"The hardest lesson a young lawyer has to learn is that Justice is not only blind, but has no sympathy. I know how you feel about Joaquin. Society owes him a debt impossible of payment. But law and justice are possessions of society, not the implements of an individual. When there is murder, motive has no weight in terms of justice except as an adduction of further proof of guilt."

"Words, Judge," Mike said. "Let's keep them simple. Joaquin is my friend. That's enough for me."

Jeffers shrugged and watched Mike slice a panful of strips from a hoarded side of bacon. When he shoved the pan onto the fire, the old man heaved to his feet.

"You're a barbarian in a lot of ways," he said. "Why do you have to fry good bacon so damned crisp? It's as uncivilized as your ideas on the obligations of friendship! Here, let me mind it."

• FOURTEEN •

Felicia Peyton gave over trying to straighten the disarray of the cabin. She returned to the mirror, brushing a strand of hair from her eyes. What had happened here on their claim during the visit Angus and herself had made to the Princesa meant nothing. The sudden raid, the violence, the ransacking of her cabin could find no place in her sickened mind. It was too full of what had happened on the Princesa, of what had been happening to her for a long time without her knowledge.

She stared at the face in the mirror. It was no different. It was a woman's face. But the creature behind it was not a woman. Behind that mask was a creation of her revenge. She had married Angus to torture him, more than she had married him for his help in repossessing the Princesa. She had married him to hold her womanhood out to him and withhold it; to watch him hunger and be unsatisfied; to watch him worship, and then destroy the thing he worshipped. And she had succeeded too well. Cultivating male habits and appearance to taunt Angus, she had shattered something within herself.

The door swung open and Angus came in from the creek. He flopped wearily into a chair.

"It was Murietta, all right," he said. "With about twenty men. He was recognized by several who knew him. Everybody along the creek is stirred up by the raid and the killings."

"Was anyone else shot but Steve and Bowling, here at our place?"

"No. Apparently Murietta didn't fire on anyone else. Just our crew."

"Where are Collins and Morgan?"

"Hiding in the hills, I guess. They were pretty badly frightened. Murietta looked all over for them after he'd shot Steve and Bowling. They were lucky to get away. I doubt if they'll ever come back."

"So we lose our crew and a hundred ounces of gold— and have the cabin torn up, too! What has Murietta got against us?"

"Nothing," Angus said. "I heard the story this morning. His wife was killed near here last fall. A few days ago Bowling and Morgan got drunk down at Freezer and boasted how they—together with Steve and Collins—had given a Mexican whore all she could stand. Murietta heard about it, I guess. It fitted the way his wife died. He came looking for our men. And he got two of them."

"When are you starting after these *bandidos?*" Felicia asked.

"Murietta's bunch?" Angus was surprised. "I'm not going after them."

Felicia looked at her husband with a rising gorge of distaste. He was so shrewd in so many ways and so emotionally helpless in others. His sympathy for Murietta was apparent. She felt the same sympathy. But Murietta's raid afforded an opportunity, and sympathy would not destroy Mike McGann for them.

"You're going to let this crazy *paisano* ride off with our gold after killing two of our men and driving the other two off? Is this the way you're going to build respect among the miners—the way you're going to make them believe you stand for law and order and individual rights? Do I have to show you every step of the way, or are you going to keep on making a fool's mistakes, like our ride to see Miguel McGann?"

"Nobody could catch Murietta now," Angus protested. "Be reasonable! He's had a twelve-hour start. He's clear across the Princesa by now, holed up somewhere in the mountains. By the time I could get a posse together and ride around McGann's boundaries, the trail would be completely cold!"

"Don't go around the Princesa. Go across it, like Murietta did."

"Murietta's a friend of McGann's. They'd let him across, but not us."

"How can Miguel stop you, if your posse is big enough? Get McGann's sheriff, too. If enough miners demand it, the Sheriff will have to go with you. McGann can't stop you if you're chasing bandits with his own law."

"He'd try."

"Seguro!" Felicia snapped impatiently. "That's the point! And how many enemies would he make, doing it? How much respect would there be left for his attitude toward his own government and laws—the very things he's been using to keep miners off his land?"

Angus rose and looked at her for a long moment.

"Well?" she asked.

He nodded slowly, turned, and took his rifle from its rack. He came back to her and put his hand on her shoulder.

"Someday maybe I'll forgive you for marrying me," he said.

"Someday we'll have the Princesa. When we do, maybe I'll forgive you, too."

'I wish I could believe that."

"Don't you?"

"No, 'Licia."

"But you can't keep from hoping, can you?" she asked wickedly.

"No," he agreed. "I can't keep from hoping."

He tucked the rifle beneath his arm and pulled open the door.

Maria came down alone and afoot from the mine, carrying a small bundle over her shoulder in a shawl. Beatriz made her sit on the veranda, the two of them sharing a pot of tea, while Mike and Jonathan Spier moved Alice Abernathy's trunk from the back bedroom and loaded it on the top-cart.

When the trunk was stowed, Alice emerged from the house. She paled a little when she saw Maria on the veranda, then went on out to the top-cart without a good-bye. Mike reminded Spier to have the cart back early, as Jeffers was determined to start for the Coast as soon as he could complete packing. Spier nodded and drove off. Beatriz went into the house to see to the room Alice had vacated. Mike dropped into her chair, intending to offer some kind of welcome to Maria, but Benson came around the corner of the house from the office. He stared after the cart for a moment, then came on over to the table.

"Good riddance, if you ask me," he said.

"Nobody asked," Mike answered.

"So they didn't."

Benson grinned and subjected Maria to an all-inclusive survey.

"We'll see you don't get lonesome down here," he said to her. "We take care of our women, down at this end of the Princesa. If you get lonesome, you just let me know, eh? We'll make out fine."

"Beatriz probably wants you in the house, Maria," Mike said quietly.

The woman rose and hurriedly left the veranda, eager to escape Benson's meaningful eye. Mike scowled at Benson.

"Now—what was on your mind when you came around here?"

"We've got nearly eight hundred ounces of gold out there in the safe. Something's got to be done with it."

"It'll get spent soon enough," Mike said.

"Sure," Benson assented. "But you can't be shipping around thirty- and forty-pound lots of raw gold to cover purchases. That ought to be handled with drafts and letters of credit."

"I've been thinking about that," Mike agreed. "Seems like by now there ought to be some kind of a bank in San Francisco."

Benson nodded.

"I'd like to take the gold out with the Judge and see. Think you can trust me, Mike?"

"There's one way to find out."

115

"If you guessed wrong, it might cost you upward of twelve thousand dollars."

"That isn't much to what it'd cost you when I found it out, Ben. Better get a move on if you want to be ready when the Judge is."

They were at the noon meal when Spier brought the top-cart back down from the mine. He came in and handed Mike a dirty envelope, crinkly with the mineral it contained.

"Dutch said to give you this."

Mike put the envelope into his pocket and took the freighter out to show him the crowned half-trunk Benson was using as a treasure chest for the gold shipment. When he returned to the table, Beatriz looked up at him. She pointed to the envelope.

"What is it, Micaelo?"

He shook out the contents of the envelope onto the tablecloth—half a dozen thick, entwined, fibrous threads of gold.

"Dutch has found his vein," he said.

"That means his stamp mill can finally go to work and at last there's a chance it might earn its cost back," Benson said with satisfaction. "It's about time."

Spier came back in to announce the cart was ready. They all went out onto the veranda.

"How long will it be, Princess?" Jeffers asked Beatriz as he gripped her hand in farewell.

"About five months," she answered. "Midwinter babies are strongest. We planned it that way."

"Like hell we did!" Mike protested.

They all laughed.

"I'm going to buy the Princess a present in San Francisco," Benson said. "Don't try to order me out of that, Mike."

"I won't, Mike agreed. "So long as you use your own money."

The two men piled up into the top-cart. Spier shook off his lines. The cart rolled past the end of the veranda and pulled abruptly up. Its three occupants scrambled hurriedly down. Mike ran toward them.

Two horses were jogging into the yard. Romero, hatless and frightened, rode the first and led the second, across the saddle of which was limply sprawled McCracken's big frame. One shoulder of the uneasy horse was covered with the Texan's blood.

"*Muchos hombres*," Romero stammered. "Many *yanqui* miners on the ridge. We go to stop them and they shoot at us!"

Mike lifted McCracken's arm. He had a badly torn wound in the heavy muscle plating his breast, but the bullet had struck at a shallow angle and there had been no penetration of the ribs. The greatest danger from it appeared to be the staggering quantity of blood the Texan had lost. Mike slid his shoulder under the wounded man and gently pulled his weight from the saddle. Benson moved quickly in and took the Texan's feet. Mike flung an order at Romero.

"Get Dutch, at the mine. Pick up Haney and his helper at the sawmill and Alex and Forrest at their claim."

Romero nodded and vaulted back onto his horse, spurring hard out of the yard. Mike turned his head to Spier.

"Light out for Freezer. Get Ed Finney and every man who'll ride with the Sheriff. Get them back here as fast as you can. Take Mac's horse. The blood may convince them we need them in a hurry."

Spier left the laden top-cart where it was and pulled up into McCracken's saddle. Mike nodded to Benson and they carried the unconscious Texan into the house. Fortunately Beatriz had water on the stove for the noon dishes. She brought a steaming pan of this and another empty basin and a stack of the spotless white cloths a woman always seemed able to lay hand to in an emergency. Mike turned his attention first to his hands. As he scrubbed them he became aware of Benson and the Judge, hovering anxiously back out of the way.

"Get out of here!" he exploded. "On your way. Now!"

"You're going to need us, Mike," Benson said.

"I'll need you more later. You've both got work to do. Get at it while you've still got a chance."

"We can't leave you now!" Jeffers argued heatedly. "Use your head!"

"Use yours! I don't know what this means, but whatever it is, I want them believing in Monterey and San Francisco that there's no trouble on the Princesa—no trouble in Delmonte County. If it got around there was, everybody'd head this way for the easy picking. It's up to you to see they don't. And you've got a trunkful of our gold in that cart. Get it out of here now!"

Benson and Jeffers looked helplessly at Beatriz.

"Take care of yourselves," she said quietly. "We'll be all right."

Mike did not see them go. He was already cleaning Mac's wound. Moving the man had started the bleeding again, a slow welling with a lazy, fitful surge which betrayed the ebbing pulse. And the torn condition of the wound made closing it difficult.

"Get some bottles. Fill them with the hottest water they'll hold. Stack them around him. And keep them hot. If he chills, he'll die sure. Brandy, too. Hot brandy."

Beatriz and Maria whispered softly from the room as Mike turned back to his task, ripping cloth to make a compress and a pressure bandage to the best of his ability. Before he was finished, Beatriz brought a steaming brandy mug to his elbow. He carefully raised the wounded man's head and got a little of the liquid between his teeth.

Slowly the blue which had been darkening about Mac's lips began to recede and his breathing began reaching more deeply into his lungs. Mike saw Dutch Abernathy and Alex in the doorway, watching with awe. He straightened.

"Keep him warm and quiet," he said swiftly to Beatriz. "More brandy, a little later. Some broth, after he's slept, if I'm not back and he'll take it."

She nodded, then caught Mike's arm sharply. McCracken had opened his eyes.

"Made it, hunh?" the wounded man whispered reedily. "Peyton! Son of a bitch!"

His eyes searched for and found his gunbelts hanging across a chair where Mike had flung them.

"Guns," he whispered, "beat a rifle. You take 'em, Miguel. . . ."

Mike picked up the belted weapons.

"I showed you," the Texan's whisper continued. "Now, damn you—use 'em!"

Mike dragged the pistols from their holsters and shoved them into his own waistband. Mac did not see this. He was looking up at Maria, bent over to tuck another hot bottle under his shoulder. Mike pulled Beatriz with him to the door.

"I'll leave Alex with you. We'll keep them away from the house. When Ed Finney and the bunch from Freezer show up, send them up Delmonte Creek after us."

"What is it—what do they want, Mike?"

"I don't know. We'll find out. But if they get a chance to see how much unworked gravel we've got up here, nothing can keep them out. That's what counts—turning them back before they've had much chance to look around."

"You promise to be careful?"

"I promise."

She kissed him and turned somber-eyed back toward Mac's bed. Mike strode through the house, picking up a queue of others who followed him silently onto the veranda. Alex, Romero, Haney and Bill Catlin, his helper at the mill, Forrest, Dutch and Pepe. All were white-faced and all were armed but the boy.

"Know where my rifle is?" Mike asked Pepe.

"*Si.*"

"Know how to use it?"

"*Si.*"

"Get it and go back up to the mine. Stay with Mrs. Abernathy. Shoot any stranger on sight. Keep on shooting until you run out of powder. Understand?"

"*Si.*"

Pepe disappeared into the house. Mike eyed Alex. "Same orders for you. Only you stay here. If anybody shows up here, keep them away from the house."

The Indian nodded and moved with grim, proprietary purpose to a position near the door.

"The rest of you, let's go!"

Romero caught Mike's arm.

"I think I could find Joaquin. *Patrón.* He has many men. He is our friend. He would help us."

"We don't need him and we don't want him."

"That's confidence—when you don't even know what you're up against yet!" Dutch said.

"Want to stay out of it, Dutch?"

"Yes. But I'm not going to."

"Then keep your mouth shut!"

Mike strode the length of the veranda and pulled onto Alex' pony. McCracken's guns, tight against his belt, dug reassuringly into the flesh of his belly. He reined the Indian's horse about and set his spurs.

• FIFTEEN •

They rode swiftly for the ridges. Romero regained courage with the reassurance of four men and his *patrón* beside him in place of the gravely wounded man with whom he had ridden down the slopes. He led the party at a tangent from Delmonte Creek toward a high park where he and McCracken had encountered the party of miners. Approaching this, Mike halted the company and took Dutch ahead to investigate. Curiously, the miners were still there. They had dismounted and sprawled out under trees on the far side. Mike saw Peyton almost immediately. The man was in motion, drifting from one group to another, with a few words for each.

"Go back to the others," Mike told Dutch. "Get this straight. Have them scatter and find good cover, but keep out of sight. I'll give them ten minutes to get set, then I'm going in."

"Alone?" Dutch grunted. "You're crazy. You've got to show the biggest force you can to get those jumpers to even listen."

"I can't wait for Finney and whoever he brings from Freezer. You boys keep this outfit covered. If a single shot is fired, cut loose and knock down every man you can hit!"

"Wait a minute, Mike! If it turned out these men are on some legitimate business and we shot them up, you'd be in great shape!"

"If they're legitimate, there won't be any shots fired. I'm just trying to give myself a chance to get clear if they open up on me like they did on Mac and Romero."

"Mac probably asked for it!"

"I won't. Ten minutes, Dutch."

Abernathy eased back off toward the others. Mike waited. He saw now that three or four men had drifted down the little trickle which drained the park and were huddled about one man working a pan with the peculiar rolling, rocking motion of an experienced prospector. Mike's lips tightened. These were the empty acres of the Princesa. Haney cut no timber here. No claims were leased here yet. None were worked. There was only Mc-Cracken's crown-branded cattle, grazing through the underbrush. Because they were empty acres, unmarked by their owner, mining men would hold they were open, subject to any man's claim, if gold could be proved on them. For every yellow fleck appearing in the pan now working in the park, there was greater certainty of a clash.

Once Mike caught a glimpse of Romero, carrying his rifle high and working into a deadfall tangle, far off to his left. However, he was not seen by the miners. Two or three more of these had risen and gone down to the group gathered about the man with the pan. At the end of a carefully generous ten minutes, Mike let his horse out into the open at a deliberate walk. He was seen almost immediately. The restlessness of the idling men fell away in relief. A few still sprawled lazily. Those with the gold pan paid Mike no attention. Most of the others rose and gathered around Peyton. Mike rode toward this group.

He was almost onto it when Ed Finney and another man came out of the timber, where he had not seen them. The sun winked on the Sheriff's badge and Mike knew Spier's ride to Freezer on Mac's bloody horse had been useless. Peyton had anticipated him in this. But Peyton had over-reached. Finney was the Princesa's sheriff. Mike pulled up and looked down at Peyton for a long moment before speaking quietly to Finney.

"These men are several miles inside of my boundaries, Sheriff. Get them off."

Finney looked uncomfortable.

"This is a posse, Mr. McGann," he said.

"Thirty-eight sworn deputies," Peyton added. He smiled. "Every one a law-abiding citizen of Delmonte County."

"We're trailing Joe Murietta," Finney explained. "Him and his gang killed two men at Mr. Peyton's camp and cleaned him out of dust."

"What happens at Peyton's camp is no concern of yours, Ed—or of mine. It's outside of the county."

"Just a few rods," Finney protested. "We got to stick by our neighbors."

"Not when they're trying to stick us!"

"Who's trying to stick who?" a man growled.

He waved his hand toward the group about the gold pan.

"They got color over there. Better color in half an hour than some of us have ever seen. You say this is your land. I say, where's your claim-markers and your development work?"

"Yeah!" another cut in. "You think you're God or something, McGann? Claiming to own the whole damned mountain! What's under the ground don't go with what's on top of it. In every other district, a man's entitled to a hundred and a half by three-fifty of gravel—feet, too—not miles! And he's got to work it or lose it!"

"This isn't a district," Mike said steadily. "It's a legally organized county. And I own all the rights to every foot of it. We've been through this before. I'm reminding you again, Sheriff—these men are trespassing!"

"You're denying fellow citizens a right to cross your land in pursuit of a murderer and a thief?" Peyton asked.

"You weren't pursuing anybody when I rode up," Mike said. "You were deliberately waiting for me."

"I made them do that," Finney said. "We had a brush with McCracken and one of your Mexicans. I didn't want that kind of trouble to go any farther. I figured you'd be here pretty quick."

"And so now what, Sheriff?"

"Join us. Help run Murietta down."

The man with the gold pan came up in time to hear this.

"The hell with that, Sheriff! Look at this!"

He held up the pan, slanted into the sun. Even from his saddle Mike could see the flecking in the residue coating the bottom.

"We're locating, right here!"

Others echoed the same intent. Mike rose angrily in his saddle.

"Any man that tries to stake a claim is measuring his own grave!" he said.

Faces darkened. Men shifted and Mike saw rifle barrels slanted in his direction.

"One of your men tried talking that way, earlier. He ain't talking so good, now!"

"Don't drive us, McGann."

"We don't give a damn for you or your Spanish title."

"This is U.S.A. now, and there's room for us all here."

Mike looked at Ed Finney.

"County law recognizes Spanish grants as legal, boys," the Sheriff said carefully. "If you want claims, Mr. McGann'll lease 'em to you."

"Payin' him for what God put underground for us? To hell with that!"

"It's the law," Finney said stubbornly.

Peyton drifted over to Mike's stirrup.

"Better face the inevitable," he said. "These men are right and you're wrong. What's a few hundred acres out of forty thousand?"

"How many?" a man asked in outrage.

Peyton rolled out the enumeration with enjoyment.

"Forty thousand, three hundred and eighty."

"Jesus! That much? And he's bellyachin'!"

"Let's get to markin' out claims!"

The man with the pan dropped it and a knot of them started moving away. Ed Finney thumbed back the hammer of his rifle.

"I told you what the law is," he said.

The men looked at the steady rifle. They looked sullenly at Mike. Peyton moved toward them.

"Maybe we can't buck the law, boys," he said, "but we sure as hell can change it."

The man who had dropped the pan brightened,

"You got something there, Mr. Peyton!" He swung on his companions. "Let's get back to Freezer an' have us a meetin'."

There was a moment of indecision, then a general drift of the miners toward their horses. Peyton smiled and moved with them. Ed Finney lowered the hammer of his rifle and looked accusatively at Mike.

"McCracken should have let us trail Murietta across the ranch. You should have. I got to see the Judge about this."

"Don't be getting bigger than your breeches, Ed," Mike told him flatly. "The Judge is on his way to Monterey. You mind your own business. Clear them out of here and see they keep moving."

Finney shrugged unhappily and rode after his posse. When he was half the way across to them, one of the miners suddenly pulled aside from the group, swung up his rifle, and fired at Mike. He tried to do it fast and rushed his aim. The bullet cut wide. Another miner angrily seized the gun and tore it from the hands of the poor marksman. Seeing he had not been touched and no more would come of it than this, Mike rose in his stirrups, waving his hand in sharp warning to his own hidden men. But Dutch and Haney and Bill Catlin and Forrest and Romero were tense and they already had their signal. They opened fire from their ring of cover.

A bullet overtook Ed Finney. Another man fell among the miners. The others raced frantically for the cover of the timber and were gone. Mike rode swiftly to where Finney lay and dismounted as the firing died for want of targets. Finney was dead. Mike rose slowly. His men broke cover and rode eagerly into the clearing, flushed with success.

"That's turning them back!" Dutch exulted as he rode up.

Mike pointed to Finney's body.

"Not for long."

Dutch and the others sobered swiftly as they recognized the dead man. Their eyes swung in unison to Bill Catlin, Haney's helper at the sawmill, who had been hidden in the direction from which this bullet had come.

"Forget it," Mike said heavily. "I gave the order. How could Bill know Ed was our sheriff, when he'd never seen him before?"

"What happens now?" Dutch asked worriedly.

"An election," Mike answered. "Peyton will see to that. Afterward, I don't know."

"You should have kept the Judge here," Haney said. "You're going to need him."

"I know. But he'll be of more use in Monterey."

"We'd better hope!" Dutch breathed.

"We'd better pray!" Romero corrected with the surety of a man who knew the efficacy of prayer in extremis.

In late afternoon Mike started for Freezer's Bar with the bodies of Ed Finney and the nameless miner who had fallen in the high park. Haney and Forrest and Dutch, all practical men, had urged the burial of the bodies where they lay. But Mike was stubborn in his intent.

A little after dark, on the downgrade to the Spittin'
Jim, he was overtaken by a purposefully noiseless company of horsemen, also coming down the ridge from the
Princesa. Many of these were *californios*, but there were a
few disreputables of other nationalities among them. He
was instantly surrounded and forced from the trail. Mc-
Cracken's guns were taken from him and death was for a
few moments very close, for these were *yanqui*-hunters
and he was *yanqui*. He had seen them and could identify
them. And he could guess their destination. They did not
intend to leave him to talk of them later.

Curiously, he was momentarily saved by discovery of
the star on Ed Finney's body. It amused these who had
scant sources of amusement that the Sheriff of Delmonte
County should be returning from his first posse raid belly-
down across his own saddle. Because of this amusement a
few listened to Mike and learned his identity and they
ceased to crowd him, then, for they were susceptible to a
man's size in spite of themselves, and he was a giant in
their eyes. He was the Princesa.

Moments later Murietta himself arrived. Mike could
not believe the change which had come over his friend in
the brief months since the terrible dawn in which he had
been forced to leave Joaquin alone with his grief. His
eyes had narrowed and deepened forbiddingly in their
sockets. His lips had thinned and grown ugly in their tightness, as though they had never smiled or kissed a woman.
He looked like a man existing on narcotics alone. And this
he was. His hatred was stamped indelibly into him.

"Go home, Miguel," he said without friendliness. "We
will take your carrion into Freezer for you."

"If you do that, they'll be saying tomorrow you work
for me, Joaquin," Mike protested. "I can't let you do it."

"Let the dogs bark any tune they please," Murietta said
in Spanish. "Why shouldn't we be your men? Perhaps you
need help. And there are many fine valleys for hiding on
your *rancho*, with no prowling miners to discover us."

"You are always welcome, Joaquin," Mike said. "We
are friends. But not these others. I want none of them."

"They are my little ones, Miguel. Where Joaquin rides,
they ride."

"Not on the Princesa."

Murietta shrugged.

"Not on the Princesa, then. Tonight you see the last of Joaquin."

Murietta took McCracken's guns from the bandit who had commandeered them. He returned them to Mike.

"Go home, Miguel!"

Mike turned his horse. Murietta signaled his men on with the horses bearing the two dead men, then reined in close to Mike.

"Once you brought me land," he said softly. "Again you came to help when even the good God could not help. I am now a man of death. When you need the help of this kind of a man, send for me."

He started away, then wheeled back.

"You will hear much of Joaquin. Already they are saying I have been in two places at once. Soon it will be a dozen. Soon Joaquin and his little ones will be the only thieves and murderers in the Sierra. The work of all will be our work. Remember that not all they say is true, my friend."

He wheeled once more and was gone. Thirty minutes later, from the crest of the ridge, Mike heard the distant bark of guns where the lights of Freezer's Bar blinked in the dark notch of the Spittin' Jim.

Beatriz was waiting up when Mike returned. Death had struck elsewhere on the ranch in the hour that Ed Finney died. Abernathy had sent word from the mine. Dutch had returned there to find Alice and Pepe in a tense state of siege. They had believed themselves under attack by the reported miners and in midafternoon Pepe had fired at a man. Riding out to investigate, Dutch had found Jonathan Spier lying a few yards from his brush-caught horse. The freighter was still alive, but he had died in Dutch's arms as he was being moved to the mine camp. Dutch had buried him. There was nothing else to be done.

Beatriz had barely finished relaying the message when Dutch himself rode in. White-faced and distraught, he hunched down opposite Mike at the lamplit table.

"Mike, I can't stand it!" he said. "I had to come down and talk to you."

"Go ahead," Mike invited.

"What do you want—what do you really want, Mike? Those men up there this afternoon weren't talking about taking everything you have away from you. Mostly they were saying you have too much for one man, is all."

"Now you think they're right?"

"I don't know," Dutch said. "But I do know two of our own people have been killed by us. Pepe and Bill Catlin are up there on the hill tonight, both sick over it. And God knows what they're talking about in Freezer, after your taking those two bodies in to them. Sure, I know you meant to be decent, but it could look arrogant as hell, too. Where can it go, Mike, but to more of the same? And there's McCracken. What's Mac think of it now?"

"I haven't asked him. He's asleep."

"Mac's got beef working for you, Mike—him and Romero. Nobody's going to want that. They want only the gold. There'll be money in beef. Good money. Haney's milling your timber into lumber at a nice profit for both of you. The claims you've leased are bringing you in dust faster than you could wash it out yourself. And I've got a hell of a lead at the mine now. Any one of these things is bound to make you rich in time. What else do you want?"

"Supposing I told you I thought you were right and that the first things I was going to give up were the mine and the stamps."

"You couldn't do that!" Dutch protested. "I've put in too much time up there. The mine is a legal claim in any district. And the mill will do a big business when others start hardrocking around Freezer. I'd fight you before I'd let you give it up!"

"Well, then, supposing I told Mac to let the cattle drift —to let the miners live on beef any time they wanted to knock one down."

"Mac'd fight, too. Especially him."

"Would Haney turn his milled lumber over to any miner that came asking?"

"These are fool questions, Mike. I was talking about you."

"I am too—and the Princesa as a whole. Each of you is a part of it. But I'm all of it, and I can't let go any more than you can."

"You make it sound right. But it's still wrong. Can't you see that? Isn't there anything I can do?"

"There sure is. Mind your own business."

"Yeah," Dutch said. "I suppose that's all."

He said good night to Beatriz and went out. Beatriz served Mike's supper then.

"Mac's better," she told him. "I think he must be made of iron. When he wakened he was clear and had no fever. Weak and hungry, of course. And he wants to move into the office while Benson and the Judge are gone."

"Then move him."

Beatriz smiled.

"I did. He's quite comfortable."

Mike grinned, then sobered.

"Dutch's trail was dragging enough already. I didn't want to tell him. But I didn't go into Freezer tonight. Joaquin took the bodies on in for me."

Beatriz' eyes widened in alarm.

"He was going into Freezer—with his men?"

"I heard firing later, from the top of the ridge," answered Mike.

"What will happen to Joaquin, Micaelo?"

"They'll catch him and hang him, sooner or later. He's turned real bad. I hardly knew him. Bad clear through."

"Couldn't you have warned them at Freezer?"

"And send Joaquin into a trap? I couldn't do that, even if he'd given me the chance."

"No, of course not," Beatriz said. "But to keep what we have here, we're going to have to do things we would never have done before. You, along with the rest of us."

"Look here, you going to land on me, too?"

"No. But I can't help thinking that if you had put Joaquin into their hands at Freezer, it would have wiped out what happened today, as far as the miners are concerned. It would have helped us a great deal."

"Joaquin was our friend."

"I know. But I can't help thinking it, just the same."

"Well, don't think it again!"

Mike picked up the lamp and Beatriz went ahead of him back to their room.

McCracken sent for his guns after breakfast. Mike took them out to the office to see what had prompted the request. He found the Texan propped up in wan comfort and the office rearranged to suit his ease. Maria had attended to this. It was not strange she felt at home here and could make another feel welcome. Abernathy had originally built this little house for her.

Mac examined the returned guns critically, wiped them on the bedclothes, and put them on the stand beside him. He looked disgustedly up at Mike.

"You're sure the gutless wonder!" he said quietly. "What you suppose I loaned you these for? If you'd used 'em, Peyton would be dead instead of poor Ed Finney!"

Mike felt a tug of weary anger but remained silent. Mac snorted.

"Miguel, either you open up the creeks so's them miners can come in an' take their pick of what sands you ain't workin' yourself, or you get holt of Joe Murietta and his boys an' hire 'em to make it so unhealthy here only dead men can get across your boundaries. Wait to fight till the miners are here on their own and we'll wind up bein' the dead ones!"

"You tried talking with guns yesterday and got a hole in you for your pains."

"Because I tried it your way—chin-talk first. I should have had my fool head blowed off for not knowing better. Nobody would have got a slug into me if I'd had a gun in my fist—or if Joe an' his boys was behind me!"

"I saw Joaquin last night. I warned him to keep away from us."

"Oh, God damn!" Mac moaned. "There's your chance an' you shoot it off in the air!"

"We'll get along."

"Sure. Just dandy. All of us. Look at me. I'm only half-dead. I'm doing fine. And you'll be next."

Mike went back to the house and sent Alex to saddle his horse. Beatriz came out and saw that Mike meant to ride.

"Where are you going?" she asked anxiously.

"Up to the stamp mill. Dutch is supposed to put his first batch of new rock through today."

"I have been thinking of Dutch, Micaelo," Beatriz said slowly. "Of what he said last night."

"What of it?"

"Are we trying to keep too much? Are we risking it all instead of being sure of a part?"

Mike gripped her elbows and turned her to face him.

"Suppose you stick to making babies and leave this to me!"

"I am your wife, Miguel!" she said sharply. "The Princesa is part . . ."

"Get this clear, once and for all!" Mike interrupted harshly. "The Princesa is mine just as you are mine. I don't share you and I don't share the ranch!"

She looked at him with hurt, hostile eyes, and went back into the house. Alex appeared, leading Mike's horse. Mike strode across the veranda and jerked the reins from his hands.

"Get back up to Forrest's claim where you belong!" he told the Indian unreasonably. "There's work to be done up there!"

Startled, Alex eyed him uncomprehendingly as he swung to leather and started out of the yard without looking back. Contrition set in but Mike grimly battled it down. If he had left Beatriz hurt and puzzled, it was her share of her own troubles. He was hewing to the same principles with which he had begun here—principles satisfactory enough to them all until unlicensed miners had set foot on the *rancho*. Now they were turning against him. All of them. And they all had to learn, sooner or later that he would give no ground. A lesson was often best learned with pain. Let Beatriz and the rest have their portion, now.

• SIXTEEN •

A quarter of a mile above the house a descending rider emerged from the timber ahead of Mike. He pulled up in astonishment. The rider was a familiar figure—one which should have been a long fifty miles out into the San Joaquin, riding the top-cart to Monterey.

"What the hell is this?" Mike demanded as Judson Jeffers rode down on him.

"Let's go on to the house, Mike," Jeffers said. "I've got to talk to you."

With an infuriating mixture of anger and unease building in him, Mike sawed around and rode back down the trail with the Judge. Beatriz and Maria came curiously out onto the veranda as they rode up and dismounted. Mike saw Alex lingering at the corner, drawn by the same curiosity.

"Blast your worthless red hide!" he shouted. "I gave you an order!"

Alex dodged alarmedly from sight. Jeffers looked sharply at Mike, then crossed to grip both of Beatriz' hands.

"Nothing really serious, my dear," he said. "Just some differences to be ironed out. Politics in California seem greatly to resemble the weather here. They change rather abruptly. If you'll forgive us, we'll go around to the office. I'll feel more comfortable there."

"Of course," Beatriz agreed. But the frown did not leave her eyes.

"Mac's moved in out there," Mike told the Judge.

"Good," Jeffers said. "I respect his judgment in most things. You should, too, Mike."

They went around the house and into the office. Mac's eyes widened at sight of the Judge, but he seemed to sense surprise and greetings were superfluous now. Jeffers dropped into a cowhide chair he had worn by long occupancy to the comfortable contours of his own backside. He sighed and sailed his hat onto the table.

"When you rushed us both out of here yesterday noon, Mike, Benson and I both felt one of us should take a look at what Mac's collision with those miners had done to the situation at Freezer. Benson had that gold to get through. That left it up to me. I got into Freezer about midafternoon."

"Well?"

Jeffers drew a long breath.

"To put it bluntly, Mike, our house of cards has fallen in on us. We knew it would eventually, of course, even when we were putting it up. Delmonte County was designed just to give you sanction and recognition of your rights and title. That had to change, sooner or later, quite naturally. Governments built for one man never last. I had hoped the change would not come this soon, but it has. Now we have to think about the permanent structure of the county. That's what I have to talk to you about."

"Talk, then!"

"There was a mass meeting at Freezer's Bar last night. Eleven hundred and some odd men put their names or marks on the rolls."

"Eleven hundred!"

Jeffers nodded.

"That's how much our original hundred-odd ballot list has grown, Mike. Of course, only part of it is natural influx. Peyton has been quietly working a very interesting device. He's been paying passage from Sacramento City or even San Francisco for any man who'll come to Freezer's Bar to prospect. He calls the operation the Miner's Benevolent Fund. What it advances to each individual is supposed to be repaid. It's making him a lot of friends where they'll count, and it won't cost him too much money in the end. Most of it will be repaid."

"How?"

"He's promised every man who takes one of these so-called loans a chance at an available claim. They'll repay him from the gold they'll pan."

"Available claims near Freezer?" Mike snorted. "Why, he can't deliver on that! There's practically no open gravel on the upper Spittin' Jim or the Conejos, either one."

"The claims he's promised aren't on the Conejos or the Spittin' Jim, Mike. They're on the Princesa."

"Holy Jesus!" McCracken exclaimed. He swung on Mike.

"And you could have nailed Peyton yesterday!"

"So could you," Mike reminded him.

"Privately and unofficially, you both probably made a serious mistake in not doing just that," Jeffers said. "But that's water a long ways under the bridge, now. The river is moving fast."

"What do you mean 'unofficially,' Judge?" Mike asked.

Jeffers looked at his hands.

"The men in the camp seemed to take my appearance there yesterday as an evidence of good faith. . . ."

"As you knew they would!"

"As I hoped they would. Consider my position, too, Mike. What happens in Freezer and some of the other large camps in the next few months is generally going to shape the basic law and political structure of this state for generations to come. Any knowledge of theory as well as practice in political science and jurisprudence is terribly important. I have to contribute to the best of my ability."

"Big words," McCracken protested irritably.

"The exact meaning of which is that the Judge has cut our throats!" Mike said grimly.

"On the contrary, I may have saved them from stretching. Yours, anyway, Mike. I'm trying hard. The meeting last night refused to confirm my appointment as county delegate to the convention at Monterey. But it did reelect me to the office of County Judge. Then, right before a vote was called to elect a man named Sam Collins—a former employee of Peyton's—as Sheriff, to succeed Ed Finney . . ."

"Collins!" Mike exploded. "He's one of the four that boasted they did that business at Murietta's!"

"As I was saying," the Judge continued, "just before the vote was called Murietta dropped in on us. He was looking for Collins and one other man. He turned the camp upside down, but Collins kept out of sight and Murietta retreated when he found out how big the meeting was. A little later Collins was elected, unopposed. Very logically, too. The electorate reasoned a man wanted so badly by the worst outlaw in the Sierra was bound to be honest."

"You stood by for the electin' of Sam Collins?" Mac asked in disbelief.

Jeffers continued to look at his hands, chafing them a little.

"Mac, when a man moves into public office he ceases to be an individual. He becomes a symbol of the office he holds. I could cite you historic examples of some of the most reprehensible scalawags in human experience who filled public office with great integrity. Believe me, Collins has been pushed up on such a high pedestal he won't dare step off for fear of breaking his neck in the fall."

Mike had a sick feeling in the pit of his stomach. These had been clean mountains. There was a stench rising from them now. He wondered how much of it was of his own making.

"Where do I stand in all of this?"

"Temporarily in a rather bad position, I'm afraid," Jeffers said. "That's primarily why I'm here. Murietta brought the bodies of Finney and a miner named Thorpe in with him."

"He took them away from me. I was bringing them in."

"He said he was delivering them for you. Unfortunately,

he left the impression he and his men are now in your employ."

"I want no part of Joaquin. I made that plain to him."

"I told the meeting that. But there are still two dead men."

"Three," McCracken said.

Mike scowled at the Texan's thoughtlessness. It required an explanation.

"Pepe got rattled up at Dutch's camp and thought John Spier was one of a party of miners heading for Dutch's tunnel. I'd given him orders to shoot and he did."

Jeffers scowled.

"They know at Freezer you didn't kill Finney or Thorpe, Mike," he said. "You were in the open and a lot of them were watching you."

"Mike's in the clear, all right," Mac agreed. "Bill Catlin got Finney, not knowin' who he was. Romero figures he got the miner when the shootin' started. Too bad about Finney, but accidents like that happen easy."

"You'll have to bring them in, Mike," Jeffers said. "Pepe and Romero and Catlin."

"They were carrying out my orders!" Mike protested. "They didn't fire until they heard the signal I'd set—a signal some idiot from Freezer gave when he tried to shoot me as they were riding away."

"I've heard the details a little differently, but they're unimportant right now. What is important is that three men are dead. We'll have to hold a trial, Mike. I'll be sitting on the bench, and knowing the circumstances . . ."

"You're not trying any of them!" Mike said angrily. "That bunch from Freezer was trespassing and here on its own risk!"

"That's another thing, Mike," Jeffers said uncomfortably. "We had a second meeting this morning before everybody scattered back to their own claims. They don't like Spanish land laws over in Freezer. They never have. You know that."

"I don't give a damn what they like and what they don't!"

"Peyton testified at the meeting that you bought the Princesa through him before you or anyone else knew there was any gold on it. He testified you bought it strictly for ranching purposes. It seems there's a general code common in most other districts. The meeting voted to adopt it here. Under it, the only gold sands you'll own are the claims you've leased and the ledges Dutch has staked out to drive tunnels into. I'm afraid there isn't going to be such a thing as a trespass on the Princesa any more."

"That's what you think!" Mike said, rising.

He strode from the office. As he left he heard Mac question Jeffers and Jeffers answer.

"Who'd they pick for Monterey instead of you, Judge?"

"Peyton."

Jeffers followed Mike, then, and overtook him at the corner of the veranda, catching his elbow and halting him.

"Mike, listen to me," the old man pleaded earnestly. "I have my own integrity, just as I know that in your own strange way you have yours. And I know a great deal about the long history of my profession."

Mike stared at him without answering, without unleashing the bitterness boiling within him. He did not have Mc-Cracken's feral grasp of the effectiveness of force. Perhaps he did not even have the courage to apply it. He did not have Peyton's grasp of the overall scene nor his ability to select the elements which could best be made to work to his purpose. He did not have Jeffers' wisdom nor his sense of a people in motion. He had only his own basic judgment of men, individually, as enemies and friends. It was out of friends he had built, believing they were unassailable. His wall had cracked when tragedy robbed Joaquin of reason. Now even the inner circle was broken. Jeffers was no longer with him.

"I am facing obligations as painful to me in their way as yours will be to you," the old man went on soberly. "I am sacrificing companionship—the one wealth I knew very little of before I came to California. But I tell you something with all the honesty and sincerity of which I am capable. Just laws are built out of experience with injustice and the cost of a new government is sometimes very high in terms of a few individuals. I urge you to pay your share here willingly and with understanding. You will draw an immense satisfaction from it the rest of your life."

Mike pointed to the rail before the veranda.

"There's your horse. Get on it and get the hell out of here!"

Two days later, sixty men rode over the ridge from the Spittin' Jim, Sam Collins was at their head. In his pocket he carried three warrants over the signature of Judge Judson Jeffers. Twenty men went up to the mine. Twenty went to the sawmill. Twenty went to the Princesa home place. At gunpoint, fuming and helpless, Dutch Abernathy and Haney and Miguel McGann watched the new sheriff's men ride off, taking Pepe and Bill Catlin and Romero into Freezer's Bar to stand trial for the deaths of three men who had been strangers to them all.

The trial itself was held on the morning of the fifth of September, on open ground slightly downstream from the limits of the mushrooming camp. A wide flat here ran out into a loop in the course of the Spittin' Jim and there was sufficient room for the total population of the camp to gather.

Because of the roughness of the trip over the ridge, Mike ordered the women to remain on the ranch. Both Beatriz and Maria were growing large with child and he would not permit Alice Abernathy to make the trip when they could not. He came down onto the flat with Mac and Dutch and Haney riding with him; a tight group still, but not with the conviction of invincibility which had once represented the Princesa in the saddle. Mac looked wan and a little strange for the fact he was not wearing his guns. Mike had forbidden them. But the Texan was well along to recovery from his wound. He rode straight and elastic and it was he who recognized the flat where the trial was being held as the former site of Smiley Palmer's camp.

There was an hour-long wrangle for the honor of appointments as bailiff and recorder, and a persistent rumor circulated that the prisoners had elected to waive defense and throw themselves upon the mercy of the court. Remembering Jeffers' mention that he knew the circumstances of the so-called murders, Mike hoped the rumor was true. The trio of prisoners would certainly fare better by putting themselves in the Judge's hands than by facing a jury of impaneled miners. Through all the preliminary delay, Jeffers sat in great dignity on his improvised platform, banging with a miner's hammer on the stand before him when disorder became too general. In midmorning a grizzled miner finally rose and cleared his throat self-consciously.

"Hear ye! Hear ye!" he sang out in a cracked voice. "The County Court of Delmonte County is now in session!"

He sat down and the prisoners were brought up through the press from the rear of the crowd. They passed quite near the quartet from the Princesa, but Mike was unable to catch the eye of any of them. Their hands were bound, but they did not seem to have been badly treated. Strangely, the only one who appeared frightened in this gathering of his peers was Bill Catlin. Pepe walked erect, scorning the elbow-gripping hand of the miner escorting him, a proud and fearless man for all his fourteen years. Romero, following next, eyed the faces about him with a quiet curiosity. Catlin, the Yankee among Yankees, was the only one who was frightened.

It was significant, Mike thought, that Sheriff Sam Collins was not in evidence. Here was proof of the unease the name of Joaquin Murietta was already stirring in the minds of men who had cause to fear him. In a way it was a great pity that Joaquin would not be present. There could be no question of outcome then.

The trio of prisoners were arraigned before Jeffers, who rose to his feet. A hushed, eager and expectant silence fell over the crowd also. The Judge began to speak in a great, rolling voice Mike had never before heard him employ.

"You, William Catlin, are charged before this court with procuring the death of Edward Finney by gunshot on the Ninth of August, last. You, Enrique Romero, are charged with procuring the death of George Thorpe by gunshot on the same date. You, Pepe Abernathy, alias Juan Doe, are charged with procuring the death of Jonathan Spier in the same manner and on the same date. It is the duty of this court to advise you severally of your rights. You are entitled to representation by counsel of your own choice. . . ."

"Save it, Judge!" an impatient man sang out. "They made their choice. Let 'em stick to it!"

Jeffers looked piercingly out over the crowd.

"Bailiff, remove that man from the hearing of the court!"

The official pushed importantly through the crowd to the man and hustled him off toward the creek. Jeffers waited patiently until the stir quieted before again addressing the prisoners.

"You are likewise entitled to enter testimony in your own behalf before a jury of your peers, to subpoena witnesses, and to enter plea according to the Constitution and laws of the United States. You have stated a desire to waive these rights and to throw yourselves upon the mercy of this court. Is this still your desire?"

Each of the prisoners nodded affirmation.

"Makin' a hell of a show, ain't he?" McCracken asked uneasily. "Why don't he just turn 'em loose an' be done with it?"

"This is best," Dutch Abernathy said. "He's making it all good and legal so there can't be any kick later."

Two or three nearby miners turned to scowl at them. Beyond the miners Mike saw Ma Finney's wide figure, empty-faced and wholly engrossed in the two men and the boy before the platform. Dutch and Mac fell silent again.

On the platform, standing against the morning sky and looking compassionately down at the prisoners, Jeffers was a magnificent, leonine figure. He seemed a personification of Yankee wisdom and Mike felt a momentary surge of pride in membership in a race which could band together like this and rise to the dignity and integrity of tradition on a frontier so remote from centers of law and government. Dutch and Mac and Haney and himself were of the Princesa. There were many in the crowd packed about them who hated them and hated the ranch. Yet they were all gathered in this common truce to pay homage to justice. There was a memorable quality to the whole scene. Jeffers raised his head after a moment to address the crowd.

"Gentlemen of this court, I now face the most solemn duty known to man—the passage of judgment upon fellow human beings. I have before me the responsibility of protecting at the same time—to the best of my ability—the rights of these accused men and the sanctity of the laws by which we all must live.

"By their own admissions these men are each guilty of taking a life, an offense against society generally covered by a series of terms ranging from justifiable homicide to murder in the first degree. In a more ordered society than ours, such degrees of guilt can be precisely determined and sentence fixed as precisely. However, in Delmonte County we are not ordered but are striving for order. We

138

do not even have a state government on which we can lean for stability. And we are as distant from the Federal bosom as the District of Columbia is from the summits of the Sierra. We alone are the government and we are the law. We alone must preserve our peace and our lives. And to do so, one of the presumptions we must make is that when one of us dies at the hands of another, the crime is murder.

"Therefore, in all conscience, having found you, William Catlin and Enrique Romero and Pepe Abernathy, guilty by your own admissions, I have no recourse but to sentence you to be hanged by the neck until dead, and may God have mercy on your souls!"

Incredulity slammed into Mike with the impact of a bullet. He saw the rounding disbelief in the eyes of Dutch and Mac and Haney. Silence hung over the crowd for a moment, then a cheer burst from the throats of the miners. The sound freed springs writhing to enormous tension within Mike. He lunged forward, not knowing if the others were with him and not caring. A miner was in his way. He hit the man with the point of his shoulder and the miner went down, yelling angrily. Another turned and seized him. Mike broke the skin on his knuckles against this one's teeth and went on. The front ranks of the crowd had surged past the prisoners and the platform and were already starting to slant up poles cut beforehand and lying back of the platform. Holes had been dug in readiness, also, into which the butts of the poles could be slid. Angry shouts sounded behind Mike as he reached the platform and bounded up onto it.

At the base of the platform, where the prisoners and their guards stood, Mike heard a flesh blow and a man's hurt grunt and McCracken's wicked voice.

"Stay put, you bastard!"

Then Mac himself grunted and a man dived belly-first after Mike, snagging his ankles and tripping him before he could get around the stand to reach Jeffers. There were suddenly a dozen miners on the platform, piling into him. He was dragged across the rough planking and spilled back to the ground. A man stamped at his face, missed, but tore his cheek. A boot plowed into his ribs, awakening the old agony Fiero had once delivered to him. He was jerked to his feet. His arms were twisted high up into his back. A rope bit deeply into his wrists as he was bound.

There were other struggling knots of men which opened in a moment to disclose Mac and Haney and Dutch, bloody and likewise bound, so it was not only Mac who had followed him, after all. Catlin and Romero and Pepe were pushed up onto the platform, then Dutch and Haney and McCracken, finally Mike himself. The seven of them faced Jeffers and the sea of miners pressed against the platform from all sides made further resistance impossible.

The poles at the back were up now, and men were scrambling up both of them to lash a crosspiece in place before those on the ground were even finished tamping the uprights securely into the holes in which they stood. Mike glared at Judson Jeffers. The old man was white-faced with strain and kept his eyes averted from the three he had sentenced. Especially from Pepe. But Jeffers' jaw was set hard and Mike turned away from him, bellowing out to the crowd.

"Listen to me. God damn it, listen to me!"

Somehow his raging voice reached them and they ceased their excited milling and turned their faces up, although those rigging the gallows over his head kept eagerly on with their work.

"Hang—hang—hang—that's all you want!"

He knew he was screaming. He knew this was no man's voice. These were no man's words. There was no dignity in this. There was no effectiveness. This was agony and the crowd was whetted for it. They saw, rather than heard. And they relished. But still the words tore from him.

"Hang these men! Hang anybody! Hang babies! Hang women! One of them is a baby—a child—a boy. Hang him, anyway! If you've got to hang somebody, hang me, if you're men enough! I gave the orders for Finney and Thorpe and Spier to be shot. I was a fool not to have ordered you all shot, one at a time, when you came here. By God, I wish I had!"

Behind him Jeffers' hammer banged thunderously on the stand.

"Order! Order!" the old man roared.

Mike's voice soared over roar and hammer alike.

"You call this a court? You call yourselves men? You call this law? You're hanging these men and this boy because you want gold—gold that's on my land. All right,

140

you maggot-bellied, rotten, gold-hungry sons of bitches, come get your gold! This boy and these men belong to me. Turn them loose. I'll buy them from you. Turn them loose and take the Princesa. Every damned foot of it. But turn them loose!"

Jeffers continued hammering furiously on the stand.

"McGann, so help me, I'll hold you in contempt!"

"You miserable, glory-hunting old bastard, you don't even know what contempt is!"

"Shut him up!" a man shouted in the crowd.

Others took up the cry. A rock sailed up and in, Mike was hampered by his bonds and could not avoid the missile. It struck his head a heavy, glancing blow. He fell to his knees and came up again, reeling into the prisoners. Romero caught him with one shoulder and steadied him.

"You promise too much, *Patrón*," he murmured softly. "What is the difference if another *californio* dies?"

Mike staggered away. More rocks were flying. He saw Dutch Abernathy pulling at Jeffers.

"Not Pepe!" Dutch was crying. "He's my son, I tell you!"

A hammer handle came flying end over end up out of the crowd. It struck Mike across the bridge of his nose and the line of his brows. He dropped instantly into a deep, sighing void as though a trap had been sprung beneath his own feet.

Much later Mike roused, sick and bruised and washed limply of emotion, to find Beatriz beside him on a bed. His eyes were swollen shut and he could not see her. His body ached in every fiber and his head throbbed. He could not move to touch her. But he was home and she was crying—the dry, soft, endless sobbing of a grief which was not for him.

By these things he knew Judson Jeffers had stood upon his pinnacle and taught Delmonte County the sanctity of the first commandment, and execution had been done.

• SEVENTEEN •

There came a time of strange quiet upon the Princesa. There was no further challenge from the miners at Freezer, from Peyton, or from Jeffers and his law. The violent aftermath of the trial seemed to have dug a moat about the ranch which none of those participating cared to cross. But there were others who had no such qualms, perhaps because their straits were more desperate. A drift of little people began crossing onto the ranch, coming straightforwardly to the headquarters.

As it was happening in the whole Sierra, so it was happening in Delmonte County. The best of the gold sands were now occupied or held in title. As more eager miners continued to pour in, the oldest laws of nature began to function. Only the strongest could survive. Those who were displaced to make room for the newcomers heard whispers of haven on the Princesa and safety in the shadow of Miguel McGann. Mike was infuriated at first, but these were helpless ones and in the end he could not turn them away. He tried to fit them into the frame of what he was building, in whatever cranny he could find, hiding even from Beatriz how many there were; they wanting no more than a roof of sorts to replace the home taken from them and work for hands which had always known honest work. He knew that what he gave them he took from Beatriz and himself and that eventually he would have to account to her. But the boundaries were still intact and the ranch still in his hands, and by right of possession he also had right of gratuity.

The quiet influx continued until Abernathy, thin-faced and silent, was working thirty men at the mine and the stamp mill and Haney, across the creek from the stamps, complained that so much lumber was going into shacks and cabins scattered in the draws and side canyons of the ranch that he had little milled stock to ship over the ridge. Dutch and Mac and Haney knew what was happening and doubtless talked of it with disapproval among themselves. But Mike silenced them when they broached it and he kept them away from Beatriz, a task increasingly less difficult as her pregnancy advanced.

Infrequently a family came in from the South, or an honest man alone, saying that Joaquin had sent him, that life in Joaquin's camp was not for him and he had no place to go and Joaquin had spoken of the *simpático* of Miguel McGann. Sutter sent up a Dutch butcher who had come to Sacramento from San Francisco, wanting beef. With a crew of saddle-born new men, McCracken put together eight hundred fat market animals and proudly handed Mike the Dutchman's draft for sixty thousand dollars. The draft was drawn on the Miners Bank of San Francisco. Mike drew the Dutchman aside and inquired of Benson. The Dutchman did not know the name.

Benson's continued absence and lack of a report on the gold he had taken down to the Coast with him fretted Beatriz a great deal. She insisted repeatedly that Mike go to San Francisco and find him. As matters stood, this of course was impossible.

Still, there was no pressure from over the ridge. Haney, for all his complaining, doubled the price of lumber delivered to Freezer's Bar and still shipped a full wagon each day the saws spun. Abernathy timbered in the tunnel of the Lost Son—which he took to calling the mine —and the stamp mill ran to midnight the week through. Although Dutch spoke irascibly of poor recovery, the safe and chests in the office continued to fill until McCracken protested there would shortly be no room left for him to sleep there.

One night while Mike was at the mine, helping Alice and Dutch with a man who had been seared by powder in the tunnel, Maria came afoot searching for him the long way up from the house, silent tears streaming and a pathetic little bundle in her arms. Her child had come suddenly and early and she had not wanted to disturb Beatriz in the night when she was also growing a child. So she had come to Mike. Was he not the *patrón?*

Surely he was the one who could help. He could give life to the weight in her arms. It had to live. It was a boy. One had already died. This one had to live. It was not hysteria. It was faith. Faith and hope, in him, the *patrón.*

Mike hated her for it, but in the clapboard bedroom Dutch had put up next to the big tent in his camp, Mike watched Alice Abernathy gently put Maria to bed in her own bed. He watched Dutch carry the little bundle that was part of him out into the night. And he wanted to give life—this life—more than he had ever wanted to do anything. But he could not, so he spoke the empty, meaningless words which were all, two languages provided to console the inconsolable.

Three days later Alice came down to the main house, announcing she would stay with Beatriz. She brought Maria with her. Maria was ailing and must get away for a while. Mike approved. But a woman could not travel alone through the hills. Not even Maria. Not any more. And she had no place to go, besides. McCracken heard the problem and surprisingly offered to take her out to San Francisco. He had not himself been down from the mountains since his arrival and he would like to go. There was still no word from Benson and Mac felt he should be found. And gold was a problem again. The accumulation in the office was dangerous to keep longer.

In preparation for the trip, McCracken and Alice Abernathy made the rounds of the lease claims and the gravel bars below the orchards, now being worked by a crew under Mike's direction whenever he could spare the time. Alice efficiently posted the collections in Benson's ledgers and made up the levy against the sawmill for the timber Haney had cut and, balanced out expenses and profits on Dutch's mine and the stamp mill. With Maria on the seat beside him and nine dark men riding flank on the wagon, McCracken started out for San Francisco with $307,000 in gold and the Dutch butcher's draft for sixty thousand more.

Mike grew restless because he knew he was waiting. He grew impatient for word from Benson. Beatriz grew restless, also, for she was waiting, too. She knew her awkwardness and her inability to get about kept much that transpired from her. Perhaps she also knew Mike withheld what he did not want her to know. The restlessness brought friction between them and Mike began to avoid the house as much as possible during the day. In doing this, he found himself drifting from one to another of the little shacks and cabins hidden in the draws, drawn by the prospect of friendly faces and eyes which saw him as he had once seen himself. Collecting this tribute, he must spread a little largess so he could collect it again the next time he rode past. His greatest wealth was yet land and he began surveying off more scattered benches and little narrow valley floors below the mineral country and yet high enough into the foothills to have timber cover and permanent water. He began drawing deeds to these in six and eight and ten-acre tracts and leaving them behind him in token of gratitude for small friendships.

He found the accent in his Spanish, which had given Joaquin and Romero so much amusement in the beginning, was smoothing away and what had once seemed curious customs became an accepted way of life to him. He found himself helping to lay out foundation lines and he issued orders against Haney's mill for lumber wherever there seemed need for it and with no attempt to record these drafts. Presently humble men were going northward afoot every few days with scribbled notes guaranteed by his signature, to Sutter for seed and staple and hardware. Alice Abernathy, in whatever time was left her by housework, labored to keep Benson's ledgers abreast of this curious spending. She kept the obligation Mike imposed on her and said nothing to Beatriz, but she warned worriedly of expense whenever she could. However, the chests in the office were filling again and Mike smiled, his irritability gone. He was happy. And out of this happiness came something else.

When neither Dutch, Mac, Forrest nor Haney could find work for another pair of hands, Mike measured out a great, careful rectangle high on the ridge where he had once seen God in a sunset across the distant San Joaquin. Here, sworn to a secrecy which delighted them, brown men padded in a huge 'dobe pit and fall grass was carefully trod as a binder into the thick mire with bare feet, and skilled hands began patting out brick and thigh-tiles. At Haney's mill wise old eyes watched for the straightest grains and commandeered them as they came from the saws. Adze and drawknife cut cleanly of the good pine and deep-colored redwood, squaring and shaping and carving in pattern with an artistry already almost forgotten.

Mike became utterly absorbed, his one concern being that Beatriz should not know. Men from across the ridge would say he built for vanity, for no such house had ever before been raised in the Californias. It was true in a degree, but he built for other reasons, also. He built to keep busy those who had come to him, against a day when there might be grimmer work for them. And more than this, he built for Beatriz. The year was ending. With the beginning of the new would come the anniversary of their wedding. The old house had been Felicia's family's home—Felicia's, as a child. The new would belong to Beatriz, alone.

Larry McCracken and Maria returned from the coast in the second week in December, bringing Father Bartolo with them. Beatriz, heavy in her chair beside Mike on the veránda, gripped his hand ecstatically when she saw them coming, recognizing the priest at a preposterous distance.

"Father Bart! Mike, it's Father Bart! Now everything will be all right. And he must stay. Promise we'll keep him until we can have the christening."

Mike smiled.

"*Seguro, querida,*" he said. "We'll keep him forever, if he'll stay."

He knew the priest would not have left the lower valleys without purpose. Friendship might have brought him—or foreknowledge or anticipation of a need for him here. Certainly he would have much news. Mike was impatient to hear it. But he had to wait.

First to alight from the freight wagon, Father Bartolo smilingly deferred to Mac and Maria, so they were first onto the veranda. Maria was radiant as she threw her arms about Beatriz. The Coast had done much for her. Mac pushed his hat back a little so that part of his white forehead showed. He eyed Mike uncertainly, truculence ready to show.

"I'd admire to have you meet the missus, Miguel," he said.

Mike stared, slowly comprehending.

"Well, I'll be damned!" he breathed.

Mac grinned self-consciously and Beatriz cried out in delight, and it all came apart. People from the yard poured onto the veranda in welcome and good wishes. Mac was pulled down by Beatriz and turned crimson with a kiss. Hands were thrust at the Texan and he shook them blindly, hardly identifying their owners. Mike drifted aside as opportunity afforded. He was astonished that Mac had done this, but there was no questioning his happiness—or Maria's. And Mike found pleasure running deeply through him. These were his people. More and more he was finding new dimensions by which to measure the Princesa. Good for his people was good for him, also.

In a few minutes Father Bartolo disengaged from the press about Beatriz and the newlyweds and came over to Mike. The priest glanced back at Mac and Maria and smiled.

"You will forgive them, Miguel?" he asked.. "They did not go straight to San Francisco. They came first to Monterey, to me."

"You married them?"

Father Bartolo nodded.

"How the hell did you ever get a confession out of Mac?"

"So often the difficult thing turns out to be simplicity itself, Miguel. He brought Maria to me and told me of their love. And he asked to embrace the Church."

"The devil he did!"

"He had what seemed sufficient reasons. He said, 'I'm no expert on this religion business, Padre, but I'll settle for Maria's God. If he's made her the kind of a woman she is, then He could sure do a job for me. I'd admire to be the same kind of man—for her.' That's all there was to it."

Mike glanced again at the group of well-wishers. It parted a moment and he caught a glimpse of Beatriz, flushed with Maria's happiness. He nodded at the priest.

"I guess I understand what Mac was saying," he said.

"Beatriz looks magnificent," Father Bartolo said softly, his eyes warming.

"The waiting's hard for her."

"Only because she is impatient. Pregnancy is the time of a woman's greatest beauty."

"I know men who would give you argument on that."

"Husbands, maybe," the priest answered with a gentle malice. "But it is the great beauty, nevertheless. Beauty of body and beauty of spirit."

He paused thoughtfully.

"Sometimes I think a man lives only half a life. He takes away but does not give back. It is a woman who leaves the world a new beginning to take the place of the start she herself used up at birth. And birth itself—it is the greatest miracle of all."

"Seems pretty mechanical and predictable to me," Mike said.

"Would you so describe the act of conception, Miguel?"

"Probably, once. Not now."

Father Bartolo smiled.

"You learn, Miguel McGann. You have learned a great deal since I first saw you. Some day it may be my privilege to have a very wise man for a friend."

"Or a very dead one," Mike corrected dryly.

"That is also a possibility," Father Bartolo conceded. "It depends on how much your wisdom has grown. I think. That and how many friends you have made. You will need them all. That is why I am here."

"What's happening on the Coast? We don't hear anything here."

"I can tell you of Monterey. The new constitution was drawn, adopted and ratified a few weeks ago. Angus Peyton was very prominent in this as the delegate from here, although I suspect his contributions at the convention were actually the work of your Judge Jeffers."

"Probably," Mike agreed. "That glory-hunting old bastard would write history, if he thought he could get away with it!"

"I shouldn't wonder but what he is writing history," the priest said quietly. "It is dedicated men like Señor Jeffers who seem to succeed in writing the most important chapters in the book."

"In blood!"

"It's a very legible ink, Miguel."

"You actually think Judson Jeffers hanged that boy and those two men of mine to protect his damned law?"

"God, Himself, so wrote—in His own blood—to protect and build belief in His laws."

"Jeffers isn't God."

"No, of course. But perhaps there is more of the godly in him than you suspect. To be a judge is not easy. And there hasn't been any more violence here."

"There will be," Mike said.

"Not if you have Señor Jeffer's courage, Miguel."

Mike snorted derisively.

"The uncertain time is already past for California," Father Bartolo went on. "We have us a government now. With ratification of the constitution, Captain Sutter's lawyer—Señor Peter Burnett—was elected provisional governor. Peyton and fifteen others were elected to the territorial senate, along with thirty-one assemblymen. Many have Spanish names, Miguel. It will be a fair government."

"With no connection with the Union."

"When the legislature meets to inaugurate the new governor, it is expected it will elect Senators to Washington. Probably General Frémont and a man named Gwin. General Riley, the military governor, is then expected to resign. An admission act should follow very soon."

"And somewhere along I'm expected to open my ranch to the wolves Peyton has brought in here on the leash of his fake loan fund! Look, Padre, if we're going to hold to Jeffers' inflexible kind of law, the whole thing's illegal! Until Congress passes that admission act, there can't be any state out here, regardless of how many votes are cast and who's elected. Generaly Riley can't resign. The new government can't operate. And I promise you, miners can't come onto my land!"

"They will try, Miguel. They will believe they have the right."

"They'll find out different!"

"It would be better to use wisdom," Father Bartolo said sadly. "I will pray for that."

He moved away. Mike saw that McCracken had succeeded in extricating himself from the thinning group on the veranda. Tilting his head sharply in signal, Mike went around the house to the office. The Texan followed him. Inside the office, the ledgers were open where Alice had been working on them. Mike pushed them aside.

"Did you see Benson?" he asked McCracken.

"Yeah. I saw him. Sends you his regards. The missus, too."

"You delivered the gold to him?"

"Sure. And collected that Dutchman's draft, too. Brought back a deposit against a thousand more head of cattle for driving in January. At a price seven dollars a head better."

"Good. What's keeping Benson on the bay?"

"He's some busy," Mac said uncertainly. "Quite a town that San Francisco's growing into. Benson's getting your fingers into a mess of pies down there."

"He's supposed to be starting a bank."

Mac looked surprised.

"You know about that?"

"Of course," Mike said. "That's part of the reason I sent him down there."

"Beatriz doesn't know about it. Never occurred to me you did."

"There are a number of surprises I've been saving up for Beatriz this winter."

"Well, this bank of Benson's is the damndest thing you ever saw, Mike. Business piling up so fast he's handling gold and money with shovels. Really. Hardly time to count it. The Sierra Pacific Bank."

"How deep has he involved the Princesa in it?"

"You know me an' figures," Mac said. "Way I get it, you're in to the hilt, though. Seems reasonable. Benson sure didn't have any money of his own to open up with. And he's got competition, too. Fellow named Wright's got the Miners Bank. Soldier Bill Tecumseh Sherman's representin' an eastern outfit, an' even the Rothschilds have moved in. It's a scramble, but Benson was in first and he says he's keepin' ahead."

Mike nodded. There were so many other questions to ask; queries concerning special instructions he'd sent down to Benson by messenger in recent weeks; hopes and plans Benson would understand; things Benson could do. But they would make no sense to Mac, any more than they would have to the rest of them here on the ranch. And Benson would have said nothing to the Texan about them. In fact, he would say nothing to anyone until the orders were carried out and the big try had been made. Benson hated reports of anything but success. It was because of this and the fact he had not heard from Benson that Mike worried. It appeared he would still have to worry for a while.

"I hope he hasn't tied up all of our profits too tight," he said to Mac, thinking out loud more than anything else. "We've got eighty families on the ranch now and a lot of expense. And I don't know what kind of trouble lies ahead. Having enough ready money available when I need it could make or break me."

"Hell, Mike, there ain't such a thing as ready money in this country, if you mean cash," Mac said. "You ought to see what they're tradin' with in San Francisco. Benson and some of the other banks are issuin' paper money—drafts of their own. But there's even wire in circulation —gold wire—cut in lengths worth a dollar—and shorter lengths for smaller change. Bit pieces, they call them—two bits for a quarter, four for a half, an' so on. It's the only money in the world a man can pick his teeth with. An' no chance of gettin' a mint of regular coinage until we get into the Union. Either you got raw gold or you got credit. You, now—you got credit."

"Credit? Benson took over that gold shipment you took down, too?"

"I couldn't stand around San Francisco with that freight wagon sagging under three hundred thousand dollars in gold, Mike. That's a rough little ol' town. I had to put it some place."

"Naturally. But on deposit."

McCracken shrugged.

"Me an' Maria an' the padre put our heads together an' done what we thought was best. Benson was stretched pretty thin. That wagonload would take the pressure off—put him out ahead of his competition. An' he had a big, short-term loan coming up—high interest an' plenty of security—that he wanted to cover. Said you'd want him to do that if he didn't do nothin' else. So we let him have the gold."

Mac pulled a bulky package from his pocket and tossed it down on the table.

"Here's the papers on the deal."

Mike transferred the package to his own pocket. He was committed, now. There could be no doubt what the big loan was. In a way, he was pleased with his own shrewdness, his own anticipation. But now the risk was engaged, he was frightened, too. Benson and the bank and the loan were in San Francisco, where he was not in touch with them. And Benson was not in touch with day-by-day events in the hills. So much could go wrong. He was grateful anew that he had never mentioned to Beatriz the orders he gave Benson.

"Any objection to me an' the missus movin' back in here, Mike?" McCracken asked. "We sort of got acquainted while she was healin' me up out here, an' her two babies is buried over there under the trees."

Mike shook his head absently.

"Go ahead."

He left the office. At the side of the house, Mike paused and opened the packet Benson had sent up from the Coast. There were a number of documents. There were receipts and weight slips totaling nearly five hundred thousand dollars, the gross revenue of the Princesa in gold. There was a duplicate of the Dutch butcher's letter of credit, endorsed as collected. There was a thousand dollar letter of deposit from the same Dutchman against the future order of beef. There was a testament of the receipt of a loan in the amount of four hundred thousand dollars, dated December 12, 1849 and executed over Angus Peyton's signature, with his wife as co-signer. Benson had certainly pushed all of the chips onto the table.

Mike supposed he should feel elation. Somehow he could not. A recurrent dream had troubled him—that the Princesa was only a vapor, and that he had no more than he possessed the day he had first sailed from Boston. It frightened him. If the plan Benson was operating for him in San Francisco failed, that dream would be too true. Even to Beatriz. Certainly she would not stay with a man who deliberately destroyed his own long dreaming in a reckless gamble.

• EIGHTEEN •

Miguel Ramón de Balanare McGann was born at eleven on the night of December 31, 1849, after seventy hours of labor which left Beatriz a wrung-out shadow seemingly shrunken again to small-girl size in the great bed. Mike, hollow-eyed with sleeplessness and her relived agony, multiplied by his guilt and his helplessness to relieve the suffering for her, looked wanly down at the small, ugly red thing Maria brought blanket-wrapped in her arms to him. Father Bartolo's miracle was bright in Maria's eyes, for this child was whole and lived, making small kitten sounds, face contorting ludicrously with use of yet unfamiliar muscles. This child lived and hers had died and Maria cooed with sad, radiant wonder. But Mike could see only one thing. He could only see Beatriz writhing through all of nearly three days. He could hear in the infant's mewing a faint echo of her moans—pleas to him, to Father Bartolo and to her God for surcease from her agony.

This was no miracle. An all-merciful God would have delivered her easily and readily and in an hour's time, without racking a blameless body beyond endurance. Love was gentle and beautiful. Birth was neither. This was, as it looked as if all things on the Princesa were to be, born of suffering and rending, in defiance of planning and dreams. Mike loved Beatriz. He would not have knowingly brought her to this to work a thousand miracles.

Maria put the child in his arms as she had once put a dead thing from her own body.

"He is your son, *Patrón*," she said softly. "Take him to her."

He carried the bundle awkwardly back through the house to the bedroom where it had begun. He stood there above the bed in a room to which the strange, elusive odor of great suffering yet clung. He looked down at the deep, dark eyes which seemed to stare up disembodied

153

from the pillow at him. The stare warmed to a wonderful look as Beatriz became aware of him. The weary, bloodless lips smiled.

"Hello—Father McGann!" she whispered.

Mike looked again at the bundle in his arms. A tiny red hand, minutely detailed, even to nails and creases at the knuckle joints had reached out to catch a button on his shirt. The grip clung stubbornly, with the stubbornness of the McGanns.

"Isn't he beautiful, Micaelo?"

"You, *querida?*" he said hoarsely. "You . . . ?"

"All right," she answered softly. "Just clumsy. So new to it. Much easier next time. I will be an old hand at it. But, Micaelo, isn't he beautiful for a first try?"

Tears burned unexpectedly under Mike's sandy, sleepless lids. He blinked them away and saw the tiny fingers still retaining their grip.

"His mother's son," he said.

"Yes. My son. God has been very good."

She closed her eyes and Maria came in. She took the infant and shooed Mike from the room.

On the veranda were gathered Mac and Dutch and Father Bartolo. Haney and Forrest and one or two others were lingering hopefully in the shadows of the yard. They all remained expectantly silent when Mike emerged from the house. Finally McCracken grew impatient.

"Well, you tightwad bastard! You could buy us a drink, you know!"

Mike looked at them, at their prideful commendatory faces, and suddenly the ice of fear which had encased him throughout the long terror of Beatriz' labor sloughed from him. The midnight was past and the new year was begun. The Princesa had an heir.

"I'll drink the lot of you blind!" he boomed.

He turned back into the house. The others trooped in after him. They drank and talked and drank again and Mike very nearly succeeded in his boast. Only Father Bartolo remained upright, caressing the shoulder of a brandy bottle and staring pensively into the embers of the fire in the gray dawn light, when Mike finally fell from his chair.

There was no word from Benson on the Coast, nor of Peyton and Felicia as the first days of January passed.

Beatriz mended quickly, coming onto the veranda in the afternoon sun to cradle her child there, so *mamá* and *mamacita* from the small houses in the lower canyons could file past in delight and view the *patronito* of the ranch. Mike was uneasy over this, certain Beatriz would call him to account for the great increase in staff and residents on the ranch and the expense involved, once she started adding these friendly visits into a total of the families. But apparently it did not occur to her.

At Freezer and along the crowded Spittin' Jim, more debtors to Peyton's Miners Fund arrived daily until the valley across the ridge became one huge, restless camp and the *vaqueros* and tenants of the ranch took quietly to bearing arms of their own accord wherever they went. Mike thought occasionally of gathering what force he could and crossing the San Joaquin to Monterey in a demonstration to hurry the impending admission question and consequent stabilization of law and internal order. But with the thought necessarily came self-recognition of the uselessness of the gesture.

Others were also thinking and worrying. Mac came sheepishly one morning to admit he had sent a man far into the South in search of Joaquin. The man had brought what was bad news to Mac. Murietta and his men had vanished somewhere into the southern Sierra, hard-pressed by two vengeful posses, and it was unlikely they would soon reappear. There could be no immediate help from Joaquin, however grave the need for it might be. Dutch disappeared for nearly a week and returned angry. He had ridden in his best clothes to Sacramento to persuade Captain Sutter to form a union between the Princesa and New Helvetia for their common defense. The Captain was now so desperate and despairing of justice that he was placing his last hopes in the Congress of the United States. He was in fact preparing a memorandum to be introduced as soon as admission was accomplished, begging Congress for redress. This was absorbing his time and interest and he could spare Dutch little time.

As a result of their separate efforts, Dutch and Mc-Cracken were of the opinion that a strong alliance, such as either Murietta or Sutter would have provided, might have made it possible for the Princesa to hold off the miners centered at Freezer, once they started to move.

Without such an alliance, even the strong force Mike had been gathering would be of little use. In fact, most of the camps across the ridge were already on Princesa territory as it was, and their occupants already in trespass.

Surprise was the one effective weapon left. To hit first and hard and take the fight from the miners before the fighting really started seemed the only answer. The blow must be struck before Peyton returned to the mountains and unleashed the avalanche he had assembled. Both men pleaded urgently for this. Mike listened, weighed their arguments and refused. He ordered Dutch to shut down the Lost Son and the mill, and he set Alice and Dutch together to recording in ledger and on plat the eighty-some-odd little grant deeds he discovered he had given to various Altamiras and Crespis and Bernals and Zalcolas.

In the midst of this work, Beatriz came idly into the office, saw it, and asked questions until she had the truth. She waited until night, when she was alone with Mike, to call him to account.

"What difference if Felicia and Angus bring miners onto the ranch or not?" she asked bitterly. "You don't think of me. You don't think of little Miguelito. Only of yourself. You burn all we have to make a flame which will throw your shadow big in your own eyes! How much is left of the ranch when you give it all away? I could forgive myself for marrying a rake or a drunkard or even a beast, Miguel. A woman sometimes makes such mistakes. But not a fool!"

She had never spoken so to him before. He tried to think it was an echo of the strange complexities of her confinement. But he knew better. He tried to be angry and failed in this, also. He tried to defend himself against hurt but could not. He knew she could be right, and so denial was impossible. Even his defense was uncertain.

"These are your people," he said. "What is the saying: 'Whatever ye do unto the least of these . . .'?"

"That isn't a saying!" she snapped. "It is the voice of God."

"I know," Mike said quietly.

"You are not God!"

"Sometimes I wish I was."

She made a face of angry irritation.

"You talked a big dream. A dream that would make whatever had happened before as nothing. I believed that.

But you are no better than my father——than Felicia Delmonte's father. You cannot keep what you have. You must give. You must be the *haciendado*, the *rico*, the *gran patrón!* You can't make everyone happy, Miguel. You can't give of what you have to all who come asking."

"There are only eighty families," he answered stubbornly. "Not one of them has asked for anything but honest work for their hands, to feed themselves. Would you have turned them away?"

"I would not give them land."

Mike looked at her. He supposed he should have known that she would cleave like this to the land above all else. It was his fault. He should have consulted her. But he had believed that what he could give she could give, also. He looked at her, but a silver sheen of wonder was rent forever. She was the woman he had married, the woman who had borne him a son. But she was not a wonder. Only a woman. A woman with a claim upon him, but no claim upon the Princesa. The *rancho* was his. His alone.

"What I do stands, Beatriz," he told her. "We'll talk no more about it."

She looked at him strangely for a moment, then lowered her head.

"*Sí, Patrón,*" she said.

That night he slept in the bunkhouse among crewmen who avoided him for the embarrassment of his presence among them. He waited through the night for Beatriz to send for him. She did not do so. He breakfasted alone in the morning. She made no appearance with the afternoon sun on the veranda. Word traveled swiftly across the ranch. The little people from the lower canyons, knowing they were not wanted, ceased coming to the Princesa yard.

When Abernathy and Alice were done with platting and recording the grant deeds to the little tracts of lower land, Mike entrusted them to Father Bartolo. The priest carried them across to Freezer and turned them over to Judson Jeffers, securing from the judge a receipt acknowledging them part and parcel of the official records of Delmonte County. It seemed certain they would stand thereafter, since not one of the homesteads covered earth conceivably overlying traces of gold and they should therefore be immune to disturbance.

Mike felt the better for this. It was his tender of payment for the services of those who had joined the Princesa—paid in full and in advance. He wanted Beatriz to understand this, but there was no way he could explain without making overtures, and a strong and grieving pride would not let him do this. He returned to his waiting, keeping away from the yard as much as possible and with his eyes constantly turned toward the ridge, beyond which lay the restless camps along the Spittin' Jim.

Although Mike himself lost heart and almost all interest in the structure rising in the upper meadows, Father Bartolo became immensely engrossed in it. The priest unabashedly admitted to a genius at architecture and structural supervision, claiming credit for the preservation of some of the most noteworthy buildings raised by his order in the twenty-two major establishments of the mission chain —works of substance and beauty now far gone toward ruin since the secularization order of the Mexican regime. Although Mike dully tried to dissuade him, the Franciscan spent every available hour at the meadow. What had seemed in the beginning necessarily the work of many months rapidly began to take on the finish of detail and trim. What had chiefly been meant to be substantial and comfortable acquired beauty and great charm under the Father's shrewd direction. To Mike in these weeks it was a monument to something which no longer existed and he avoided the site as assiduously as he did the home place.

In this time Sutter sent an urgent request for gold to cover purchases made at his fort by *vaquero* families against the Princesa account. It was a staggering total, and for the first time Mike began to see some justice in Beatriz' unreason. It grieved the Swiss captain to make demands on a neighbor similarly bedeviled, but ready money or its equivalent was still his desperate need. He wrote that in a few more months he believed himself certain to emerge from his morass of debt as the rich man he knew himself to be and he could then send for the rest of his family—a thing long dear to his heart.

Knowing the Swiss was doomed and nursing a fear that he himself might be, Mike emptied the chest in the office again, even to modest shares apportioned to Dutch and Mac and Benson, to meet Sutter's request. There was a small overage, which he directed Sutter to apply to glass and such household furnishings of a suitable quality as the Swiss might be able to supply. His own interest was so low he did not even specify details.

He sent the gold across to Sacramento City with Dutch and Alice, refusing to trust McCracken's mercurial nature. The Abernathys would be able to side-step trouble along the way. In case they could not, he sent twenty *vaqueros* with them. The party crossed to Sutter's without event. They returned with a wagonload of elegance Sutter had acquired for himself and which he now had neither the funds nor the leisure to enjoy. Mike sent the wagon onto the upper meadow without even examining its contents. Father Bartolo went up the ridge with it, still jealously guarding the secret from Beatriz, and there he fell to work again, wearing further calluses onto hands long thickened by the hard labor of love.

On the nineteenth of January, Mike received word all was in readiness on the meadow. He reluctantly entered the house and proposed a drive to Beatriz—an airing for the baby. She agreed with eagerness, but with no sign of awareness of the estrangement between them. In fact, no such estrangement seemed to exist, as far as she was concerned. Mike began to wonder if he had become lord and master in his own house since their quarrel over the grant deeds, without his having realized it. Somehow he hoped not. He did not want his lordship to go too far. Better to have quarreled and be estranged than this.

If Beatriz noticed the emptiness of the lower yard as they started up Delmonte Creek with their son between them on the seat of the top-cart, she said nothing. If she missed the usual familiar faces to see them off, she said nothing. She seemed wholly engrossed in being again with Mike—in escaping the house for the first time since her confinement—in the joy of taking her blanket-wrapped first-born out across a beloved land which would one day belong to him.

She was so bright and eager and it was such a relief to have the tension gone from between them that Mike began to recapture his own first excitement when he first drew plans on meadow sod up the ridge. He drove by a circuitous route which kept the big house behind a tongue of timber. It took time and Beatriz began to protest the lateness of the hour with the baby but he kept on until they could look back across the San Joaquin. Here she would have had him stop, for a sunset was building in the vast visible distance, but on a promise of a better prospect beyond, Mike turned through the screening trees. They emerged suddenly into the slanting meadow where the big house stood, looking out over half of the world.

They were all there before the tile-floored gallery extending across the front of the house, both upper and lower floor—nearly three hundred of them. There were women and older children and their men; men with hands rough with splinters caught in stoning the planks of the floors smooth; men with nails clay-encrusted from glazing in precious window glass; men whose handprints would outlast their own lives in the 'dobe of the bricks. There were Dutch's miners, Haney's sawyers, McCracken's *vaqueros;* those who owed the roofs over their heads and the labors they performed and the full bellies of their families to the *patrón* of the Princesa.

Beatriz looked from them to Mike. He thought some understanding was in her eyes now. He was not sure. It was only that he wished to believe it. He drove up to the gallery through a passage opened by those who had come to warm the house. Beatriz stared with incredulity at the faces and the lamplight within and the great, carved, double-hung doors standing open in invitation.

"For—for me?" she breathed, so low he could barely hear.

"For you," he agreed.

Then, because he had long ago thought of this hour and rehearsed it and what he would say and what he would do, and because if he was going to be a fool he might as well be a whole fool, he said the rest of it.

"If we could have built a road up a higher mountain, it would be there. If we could have cut longer logs, it would be bigger. Because of you."

"It's a dream," Beatriz said. "Please don't waken me."

"Maybe the dream has been the last few weeks," Mike suggested. "Maybe we're both wakening now."

"Yes," Beatriz answered. "Yes, Mike!"

Only her eyes spoke after this. They were enough. Weight slid from Mike. Guilt slid with it. Maybe he was fool enough to quarrel with her, but it would be the same again. Her eyes said it was the same. As her eyes had

160

spoken of their son when he had first brought the baby to her, so now they spoke of the house. Mike felt a moment of deep jealousy. Here was a woman's world. A man and a child and a house encompassed it. A woman did not want beyond this. Beatriz did not really want beyond this. She was not troubled beyond this. It showed in her eyes. A woman knew contentment this easily. A man was not apt to know such contentment as this in a lifetime.

Alice Abernathy came from a group of the first Princesa people, under the gallery. She reached up and Beatriz surrendered Miguelito to her. Rising then, she swayed down into Mike's arms. He held her high and tight against him and crossed the gallery. Father Bartolo stood at the great doors in the humble vestments of his order, and Mike set his burden down. They knelt, with the others kneeling behind them, while the little priest earnestly besought the Spirit of God to enter the house before them and abide in it always.

Mike lifted Beatriz again and strode with her over the threshold and set her down within her new home. Framed in the doorway to those outside, she continued to hold him about the neck and drew his head down and kissed him. The others, watching, had a long wait, but they made no sound until the kiss was done. Then they shouted, cheering wildly, and a song began. Mike led Beatriz through the house.

Her eyes strayed round in wonder and finally they came to the big upper room in the front corner where opposing windows looked out with equal freedom upon the sunset glory of the San Joaquin and the red snow summits of the great Sierra. Here was a crib, and Maria waiting, and Alice brought the baby. Miguelito was dressed in nightclothes with much fussing, and snugly blanketed. Alice left and Mike did not think Beatriz had seen his last surprise. Then Maria also left and Beatriz crossed at once to the bed, a hand reaching out slowly to lift an edge of its covering.

So many things a man remembered poorly, even those things from the beginning which he wished to recollect in entirety. Mike had tried hard with this, drawing sketches a hundred times to catch every detail in a pattern already faded when he had first seen it. And Alice Abernathy, with the needle of an artist, had been faithful to the best of the drawings. Beatriz felt the texture of the material and the piecings and the stitches and her hand knotted suddenly in the coverlet, knotted tight and hard. Mike knew then she remembered well enough the covering beneath which he had slept that first night in Monterey.

He went quietly across to a corner stand where stood a heavy silver goblet quietly purloined from the battered old portmanteau with which Beatriz had arrived on the Princesa. And Mac had performed a special mission in San Francisco. He had found a dealer in vintages who carried a precious stock. Mike drew the cork from a bottle of Valenciano also on the stand, filled the Balanare goblet, and carried it across to Beatriz.

"Welcome home," he said.

She drank of the goblet and raised it to his lips. She choked and was crying. Mike reached under the near pillow and drew out an open-mouth pouch with a flourish which flung minted gold to the floor in a spray about their feet.

"Let's go to bed," he said.

Beatriz laughed through her tears, happiness welling up, and she flung her arms about him.

"With Miguelito not yet three weeks old?" she said.

"I just wanted you to know I remember," Mike told her.

She looked at him, shaking her head with a new gentleness.

"Poor Miguel," she breathed. "You would be so harsh and cold and invincible—and unforgiving. And you can't. Not even when you have convinced others you are. Not even when you have convinced yourself. It is an impossibility. I should have known it. I am sorry for what I have said to you, Micaelo—sorry—sorry!"

Her lips moved, restlessly, hungrily over his face, then she broke away again.

"They wait for us below to dance, Patrón. I could dance a little, I think."

Mike turned slowly with her toward the stairs. He wondered if what she had said was true. Was invincibility impossible for him? Was it true he would not hold the Princesa? Somehow tonight it made little difference. Tonight there was music below the stairs and there was music in him, also.

Dancers spun on the solid floors of the new house until the morning sun was high, and all through the night the winter chill of the Sierra could not enter.

• NINETEEN •

Three days after the housewarming, the big storm of the winter came in from the North, where it had been lurking against the skyline, building strength. It was nature's one annual assault against the placidity of central California weather. It came on rolling winds which gathered velocity in the sweep across the northern end of the Central Valley and piled against the foothills of the impervious Sierra in an incredible turbulence of updraft and back-current and gust. Rain was in the dark underbelly of the boiling cloud masses riding the wind, and snow and sleet lay above this in the structure of the storm. The barrier of the mountains was so steep and the changing currents it caused so violent that whole islands of cloud were occasionally upended so that snow briefly fell on the lowest slopes and rain washed the glaciers of the high peaks. Then the island would right itself with lances of lightning and a great blasting of thunder, and rain poured again on the frosted foothills while the summits vanished in the gray pall of blizzard.

Mostly the big storm was rain: a steady, slogging, hard-slanting fall, riding the gusts of wind; rain thirstily swallowed by the parched soil until the earth could hold no more, gathering then as surface water to tear at sand and clay and loam wherever roots and cover did not bind and protect, running yellow trickles to darker rivulets to gullies, roaring as they cut deeper channels into the permanent streams. Swelling creeks became raging mud rivers and rivers became enormous, malevolent giants, loose in the land.

Father Bartolo stood under the gallery of Miguel McGann's mansion with the wind flattening his coarse habit against him and the spume reaching him even here. Father Bartolo stood, shaking his head and watching the big storm grow even bigger with the gathering dark. Mike, watching him from the doorway, thought of the crowded camps in the run of the Spittin' Jim and the Conejos and he wondered if the little priest was speaking to God in the storm, praying for mercy for miners, or whether he was praying that this be the biggest one of all and that it wash the Princesa clean as it had been in the beginning, for the benefit of his friends. But the priest did not speak of what he prayed, or even if he prayed at all. During the night Dutch Abernathy came in with his wife, both wet to the skin and frightened. Delmonte Creek was a tiger loose in the dark. It had unhung the waterwheel at the stamp mill and carried it away. The dam which backed up the water for this and for Haney's saws, across the creek, seemed certain to go. Dutch's tent had been shredded by the wind and the roof had been carried from the frame bedroom annex. There was no light at Haney's sawmill across the creek, and no way to tell how he fared.

Beatriz, forgetting her resentment that they were there, worried for the safety of the families on the lower slopes. Mike reassured her. This was their country and those people knew it. They knew its storms as well as its peace. They had chosen their homesteads well, turning down more than one sylvan spot Mike had suggested to choose higher and more solid, if less attractive, ground. There was no new *casita* on the Princesa less secure than the big house itself.

Beatriz slept, then, and the Abernathys, and Father Bartolo. Maria could not, for McCracken was downstream at the old house and there had been no word from him. Mike did not share her concern for the Texan. The old house was secure, also, and Mac knew Maria was safe here. He would recognize the folly of travel until the storm eased.

Mike could not sleep either. He did not want to. The big storm fascinated him as all big things had come to attract his fancy; perhaps a reflection again of the bigness of the Princesa. He remained downstairs, alternating between the open gallery, where he stayed each time until chilled, and a lower window through which he could watch the outer violence while the fire at his back rewarmed him. The storm spoke to him all through the night with a thousand tongues and he tried to understand them all.

In the morning McCracken came up through the undiminished fall on a muddied horse. His Texas hat hung about his ears with the arrogance of its felt washed from it, and he was soaked and shivering. But excitement was in his eyes and Mike knew that he, too, had listened to the stirring, inciting, violent voices of the storm through the night. But Mac was practical, also, and his ride had a point beyond reassurance to Maria. He brought news. All was secure at the office and the old house. At Forrest's claim the sluices had been carried away, but Forrest himself was at the *casa* of the foreman of his shovel gang, on the slope back of the working. The dam had held at the mills, but Delmonte Creek had cut itself a new channel around it during the night. This followed the race of the stamp mill, undercutting its foundations and toppling the whole massive structure of heavy timber and iron into the current. Across the creek, with pressure against the dam thus relieved, Haney's sawmill was safe. Mac had seen Haney from the near bank and waved to him. Haney had signaled all was well enough there.

The big storm began to subside late in the third day and the morning of the fourth dawned to a steaming, blue-domed, clean-washed world. Great sheets of water lay in patches across the San Joaquin and the snow crowning the Sierra reached far down into the timber, even whitening the summit of the ridge which stood between the Spittin' Jim and the big house. Over this ridge, in midmorning, came the men of the Spittin' Jim and the Conejos and Freezer's Bar.

The first intimation Mike had that they were on the way was the arrival of a party of his own men, riding swiftly up from below, with Mac, who with Maria had previously returned to the old house, at their head. Haney and Forrest were also with them; the *vaqueros* and sawyers and Spanish miners from Forrest's claim and the Lost Son, and laborers from the disabled stamp mill; the Altamiras and Bernals and Crespis and Zalcolas, up in force from the lower slopes.

Mac wore his two clumsy-looking guns for the first time since his return from San Francisco with Maria, and an old, hot, high eagerness was up in his eyes.

"It's all of 'em, Mike," he said as he strode across the

gallery. "Except them that got washed clean to hell during the storm. Half the buildings in Freezer is gone and the Lord knows how many of the camps along the creeks. They're comin' to stay—packs on their backs an' guns in their fists. I've had Sespi Bernal watchin' from the summit the last couple of weeks. He just brung me word."

From wherever *casitas* lay, other Princesa people were coming in, angling across the meadows to converge on the big house, in answer to the message which had raced across the *rancho* saying that the *patrón* had need of them. Looking past McCracken's shoulder. Mike could see them on the grass and emerging from the timber.

There were more than a hundred men when they all assembled, drawn by an old bond of the country which made a man his neighbor's ally in any foreign trouble; a hundred men to whom the conflict between Spanish and English tradition in land laws meant nothing except in terms of their own loyalties; a hundred men who had seen governments and their statutes overthrown by violence twelve times within their own memory; a hundred men filled to the brim with accumulated bitterness and needing only another incident to spill it over.

Mike turned back into the house, followed by Mac and Haney and Forrest. Beatriz and Father Bartolo and the Abernathys were already in the living room. Mike thought of the faces which were absent: Benson and Judson Jeffers—one certainly a traitor, in his own way, and an enemy; Joaquin and Romero; Jonathan Spier and Pepe and Bill Catlin. All gone past returning. But the others were here. All of them but Maria, and Mac would speak for her.

Looking at them Mike felt strangely alone, as alone as he had felt the first time he had touched foot on the *embarcadero* at Monterey. They were here, his wife and friends, but they were apart. They were waiting for his decision. This was the lonely thing, this making up of his mind.

"It means Peyton is back from the Coast," he told them quietly. "It means that what we all knew was coming is finally here. Peyton and Jeffers, with his damned law, have been planning it a long time. They've probably got every detail worked out. There isn't much we can do but fight."

"But Mike," Dutch protested nervously, "you can't let them pen us up here. Not with the women—my wife and yours—even your baby!"

"They will be all right if we win, Dutch. And I don't intend to lose!"

"I'm not sure trying to defend this house is the soundest military strategy, Mike," Father Bartolo ventured mildly.

"The hell with strategy, Father Bart—and what you know about it, either! Call it my castle—call it anything you like. But we're holding the house."

Mac grinned at him.

"We'll make it easy, Miguel," the Texan told him. "Recollect the surprise me an' Dutch argued for? The storm did the same thing. Them pick-swingers have been hit hard, flooded out. That'll have softened them up. Now we belt 'em once hard enough to make 'em know we mean business an' we'll have their backs broke."

Father Bartolo shook his head sadly at them all.

"It is not unusual for a priest to find himself in a position where he must stand with one army or another," he said unhappily. "I am a man of God—an impartial God —but nevertheless I am a man. I will pray for you all. I could not do otherwise. The judgment must be God's."

Beatriz came to stand beside Mike while the others waited.

"Will we lose it?" she asked. "Will we lose it all?"

"We won't lose anything," Mike said. "Bring the men in. Push the furniture back and put them at the windows, Mac."

McCracken headed swiftly for the door. Mike led Beatriz to Alice Abernathy.

"You and Alice get Miguelito and the house women. Go to the cellar and stay there until I come after you."

"Miguelito will be safe with Alice and the other women," Beatriz said. "I stay with you, Miguel."

Mike started to protest in swiftly flaming anger, but a distant shot crashed and Mac commenced shouting urgently on the gallery and the Princesa men poured in through the door, scattering quickly through the house. Mike ran to a window and saw men at the edge of the timber across the meadow on the side lying toward Freezer's Bar. He wheeled back to the room. Those from outside were now all safely within the walls. The halves of the great double door were slammed to and Mac was dropping the bar in place. The Texan ran across to join Mike at the window.

The miners were free of the timber now—a long, ragged line, an incredibly long line, five or six men deep. They bore packs and tools and weapons. They were invaders, as Mac had promised, bringing their possessions with them. They would not turn back. There were pack animals behind the lines, a few carts, two wagons, heavily loaded. And an occasional woman. Mike thought he recognized Ma Finney's stocky figure. A few women and how many men? Six hundred—eight hundred? Even the thick-walled bulk of the house seemed small in the face of such an advance. It was understandable now that a man of Peyton's wealth had still been forced to borrow to bring such a party together.

McCracken faced Mike with the old recklessness. He wore the old humorless, eagerly anticipatory grin. And he was walking again on a cat's feet, winding the spring of his body tight for the release he knew was coming.

"One thing about us up here, Miguel," he breathed. "We really do things big! Look at the bastards come!"

"I want you to go out with me, Mac," Mike said quietly. "Just you and me."

McCracken's eyes widened incredulously. At the same moment a shot sounded again and a heavy rifle bullet slammed into the impenetrable planking of the front door.

"There's your answer, Miguel!" Mac snorted. "Go out to that?"

Mike ignored the warning. He gripped the Texan's arm. "Coming?"

Another shot sounded and the door shook again to leaden impact.

"Baiting us," Mac grunted.

"Let's take the bait then."

Mike crossed to the door and started to lift the bar. Mac pushed in front of him.

"They nail you and we're done, Mike!" he said urgently. "They know that as well as we do. They'd want nothing better than a clear shot at you."

"Then they're going to get it!"

Mike shoved the bar up and took hold of the ringbolt handle of the door. McCracken drove a shoulder against him in desperation, pinning him against the planking.

"You idiotic son of a bitch!" he exploded, and one hand swept for the near gun at his belt.

Mike knew how effective a bludgeon the barrel of one of those long Texas pistols could be, and he realized Mac intended to stiffen him with one swiping, stunning blow. He brought his knee up sharply into Mac's groin, slowing him, and then he swung solidly, hitting the Texan under one eye. Mac reeled back, shaken and half-blinded, and Mike pulled open the door. He pulled open the door and stepped out onto the gallery with a quiet, positive conviction no bullet would reach him—that none would be fired; a ridiculous and incredible belief—even to himself —that he was the Princesa and the *patrón* and the biggest man in the mountains, and that somehow the advancing miners would not be able to fire at him when he actually faced them.

The foreranks of the men from the creeks were within a few yards of the edge of the gallery when Mike emerged. Guns were plentiful among them and many were guardedly held at ready. But strange as his belief was, the miners seemed to hold it, also. Although several weapons started to swing in an arc toward him, the swinging halted abruptly. It was not until he had halted at the front edge of the gallery and McCracken came up beside him, blood running from a wide cut beneath his eye and both of his pistols in his hands, that Mike realized why these first critical instants were granted to him.

McCracken's eyes darted along the line of miners, instinctively searching out a man here and there, until guns yet half-raised were sullenly lowered. Mac eased then, holstered his pistols, and looked at Mike.

"Who's doing your talking for you?" Mike demanded of the miners.

"We ain't here to talk!"

"I am!" Mike snapped. "Who talks for you?"

A man pushed to the fore. A big, thick-fingered, untidy bear of a man with a nickel badge pinned to his shirt and the butt of a short pistol protruding from his hip pocket. Mike frowned as he recognized him.

"Reckon I can do what talkin' there is, McGann," Sam Collins said.

"Not with me, Collins. Not you. Where's Peyton?"

"We don't know and care less. He was supposed to put

169

us on claims up here two months ago. Instead, he kept sending more men in. He's kept us waiting long enough."

"Somebody who knows what the law is, then," Mike suggested reluctantly. "Judge Jeffers, if you haven't got anybody else."

Collins laughed shortly. His eyes touched the men nearest to him—grim men, taut men, disheveled men, as they all were.

"Too bad you weren't in Freezer the last three days, McGann," Collins said. "You'd wonder how any of us came up out of that canyon alive. A lot of us didn't. The judge didn't. He's drowned. Washed away. Dead. Him and his books and his records. The works. There ain't no more county, less'n I'm it. There ain't any law but me. And what I know didn't come out of any split-tongued lawyer's mouth!"

Mike heard a breath caught behind him. Mac heard the same sound. Both risked a glance, reluctant to take their eyes from Collins and the miners. Beatriz and Father Bartolo had come out of the house to stand on the gallery in defiance of the crowd in the foreyard and in defense of the Princesa. In defense of Miguel McGann. Beatriz was very pale but her eyes flashed arrogant fire. Mike knew he could not make an issue of returning her to the house now. She was entitled to her courage and her pride, as he was to his own. He swung back again to the miners, thinking of Judson Jeffers.

The old man was gone. The opportunity he had found here, and the challenge, were gone with him. The sacrifice he had made to the ideal of an inviolable law was gone. His records, the transactions of the county he had so carefully preserved for their historic content, were gone. Nothing remained of Judson Jeffers but the memory of a judge who had hanged a boy and two men whom he knew to be morally innocent in order to establish the sanctity of the law before others.

"Listen, all of you," Mike said slowly. "The flood didn't destroy your rights, or mine either. You're trespassing on my land. I'm reminding you I've been willing all along to lease promising claims for ten percent of their profits to any honest miner. . . ."

"Rights!" Sam Collins said loudly, so that all behind him could hear. "You got no right to lease what don't belong to you! As sheriff of this county, I'm takin' over these creeks and openin' them up!"

"You're no sheriff," Mike answered him coldly. "You're the worst kind of rotten, woman-killing murderer!"

"You damned Mexican-lover!" Collins shouted. "Standing up against white men for a bunch of slime-bellied greasers!"

"Why not?" Mike said. "There are a hundred of them at those windows behind me, ready to back me in anything I do."

Collins eyed the windows across the face of the house and subsided a little. Mike spoke directly to the miners.

"Mrs. McGann and I and the people who work for us have made a lot of enemies. But we haven't done it on purpose. I know most of you have been washed out of your camps. Some of you haven't had a dry bed for three nights and maybe no food in as long. We've never turned a person in trouble away from the Princesa and we're not going to turn you away now."

Ma Finney shoved through the men ahead of her and elbowed the dark-faced Collins aside.

"We want the creeks!" she shouted.

Mike ignored the interruption.

"There's plenty of food and dry bunk space for most of you in the bunkhouse and the old main house at the lower ranch. We can take care of a few of you here. Our people can find roofs for the rest of you for a few days. . . ."

Mike did not see Sam Collins move. Nor did he see McCracken move, either. He was suddenly interrupted by a confused concussion of gunsound. Two virtually simultaneous explosions, followed by three more swift, staccato shots in smooth succession. He was struck a glancing blow on the upper arm which partially turned him. Recovering his balance, he saw the Sheriff of Delmonte County, his lowering, smoking pistol in his hand, waddle out half a dozen steps in white-faced agony before he pitched forward. Collins rolled over onto his back to sob terribly and claw at his lower abdomen with bloody fingers.

Two or three miners started instinctively toward the fallen man. Mac drove them back with rocking guns.

"Leave the bastard lay!"

It was only then that Mike realized the infernal accuracy with which McCracken had driven his bullets into Collins' body.

"All right, Miguel?" the Texan asked without turning his head.

Mike's fingers had already probed through the rent in his shirt to find the slight, hardly bleeding flesh wound in his own arm.

"All right," he said.

"Anybody else want to make a try for the boss?" Mac invited the stunned miners.

The miners did not answer. They stood in two immobile groups—the gallery and the foreyard—watching as dark pelvic blood flowed in a great tide from Collins' body, staining the grass. The man's vocal agony continued until it was insupportable. Then, after an interminable time, it choked off and he was dead. McCracken spat and slowly holstered his guns. Ma Finney looked down at the dead man, then stepped past Mike to face Father Bartolo.

"There ain't a woman alive, Father, nor a man that's decent, either, that wouldn't say Sam got what was comin' to him. But it don't settle nothin'. You're Mr. McGann's friend. You can make him see he's wrong and we're right about the creeks and the gold."

Father Bartolo slowly shook his head. The old woman turned anxiously to Beatriz.

"You can do something with him, Mrs. McGann. Make him order the people behind you out of your house and give up their guns so we'll know the shootin's over. Most of us don't mean no harm, but you're forcin' it onto us. One man and his wife ain't got no right to all you got here!"

"My husband has," Beatriz said firmly. "He believed in it and he built it. I'll help him keep it!"

Ma Finney's face flushed darkly and her stocky body rocked on widely planted feet.

"Devil take the stubborn lot of you!" she said.

She turned, raising her voice.

"If they won't bring their guns out, we'll have to go in after them!"

The miners started forward. McCracken tensed. Mike caught his arm and checked him. The first of the miners surged about them and they were separated. Mike plowed for the door of the house, knowing those within would not fire until Beatriz and Father Bartolo and Mac and himself were safely inside. As he moved, his mind raced ahead of this instant to what would follow when the first shot was fired. Miners would die, but men within the house would die, also. Friends. Perhaps some of them closer to him than the little people who had the most lately arrived; perhaps some of them who had helped him in the building from the beginning. Suddenly he felt sick, as he had on the day when McCracken and himself had killed four men on the creek below the orchard on the lower ranch. It was a sickness which went deeper than the body itself—cowardice, perhaps. He didn't know. But he knew one thing beyond doubting. Blood and violence could not settle a question of rights. At best it could only settle a question of strength. And more than strength was involved here.

He drove forward more urgently, shouting hoarsely for attention.

"Wait!"

He reached the door and wheeled, his back against it, to face the advancing miners.

"Listen!" he demanded.

The foreranks pulled up uncertainly. Mike glanced aside at Beatriz. She was looking at him with widened, uncertain, fearful eyes. He wished he could know how she was going to take this. He wished he could know if she would understand. But there was no time to find out. He swung back to the miners.

"Most of you won't stay in the mountains. But some of you will. Those that do will be neighbors. And however we feel about it now, we'll still be neighbors. This is a rotten beginning for us . . ."

He paused, thinking again of Beatriz. But he had to go on.

"Maybe you people can't afford to wait for the decision of a court or a land commission to settle this question of claims. Maybe you're honest in claiming you can't. But I can wait. I can afford to. I know what it will cost me. But I still can afford to wait before I can fight you."

Mac pushed along the wall to him.

"Don't do it, Miguel!" he warned sharply. "Back down now and they'll stampede you sure!"

Mike ignored him.

"Go ahead," he told the miners. "Stake your claims. Work them. Keep the gold you take out. But remember I'll fight for my title when I can get the case tried."

Men stared incredulously at him. They looked at one another.

"Keep away from claims already leased by me," Mike went on. "Keep away from the homesteads I've granted and the people on them. Keep away from my mine and my mills and my cattle and you'll have no trouble from me or my people."

The miners began to break into small, astonished groups. Quiet talk began running through them. The tension which had begun to build with the first shot against the closed front door swiftly ebbed. Mike's knees were a little unsteady. He still could not look at Mac or Beatriz or Father Bartolo. He turned and hammered on the door at his back.

"Open up!" he said.

• TWENTY •

By supper the meadows about the big house were empty of miners and the gathered people of the Princesa, alike. Maria had come up in midafternoon from the lower ranch. She and Mac were at the table with Father Bartolo and Abernathy and Alice and Beatriz when Mike came in from the room in which he had shut himself up all afternoon. There was no word from Peyton—no word from Benson. Mike had not realized how heavily he had been counting on Benson—how sure he had been of his own shrewdness. The plan which he had long ago suggested to Benson, and which Benson had eagerly promised to implement, must somehow have failed to come off. Perhaps Peyton had been more alert and suspicious than Mike had believed he would be. Or perhaps Felicia had divined the quiet conniving Benson and himself had planned behind the façade of the Sierra Pacific Bank. Possibly it was even more simple—that Benson had found a greater margin of profit for himself and had failed in his loyalty. Whatever it was, it was over, now. The Princesa had been invaded at last. The big dream had crumbled. There remained only salvage.

When he joined the others, Mike found the meal had begun. He sat down, conscious that conversation was monosyllabic and related to food alone. He could eat but little and pushed his plate from him before the others were finished.

"All right," he invited them all wearily. "Say it."

They looked at him, none stirring. He forced his eyes to Beatriz. She was watching him with the same uncertainty she had shown on the gallery when he had begun to talk to the miners.

"I gave it away," he said. "The money—the real money—the gold from the creeks. I gambled it all on a chance I could trick Peyton as he tricked me in the beginning. I played on a chance of winning without guns, without battle. Maybe I knew I couldn't fight when the cards were all down. Not with the lives of others—your lives. I don't know. Benson was in on it. Just Benson and myself. Maybe that was a mistake, too. Some of the rest of you wouldn't have trusted Benson. Anyhow, I did—and I lost."

"All of it?" Beatriz asked softly, unwillingly.

"All of the money," Mike agreed. "Now we'll talk about what's left. I figured it out roughly this afternoon. Jeffers is out of it, and Benson's probably taken care of himself. Romero is dead. His folks will get his share. Pepe's goes to Maria, since she was closest to him."

"I was," Dutch corrected softly. "He was mine."

"His share goes to Maria," Mike repeated.

Dutch lowered his head.

"You talking about shares in the Princesa?" Mac asked incredulous.

"No. The Princesa belongs to Beatriz and Miguelito and me—what's left of it. These are shares in what we can salvage out of what the ranch has produced."

He saw Beatriz lose her uncertain look. He saw brightness come up in her eyes and a wave of relief. And he understood. It was not the money, then, not the gold. It was that she had been afraid he was parting with the thing he had once told her he wanted most—possession of the bulk of the *rancho*—its size and its vastness. She had been afraid of his loss, not her own.

"The wages and shares . . ." he continued. "I put away some of the first gold. It's been spent long ago, but for you. Mac has built the cattle herds. A quarter of the beef income is his—or a quarter of the herds, if he wants it that way. Dutch built the Lost Son and the stamps. A quarter of them is his. I bought a half interest in Haney's sawmill with what I put away for Benson. As I said, he's apparently taken care of himself. His share would go to Pepe, so now it's Maria's. I bought Haney's interest in Forrest's claim with what I put away for you, Dutch. So you and Alice are partners with Forrest.

"I can't pay any of you anything beyond this. But the mine will be producing again as soon as the stamps are rebuilt. There'll be a beef profit in the spring. Meanwhile Mac and Maria can draw against Haney, and Dutch and Alice against Forrest, for anything you want quickly."

Mike stopped and looked at the rectangle of faces about the table.

"Any comment?"

"No," McCracken said.

There were soft tears in Maria's eyes. Mac smiled at her and put an awkward arm about her shoulder. Mike's eyes moved on to Dutch and Alice.

"You two?"

They shook their heads. Mike's gaze challenged Father Bartolo. The little priest smiled.

"It is good for a man to put his house in order," he said.

"You think I have forgotten you, Padre?"

The Franciscan shrugged.

"The Church is accustomed to this. But you have not forgotten, Miguel. How many pieces of land have you given away to those who came here with nothing?"

"Eighty-two," Alice said. "A little more than six thousand acres of growing land."

"The best on the place, too!" McCracken added with a shadow of resentment.

"Whatsoever ye do unto the least of these, ye do unto me," Father Bartolo murmured softly. "I am content."

Mike turned last to Beatriz. She was smiling.

"I have riches," she said. "I have you, Micaelo."

McCracken leaned back in his chair, eyes narrow and appraisingly on Mike.

"Having now read your last will and testament," he said dryly, "would you mind telling us what the hell's eating you?"

"I backed down. I quit. You all stood with me because you figured I wouldn't do that, because you figured I'd fight, because I knew where I was going, because I believed in myself. Now I don't know. What I've built is falling down. One wall is already gone. Tomorrow it may be the roof. Now is the time to take what you've earned, before it is gone, too."

Mac lowered his chair legs to the floor and pushed back and went to the sideboard at the other end of the room. He came back with a stone demijohn and slopped Mike's empty water glass full of what they had come to call the Murietta brandy, although its grapes had come from Sonoma and not the little vineyard above the Spittin' Jim. The Texan put the glass into Mike's hand.

"Now ain't your troubles a hell of a note?" he asked.

Mike glanced covertly at the others and suddenly he felt ridiculous. Ordinarily it was a feeling he hated, but it was welcome now—more welcome than any other would have been. Smiles grew at McCracken's sardonic sympathy and the smiles broke into laughter as the Texan made his way from glass to glass around the table with the demijohn. Mike began to smile, also—sheepishly—and Beatriz reached beneath the table to grip his hand tightly. Dutch swallowed what was for him an unusually long drink and banged the glass down decisively.

"I'm glad something has cracked the wall," he said. "Now maybe we can settle down to business without worrying our backs stiff about the damned Princesa!"

Glasses were lifted in a toast to this and for the first time Mike realized how tightly he had bound them all to a concept which he had himself abandoned over recent months, gradually and without pronounced regret.

Felicia and Peyton and Benson, traveling together, arrived while they were still at the table, Felicia and her husband were naturally triumphant, but in a bad humor. Benson was bland, wholly without apology for the long weeks of silence and the lack of reports on the plan to which he knew Mike attached so much importance. Nor was there any evidence of guilt in his manner over the personal conversion he most certainly had made of a portion of the assets Mike had entrusted to his keeping. Instead, he affected a tremendous reaction to the new house.

"This is living!" he said expansively. "There isn't a roof like this in California!"

"I'm surprised you haven't built a bigger and better one in San Francisco," Mike growled at him. "You've sure had enough time and money on your hands for it!"

"Oh, I am building," Benson said. "Construction's under way. Ground broken and everything. On Rincon Hill. All us nabobs are building there."

Mike eyed him suspiciously. Benson's mood was too light. An inkling of something began to dawn. Mike rested back in his chair to wait—afraid to hope but doing so, nevertheless.

"Let's don't hear any more about that house!" Felicia Peyton snapped. "Delaying us in San Francisco while you argued with the architect about the plans—as if they couldn't wait better than we could!"

"Mike will tell you I am a very selfish and thoughtless man," Benson said.

Mike offered chairs and called for fresh table settings for the new arrivals, for an old custom he had once scorned had become deeply grained into him and the tradition of hospitality was inviolable. Besides, having this morning placed himself beyond damage from Peyton's miners, there was only the man himself to contend with now and it pleased him to subject Peyton and Felicia to a host's arrogance.

"I looked for you this morning with the rest of them," he said as they seated themselves.

"We would have been here . . ." Peyton said sourly. "The historic moment. The revolt against the landed overlord."

"We had it all right," Mike agreed. "What kept you?"

"Benson's damned house, for one thing—and bad luck; the storm, a drunken riverboat pilot. The stupid idiot had us aground a dozen times between Benicia and Sacramento City. Eleven days, getting up here from the bay!"

"Mr. Benson is the most obstinate traveler I've ever seen," Felicia added unpleasantly.

"I tried to explain I'm hardly responsible for river accidents and storm," Benson protested.

"I'm not so sure!" Felicia snapped.

Peyton scowled at his wife.

" 'Licia, for the last time, stop that bickering!"

"When you show some common sense. You and I both know Benson's an utter scoundrel. Why won't you admit it?"

"For an excellent reason. He's our banker."

Peyton turned to Mike, inner pleasure improving his humor.

"You actually made no effort to stop the miners from the Fund?"

"No. Not personally."

Peyton shook his head.

"Benson said you wouldn't. He said you had too much sense. I'm rather sorry. I hoped you'd fight your fool head off."

Mike saw Benson's eyes were dancing. He shrugged.

"We all make mistakes, Angus."

"Well, it makes no difference to us in the long run," Peyton said. "Of course you must know by now that Felicia and I are the Miners Benevolent Fund."

"I've known it a long time," Mike said quietly.

"As owners of the Fund, we hold a twenty-percent grubstake interest in every claim filed by men who have borrowed from us."

Mike nodded again, covertly watching Benson, pleasure growing in him with the growing realization that perhaps Benson had not failed as utterly in San Francisco as he had feared.

"I told you I'd put Felicia back on the Princesa, McGann," Peyton continued. "Naturally, our whole interest from beginning to end has been the gold. We're satisfied with our twenty percent of that. As far as the rest of the ranch is concerned, you're welcome to it."

McCracken scowled at Peyton and rose abruptly.

"Where are you going?" Mike asked him.

"I'm not going to stick here and listen to these bastards rub your nose in it, Mike!"

"Sit down, Mac," Mike told him quietly.

"Yeah, sit down, Tex," Benson urged. "You just might enjoy this."

McCracken subsided curiously. Benson leaned toward Beatriz.

"Are you aware you are married to one of the most larcenous connivers who ever lived?" he asked.

Beatriz shook her head, not understanding.

"I always thought I had a real genius for this sort of thing," Benson continued. "But Mike puts me in the shade."

He turned to Peyton.

"You're a fair amateur, too, but you've been outclassed."

"Really?" Peyton asked, undisturbed. "It seems to me I was able to finance the little loans my Fund made by securing a big loan from you. And unless I'm mistaken, the money you loaned me came from the Princesa. In other words, McGann financed the miners who took his gold away from him today."

The pressure all went from Mike, then. Benson grinned openly at him.

"We rather hoped you'd figure it that way," he said to Peyton. "It was Mike's idea. And maybe I should have mentioned this a little earlier, but the loan your Fund secured through me was dated December 12, with a term of thirty days for repayment in full, with interest. Today is the Twenty-sixth of January."

Peyton frowned, worry creeping into his eyes. Felicia stiffened.

"Those were current standard terms in San Francisco," Peyton said defensively. "You told me so, yourself. But subject to extension as required, of course. We understood that. See here, Benson, your bank can't hold us to that first term. It can't demand repayment from a state senator that high-handedly. It wouldn't dare!"

"No," Benson agreed. "The Sierra Pacific Bank is too new an institution to call a note as sharply as that on an important citizen. It might indicate nervousness and a shaky position and insufficient reserves."

Both Peyton and Felicia visibly eased. Mike thought there was something obscene in a trap which closed so slowly and inexorably. Benson smiled benignly at the Peytons.

"But you forget the function of a good bank is as a fiduciary agent as well as a repository and lending institution," he continued. "And there was a certain personal obligation on my part involved, also. My principal depositor put a great deal of trust in me at a time when he had very little justification for doing so. Therefore, I owed him a service."

Benson paused, maliciously making Peyton and Felicia wait a moment.

"The truth of the matter is that the money you borrowed was not funds of the Sierra Pacific Bank but was advanced to you out of Mike McGann's personal account, and he holds the collateral you deposited as security."

Peyton and Felicia were not the only ones at the table who were stunned. Benson winked at Mike. His smile grew happy and he borrowed a sip from Maria's brandy.

"Since the term of the loan is now two weeks past expiration, I am duty bound as financial advisor to the McGann family to counsel demand for immediate payment," he added.

"Four hundred thousand dollars!" Peyton said hoarsely.

"Exactly. Four hundred thousand dollars—every cent Mike had taken in from the Princesa—everything he had —and he gambled it on my ability to entice you into financing your Fund with it. He gambled it on my honesty and the chance you couldn't move your miners in force here in time to get back enough revenue from the creeks to repay it."

"Four hundred thousand . . ." Peyton repeated dully. "And you led Felicia and me into believing you were fleecing McGann yourself. Half of San Francisco thinks so."

"Not the half that counts. I've got a pretty good reputation as a banker already. This deal ought to clinch it for good."

"But I couldn't raise four thousand of it now," Peyton said thinly. "You—you've even got the Yankee House and my income from it impounded at collateral!"

"Mike has," Benson said.

"My only hope of repayment is from claims up here. It'll be weeks before even the luckiest of them are located and can begin to produce!"

"It took too long for the miners up here to move," Benson shrugged. "You should have been up here with them weeks sooner. That was Mike's gamble. Now the cards are his. Now he'll foreclose against the Fund, and your other property he holds as collateral."

Peyton sagged back in his chair. Felicia surged fiercely to her feet.

"You despicable thief!"

"I'm sorry you find an unfortunate partiality in my honesty, Mrs. Peyton," Benson said smoothly. "Particularly since you made so much effort to be charming to me on the Coast. But I took initial steps in the foreclosure proceedings before we left San Francisco. In my judgment—as a banker, mind you—you and your husband are bankrupt."

Benson reached for the demijohn McCracken had set on the table, and with an apologetic glance at Maria, refilled her glass and sipped it again. Mac and Dutch, looking from Mike's grinning face to the bloodless masks of Peyton and his wife, burst together into open laughter. Beneath the table, Beatriz unconsciously drove her nails deep into Mike's palm before she freed his hand and rose to circle the table swiftly and plant a kiss on Benson's cheek. Benson looked up at her with the warmth of real affection, winked again at Mike, and leaned back in his chair, enjoying himself hugely.

"I might point out, in passing, a service you have done for my client, Peyton," he said. "Mike has always been willing to lease out Princesa claims for ten percent of their production. By exacting a twenty-percent fee agreement on your loans at Sacramento and San Francisco, before the miners could get here and discover Mike's own terms, you have doubled his expected income from the creek gravels, now he's foreclosing on you. And no land commission can take this fifth share away from him, since the miners themselves will hold the titles to their claims, subject to his grubstake."

McCracken leaned forward to speak past the bewildered Maria.

"Benny, you're really a first-class, double-dealin', oily-backed little son of a bitch!" the Texan said with vast admiration.

Felicia Peyton stood beside the table, looking down at them all with a trace of the arrogance of her blood and a vestige of her pride. And if her beauty had become submerged beneath a strange masculine hardness, the regularity and strong modeling of feature were still there. She moved toward Beatriz, and Mike saw the small knife at her belt. Some instinct warned him before her hand touched it. He surged out of his chair as she suddenly pounced. The knife slashed toward Beatriz in a wicked attempt at a terrible, beauty-destroying face scar. Unable to arrest the sweep, Mike drove his own forearm in ahead of the steel, knocking Beatriz back and taking the edge of the flashing blade on the heel of his hand. Closing his fingers, he tore the knife from Felicia's grasp and flung it across the room. Clamping a napkin into his palm to stop the bleeding, he started for Felicia.

She had struck at him for the last time. With Peyton she had struck at the Princesa. This he could bear with strangely little anger. But when she struck at his wife, she freed a fury. She backed away, dodging to put the table between them. Mike flung the table aside, filling laps with what dishes had not been cleared away. Mac seized one of his arms and Dutch the other. He shook them off with a violence which sent McCracken crashing through a chair. Felicia darted past Peyton and the man stood in Mike's way. Mike hit him and knocked him back against the wall. Felicia turned, then, running in terror through the house. Mike followed her to the front door. When it closed behind her, he leaned against it, getting a grip on himself. Peyton came up uneasily, a kerchief to his broken and bleeding face. Mike stepped aside and Peyton also went out. Turning slowly, Mike returned to the dining room. Benson pushed his own brandy glass toward him. Mike dipped the napkin corner in it and wiped out the thin, deep cut in his hand. It was a trivial hurt.

"I'm sorry," he said to them all.

"Cost me thirty dollars to bribe that boat pilot every time he put us aground," Benson said. "I didn't think you'd fight the miners unless Peyton was with them. But I knew you would if you saw him stirring them up. So I had to delay him and hope the miners would get impatient enough to move on their own."

"The storm did that," Mac said.

"A fight now would have ruined the Princesa's chances in court later, Mike," Benson added. He turned to Beatriz.

"I hope you'll forgive us for keeping a few secrets from you."

"It would be very hard to refuse your forgiveness for anything, tonight," Beatriz told him.

"Well, I don't want you to think that mick husband of yours is the only one to profit from what I've been up to in San Francisco. The Sierra Pacific Bank is a legally incorporated concern in which I hold four hundred shares of stock. The other six hundred have been issued in the name of Beatriz de Balanare McGann. For your information, a great number of potentially important clients have been very reassured to discover the principal stockholder is a former Balanare."

"Thank, you, Ben," Beatriz said. "I'm sure you will make me a rich woman. But to have you back here is the most important thing of all."

Mike gripped Benson's hand with his own left, favoring the knife-cut in his right.

"I'm not quite sure what I should say. I've half a notion to take you outside and bat your teeth loose for not letting me know how things were going with you down on the Coast. I couldn't tell."

"Neither could I, most of the time, till the last minute. Mind if I get drunk? I haven't even dared to smell a bottle since I left the mountains—the banking business being pretty fast on its feet down there on the Bay. And shouldn't there be some kind of a celebration?"

The stamp mill was rebuilt and Abernathy contrived a concentrator which brought the efficiency of the yield from the Lost Son closer to Dutch's satisfaction. He and Alice spent the spring in planning and the summer in building a dainty little chalet of redwood a few yards from the site of his first camp in the timber-ringed park above the old Murietta place. Mac and Maria also built during the summer, a sprawling adobe four miles below the lower ranch, where the Texan could look out over the blending of the Princesa's best grass with the immensity of the San Joaquin.

Benson did not return to the hill again, cursing the press of business. Papers from the Bay spoke with growing respect of his bank and of him. Both Haney and Forrest went out to make a business alliance with the bank and returned separately with wives before the first fall rains.

Judson Jeffers' body was uncovered in a new placer six miles below Freezer's Bar and was identified by his watch. A shaft was raised at this spot by action of the County Board of Supervisors in memoriam to the first lawgiver of Delmonte County. Mike completed a road avoiding the hard pull of the ridge. It passed by this memorial shaft and skirted the foothills to a junction with the main Sacramento route near Placerville. Traveling this road, he took Beatriz and Miguelito to Sutter's, spending a week with the Swiss and a part of his reunited family at Hock Farm, favorite quarters of the still harried lord of New Helvetia.

Occasionally word came of Peyton. Disqualified by nonresidence, he had lost the Delmonte County seat in the state legislature. Dispossessed from Nicolo Delmonte's old home in Monterey, Peyton and his wife were living in quarters on the upper floor of the Yankee House. Benson had loudly protested when Mike released the Monterey tavern from the Peyton collateral against which he was levying, but Mike drew recurrent satisfaction from the thought Peyton now had only what he himself had wanted on his first trip to the California Coast and that Felicia was hostess where her husband had once planned to put Beatriz Balanare.

Miguelito grew and was well and with him grew the fortunes of the Princesa.

In the fall of 1850, Congress finally decided to risk addition of a state which was not identifiably either slave or abolitionist, and President Fillmore signed a belated act admitting California to the Union of her sister states. Six months later, Washington appointed a California Land Commission and Mike filed through Benson the documents supporting his title to the ranch.

Sutter, in the hands of counsel accepting fees from both the Swiss and the squatters contesting him, fared badly and moved on to the Supreme Court on appeal. The Princesa case did not reach hearing until the spring of 1853. At this time Alice Abernathy drew a report showing revenues of nearly thirty thousand dollars a month after partnership divisions and expenses. Since the original Peyton contracts of the now dissolved Miners Benevolent Fund did not involve title—the claims belonging outright to the miners themselves—there was no contest of the Princesa before the Commission. Some commissioners, however, found fault with Abernathy's survey, which had sprawled the grant out in tentacles to embrace all possible gold-bearing sands and ledges. A boundary realignment was ordered. Abernathy was permitted the field work on this, and when it was complete, virtually all exclusions from the original survey were made up of claims and homesteads Mike had relinquished.

In midsummer a federal patent was issued, securing title to thirty-one thousand acres of grazing and timber land, including the Lost Son and two other equally promising ledges Dutch had long ago marked for future development. One shipment of gold, totaling a little less than eleven thousand dollars, was lost to bandits about forty miles north of Freezer's Bar. John Finney, another of Ma's boys and successor to Collins as Sheriff was certain the theft was the work of Murietta and Three-Fingered Jack. Mike doubted this and wrote the loss off. Joaquin had become the scourge of all the Central Valley, but he had once been of the Princesa and would not harm his friends —if, indeed, he was still alive. He was later reported on the same day a hundred miles to the south.

With the passing of the State Capital from Monterey to San Jose and then Vallejo and now to Benicia, property values in the original capital were falling. Benson became anxious for Mike to rid himself of the old Delmonte place there. When an offer was transmitted from a retiring sea captain, Mike decided on a holiday. Miguelito was left with Alice and Dutch. Mike and Beatriz set out in a newly acquired Studebaker road wagon for the Coast.

At a Castro farm thirty miles out into the broad San Joaquin, they were overtaken by McCracken, riding more recklessly than any *californio* who ever lived. They were minutes getting his message from him, minutes in which Beatriz suffered miserably, for in these last few weeks Maria was nearing the end of her first full-term pregnancy. Finally Mac slowed to an approach to coherence.

"Twins!" he exulted. "God-damned twins! Cutest, ugliest, beautifullest little things you ever seen! One's a stem-winder an' one's a her. Christ but Dutch is mad at me!"

There was no holding Mac. He switched to a fresh horse and headed back for the mountains at a full lope in the gathering dark, thereby scandalizing Señora Castro, whose hospitality he thus offended. But then, a man with twins— could such a man be sane at a time like this? She decided Mac was blameless under the circumstances and so was mollified.

Father Bartolo was no longer at Monterey. His work and a steady tithe of funds from the Princesa had taken him some months before to Santa Barbara, where he dreamed of aiding his order in the development of a seminary. There was no one in Monterey. No old friends. Not even for Beatriz. But the Princesa and the name of McGann were already legend and invitations poured into the hotel, a much newer structure than the one Mike remembered.

However, accommodations here were as bad as those in the old one and Mike accepted the hospitality of an English friend of his buyer, who had acquired a little of the land and the fine house of one of the old *ranchos*, south of town.

Their business done, Mike and Beatriz drove south through the streets shortly after sunset. They found themselves caught up in a current of excitement, more people on the street than they had seen since their arrival. They turned curiously with the current and were carried into the block containing the Yankee House, garish as always and ablaze with lights. The crowd was pouring in through the tavern doors and a similar crowd was pouring out. Mike hailed a man passing the wagon.

"What's going on?"

"Murietta," the man said with excited satisfaction. "They finally got him. Down to Priest Valley. Captain Love and the State Rangers. They got his head in there in a jug of alcohol."

Beatriz caught her breath.

"No, Micaelo!" she cried. "Not like that!"

Mike understood her horror and her sadness. They remembered a kind and happy man. He handed her the reins.

"I'll see."

He crossed the walk and pushed into the Yankee House.

The crowd was knotted about an exhibit about halfway up the principal bar. As he moved toward this. Mike's gaze swept the room. He discovered Peyton almost immediately—a bloated, pouch-eyed man alone at a table in a corner with a bottle and a small glass before him. He needed no second look to know Peyton was drunk, soddenly, hopelessly, deliberately drunk. The man occasionally surveyed the room but he saw nothing, only the bottle before him. Mike elbowed through the crowd at the bar.

A strange, hideous, impersonal thing floated in an alcohol tank on the counter; a thing of pickled bone and flesh and hair resembling more a caricature in wax than anything which had ever owned life. He looked at it a long moment with great sadness, then turned back toward the door. At the foot of the stair, near the entry, he pulled up sharply to avoid collision with two women descending the steps from the floor above.

One was a frilled, busty, bustled girl with a wanton's easy, accentuated grace and addiction to color, who glanced sharply at him in the habitual, instinctive appraisal of her kind; the other, a thin, brittle woman with an imperious carriage from which the life was gone, did not see him. Her eyes, metal-hard with something hungry and ugly, were turned toward the wanton and one of her thin arms was about the narrowness of the accentuated waist. They passed and Mike stepped with relief out into the clean, fog-washed evening air.

"Joaquin?" Beatriz asked in a small voice as she handed back the reins.

"No, not Joaquin," Mike answered her gently, with the utter guilelessness of complete honesty. "I think our friend died a long time ago. It was not Joaquin."

He spoke gently with the reins to the two spans of Princesa horses in the harness. The wagon rolled on down the street. At the end of the block they turned. Open country lay off to the East, where the Sierra lay. And the moon was silver.

"Micaelo," Beatriz said suddenly, "couldn't we start for the mountains now—tonight?"

Mike glanced behind him into the body of the wagon, packed with their luggage and the necessaries of travel.

"Even the Studebakers don't make their wagon beds as comfortable as an Englishman's featherbed."

"Won't it be even better, with the moon?" Beatriz asked.

"We have the mattress. And I—I packed the coverlet, Micaelo."

Mike grinned at her and snapped the reins smartly and the Princesa horses surged into an eager trot, knowing they started for home.

Tom W. Blackburn was born on the T.O. Ranch near Raton, New Mexico, where his father was employed as an engineer. The T.O., which controlled such a vast domain it had its own internal railroad system, was later used as the setting for Blackburn's novel, *Raton Pass* (1950). Tom eventually moved with his family to southern California where he attended Glendale Junior College and then UCLA. In 1937 he married Juanita Alsdorf and, surely, she was the model for many of his notable Spanish and Mexican heroines. Blackburn first began writing Western stories for pulp magazines and, in the decade from 1938 to 1948, he contributed over 300 stories of varying lengths to such outstanding magazines as *Dime Western*, *Lariat Story Magazine*, and *Western Story*. Also during the 1940s he worked as a screenwriter for various Hollywood studios, a circumstance which prepared him to adapt his own Western novels into screenplays, beginning with his first, *Short Grass* (1947). Blackburn's longest affiliation was with the Disney studio where, for a time, he was best known for having written the lyrics for "The Ballad of Davy Crockett," a popular television and then theatrical series based on the exploits of this legendary frontiersman. In his Western novels, Blackburn tended toward stories based on historical episodes, such as *Navajo Canyon* (1952), centered on Kit Carson's roundup of the Navajo nation during the Civil War, or *A Good Day to Die* (1967) set during the twilight years of the great Sioux nation and the massacre at Wounded Knee. Perhaps his finest achievement as a novelist is the five-part Stanton saga focused on the building of a great ranch in New Mexico from the Spanish period to the end of the Nineteenth century. Following a stroke, Blackburn came to spend the years prior to his death in 1992 living with his daughter Stephanie in Colorado, surrounded by the mountains he had always loved. Tom W. Blackburn's Western fiction is concerned with the struggles, torments, joys, and the rare warmth that comes from companionships of the soul, the very stuff with is as imperishable in its human significance as the "sun-dark skins of the clean blood of the land" which he celebrated and transfixed in shimmering images and unforgettable characters.